Chasing Windmills

Chasing Windmills

Catherine Ryan Hyde

DOUBLEDAY | FLYING DOLPHIN PRESS

New York London Toronto Sydney Auckland

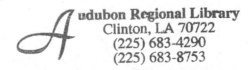

FLYING
DOLPHIN
P R E S S

PUBLISHED BY DOUBLEDAY/FLYING DOLPHIN PRESS

Copyright © 2008 by Catherine Ryan Hyde

All Rights Reserved

Published in the United States by Doubleday/Flying Dolphin
Press, an imprint of The Doubleday Broadway Publishing
Group, a division of Random House, Inc., New York.
www.doubleday.com

DOUBLEDAY/FLYING DOLPHIN PRESS and its colophon
are trademarks of Random House, Inc.

LIBRARY OF CONGRESS CATALOGING-IN-PUBLICATION DATA

Hyde, Catherine Ryan.
Chasing windmills / Catherine Ryan Hyde.—1st ed.
p. cm.
1. Teenage boys—Fiction.   2. Women—Fiction.
3. Mojave Desert (Calif.)—Fiction.   I. Title.
PS3558.Y358W56 2008
813'.54—dc22
2007013093

ISBN 978-0-385-52127-7

PRINTED IN THE UNITED STATES OF AMERICA

10 9 8 7 6 5 4 3 2 1

FIRST EDITION

For my sister Christie | 1951–2007

Chasing Windmills

Chemistry

This is the part that's going to be hard to explain: How can I tell you why two people who were afraid of everything—other people, open places, noise, confusion, life itself—wound up riding the subways alone under Manhattan late at night?

Okay, it's like this: When everything is unfamiliar and scary, your heart pounds just getting change from the grocery cashier. That feels like enough to kill you right there. So the danger of the subways at night can't be much worse. All danger begins to fall into the same category. You have no way to sink any deeper into fear.

Besides, consider the alternative. Staying home.

That's enough about that for now. I need to tell you about her.

She got on the Lexington Avenue local at . . . what was it? . . . I think Union Square. Funny how a thing like that can be so damned important, but you don't know it's important until an instant later in the big scheme of time. Then you go back and try to retrieve it. You tell yourself it's in there somewhere. But it's really in that no-man's-land of the moment before you woke up and started paying attention to your own life.

I'm pretty sure it was Union Square.

At first we looked at each other for a split second, but of course we looked away immediately. It's part of what makes us like the animals, I suppose. Ever seen two dogs circling to fight? They look right into each other's eyes. It's a challenge. So when a dog doesn't want to challenge anybody, he looks away. In case I haven't made it clear by now, we were two dogs who weren't looking for a fight.

But then, after we both looked away, we weren't afraid of each other anymore. We knew we didn't have to be. I mean, except to the extent that we were afraid of everything.

There was no one else in the car. It rumbled along again, with that special rocking, and the clacking noise, the lights flashing off now and then. And the heat. It was only May, but the heat had started early. It was after midnight, so I guess you'd think it was all cooled off by then, but it wasn't. A little bit cooler up on the street. Not so much down there. It was stuffy, like more air would be nice.

Every now and then we'd hear a noise that could have been somebody opening the door from another car. And we'd jump in unison, and look up. But it was never anybody. Just the two of us all the way to the end of the line.

Once I looked over at her while she was looking away. Her hair was dark and thick and about down to her shoulders. Her face was thin, like the rest of her. I couldn't figure out if there was something angular about her face, or something almost delicate. Maybe both.

I was trying to get a bead on how old she was. Older than me, that's for sure. I mean, she was a full-grown woman. But young enough, I guess. But maybe old compared to me. Early twenties.

Every inch of her was covered. Except her face. Jeans, boots, some kind of shawl thing wrapped around her. Seemed like too much to wear in that heat.

And a hat. She was wearing a hat over all that dark hair. A gray felt thing with a big brim. So all she had to do was dip her head an inch or two, and she was gone again. She could break off eye contact just like that. It seemed like such a great plan. I wondered why I'd never thought of it myself.

And on one cheek, a dark spot. Not exactly a bruise, but something like one. Like a shadow. Like she'd had some sort of an accident.

I think I remember feeling that it was a lovely face, but maybe I'm adding that in after the fact. It's hard to go back and describe what you thought of such an important face the first time you saw it. The memory gets colored with all those other things you felt later on. It's hard to separate them out again. But whatever I thought about her face, I noticed it. And it held me.

Then she looked up and I quick looked away.

At the end of the line, we both waited. And neither one of us got off the train.

You see, it says a lot about someone when they don't get off at the end of the line. When they just sit there with the doors open until the train starts back the other way. Right back to—or past— where they started out in the first place. That says a lot.

After the train started back up again, she looked right into my eyes. She didn't look away and neither did I.

Something happened in me. I'm not sure how good I'll be at explaining what it was. But it was an actual physical something. Something in my body. And I'm not going to go into any personal information about certain body reactions, because some things I'm just not comfortable discussing. Some things a gentleman doesn't talk about. Or, anyway, that's what I believe. But something happened in my gut. Like all of a sudden something that used to be solid in there turned to water. Hot water. In my arms, too, around my elbows. And a little bit down my legs. Especially around my knees. I remembered hearing an expression about being weak in the knees, and I guess I understood it for the first time. And there was a tingling associated with all this. A kind of all-over tingling, but mostly in my face. Which felt a little hot, like it might be turning red.

Then it was too much and we both looked away again. But not the same way we had before.

We rode like that for another hour or so, and never looked at each other after that. I wanted to look, but I couldn't bring myself to do it.

Then I woke up—which was weird, because I'd never felt myself go to sleep—and I was on that subway car by myself, and she was gone. I looked at my watch, and it was after three.

All I could think was that I wanted to talk to Delilah about this. About what had just happened. But, what had just happened? What was I supposed to say? There was this woman on the subway, and she looked at me. But in the few weeks I'd been talking to Delilah, every time I told her something I'd been feeling, she seemed to know what that feeling was. It made me seem almost . . . normal.

WHEN I GOT HOME, the apartment was dark and quiet, and of course my father was asleep. I came in on my tiptoes, even though it's pretty hard to wake him after he's taken his sleeping pill. You'd almost have to be trying. But I was careful all the same.

I looked at myself in my bathroom mirror. I wanted to look at myself the way someone else would look at me. I wanted to see what she saw.

I discovered something strange about myself in that moment. The moment I caught my own eyes in the mirror, I looked away. It was hard to force myself to look at myself. I wasn't bad to look at. It wasn't that. I wasn't the handsomest guy in the world, but I wasn't ugly. I guess I thought I looked fine. But it was almost as though I'd never really looked into my own eyes before. Like it was as hard to look at myself as it was to look at somebody else. And I wasn't sure what that meant. Unless it meant I was the kind of dog who didn't even want to challenge myself.

IN THE MORNING, I came to the breakfast table, and my father was staring at me. Taking my emotional temperature, as I like to put it. He only looked away once, to glance at his watch. That was his way of telling me I'd slept too long. If he only knew.

Then he went back to scrutinizing me again.

I hate that. It makes me feel like I guess a worm must feel when some fisherman is about to stick him on a hook. Like you want to get away, but there's no way to get away, so you just squirm. It's no use, but you do it anyway.

He said, "Good morning, Sebastian."

I said, "Good morning, Father."

I know how weird that sounds, but that's what I have to call him. He's not into any of that "Dad" or "Pop" stuff. I'm Sebastian, all three syllables every time, and he's Father. And that's not negotiable. That is one of any number of things that are not negotiable.

He was wearing his glasses at the table, his weird little round, wire-rimmed glasses. All the better to stare at me, I suppose. And some of his hair was spilling down over his forehead. His hair was curly and a little unruly, like mine, but gray. Suddenly, it seemed. Almost as if every morning you could see how much grayer it was than the day before.

And he was still studying me. It was as if he could see that something had changed in me. It was horrifying.

"What?" I said, finally, when I couldn't take it anymore.

"You seem different."

"I don't feel different," I said. Lying.

"You seem different."

"Different how?"

"I'm not sure. Like you were happy or excited about something."

Ah, yes. That. The sin of being happy or excited. According to my father, we must guard carefully against such things. According to my father, these emotions are the equivalent of dancing on our fifth-floor window ledge. Clearly inviting a nasty fall.

"Well, I'm not," I said. Hoping that would be the end of it.

It wasn't.

"I think you're taking too much sleep," he said.

"Sleep is good for you. You can tell because I've been so

healthy. Think how long it's been since I've been sick. It's the running, if you ask me, and plenty of sleep."

"There's still such a thing as too much."

I shifted tactics in midstream. "I was up late last night. I couldn't sleep. Didn't get to sleep until after three. That's why I slept in."

At first he said nothing. But I could tell by his mood that he wasn't done. You could feel it shifting around in him. You can always tell when he's mixing up another batch of something. But for a while he just stirred his bowl of cereal with a spoon. I remember thinking it must be getting really soggy.

Then he said, "What do you do? When you can't sleep?"

"I don't know. Just lie there."

"And do what?"

"I don't know. Think, I guess."

"What do you think about?"

I wanted to jump into that. I always want to jump him when he does that. It makes me want to attack. Not physically; I'm not like that. Attack verbally, the way he does with me. It makes me crazy when he tries to get inside my head. The only place I have left. But it never helps to rise up against him like that. It just never does any good.

"I don't remember," I said.

The face of the woman on the subway came into my head, fully formed, perfect. A perfect recollection. I wondered if I would ever see her again. I couldn't have imagined at that moment that I would.

I FINISHED MY LESSONS by one P.M. and went out for my run. My father frowned, the way he always did when I left the apartment to run. But he said nothing anymore. This point, at least, I had permanently won.

The whole time I was running, mostly in the park, I thought, *Please let Delilah be there today. Please.* It was like a chant that kept me going.

As I turned the final corner, I looked up at our building and there she was. Three floors up, hanging half out her window, waving at me. I smiled without even meaning to. Out loud but quietly, I said, "Thank you," and then realized I didn't even know who I was talking to.

I waited by the outside door, panting, for a few minutes, and then she hobbled down, and I held the door for her. She said what she always said.

"Thank you, child."

It's hard for her to get through the door without help. She has a bad hip, or maybe it's both of them, and she's very big, and walks with a cane. So getting through the door is hard unless somebody else holds it. Something about her hips or her back pushes the top of her body forward, so she looks like some kind of punctuation mark, though I'm not sure which one. Maybe a question mark that doesn't really curve around all the way on top. And she walks with her huge back end kind of trailing in a noticeable way. But I'm not criticizing. She's the best friend I have. She's the best friend I've ever had. Maybe it seems weird we could be friends when she's over fifty and I'm under eighteen. But we manage just fine.

We started off on our walk together. I had to remember to walk about twelve times slower than I would on my own.

Delilah took her little portable fan out of her pocket. A little plastic rocket of a fan, bright blue, with little blades like a miniature helicopter. She had to turn it on with her left hand, because she needed to lean on the cane with her right. The blades opened up like a flower and I could hear the buzz as they started to spin, and she trained the breeze onto her face and sighed.

"This weather, child," she said. "Good Lord, this heat."

She had a wonderful face, Delilah. Light-skinned black with freckles on her cheeks, and eyes the color of walnut shells, and the biggest teeth you ever saw in your life, so that when she smiled it seemed to take up her whole face. It was fun to make her smile, just to see it again. And it wasn't hard, either. Lots of things made Delilah smile.

"So," she said. "Where does that father of yours think you are right now?"

I looked down at the sidewalk and didn't answer.

"So you still haven't seen fit to tell him you made a friend."

"You don't know how he is," I said. "You don't know him."

"Not sure I got a yen to. Not sure what I think of a man doesn't want his own boy to have a single friend."

I looked up from the sidewalk and gave her a pleading look. Like, *Please. Not now. Not again.* And she caught it, and nodded, and waved it away with the hand that held the little plastic fan.

"Okay, okay, never you mind," she said.

Imagine such a thing. Being able to tell somebody what you want with your eyes. And get it. See why I loved Delilah so much? Even though I'd only known her for a few weeks.

"Something happened last night," I said.

" 'Bout time," she said.

"I'm afraid it'll sound silly. Like it was nothing."

"If it's something to you, then it's something to me."

So I told her about the woman on the subway, and the way she looked at me, and the way it made me feel inside. She listened with a little closed-mouth smile getting wider and wider on her face. Not like she was making fun of me, though. More like she knew what I was talking about even if I didn't.

When she was sure I was done she said, "Oooooh-weeee."

"Meaning what?"

"Your first dose of electricity."

"What does that mean?"

It's not that I didn't know what it meant, exactly. I'm not a complete idiot. I meant . . . what did I mean? I meant, why *that* woman? And why not ever before? At least, not quite like that ever before.

"Means you're a boy. And you're not dead yet. And you're not a little child no more."

But those were the parts I already knew.

We walked without talking for a couple of minutes. But it was still okay.

Then her fan slowed down. I could hear the sound of the blades change, and get low and sluggish. She rapped it hard on the top of her cane, and it seemed to pick up again. But a minute later, it slowed even more.

She stopped walking, so I stopped, too. She looked down at the fan like she was looking under the hood of a broken-down car. Like she would see the problem and know how to fix it.

"Bat-tries are dead. I wore the darn bat-tries down. Can't believe I didn't charge the darn bat-tries." She turned it off, sighed a very different kind of sigh from when she'd turned it on, and slipped it into the pocket of her enormous linen pants.

"I didn't even know her," I said. "I'd never even seen her before."

"That won't matter," she said. "Chemistry won't care. Two people either have it or they don't. Have it first time they set eyes on each other. Across a crowded room. Like the song says."

I didn't know what song, but I didn't ask.

A minute later, we passed by one of those stores that sell cheap souvenirs to the tourists. Electronics and postcards and little plastic Statues of Liberty. And in the window I saw they had fans. The old-fashioned, low-tech kind. The kind that fold up into a little stick, but unfolded they look like an accordion and have Chinese or Japanese art on them.

"Wait here," I said.

She looked like she could use a minute to rest, anyway. I ran inside to buy one for Delilah. Yes, ran inside. Risked the horrors of people I'd never even met. Walked right through the heart pounding. All for my friend.

It only cost me $1.99, about ten percent of my weekly allowance, but from the look in her eyes you'd have thought I bought her a new car or a mink coat. She unfolded it and hid the bottom half of her face behind it, pretend coy like a Japanese geisha girl.

Then she lowered it and laughed so loud I bet they could hear her inside the store.

"Child, if you aren't just the sweetest thing," she said, when she was all through laughing. And she put her hand on the top of my head and brought it down to her level and kissed me right on the forehead.

Then we walked on, and she fanned herself with her left hand and seemed to feel better.

"Congratulations," she said.

"For what?"

"For being alive. Hope something like last night happens to you again real soon."

One More Night

Tonight was tougher than usual.

First off, Natalie was extra fussy. She didn't want to go to bed. She's got a stubborn streak a mile wide, and I didn't get her down until almost ten. And of course this is the first of the two nights of the week that C.J. gets to stay up until his daddy comes home. Pops, he calls him now. I guess he figures that sounds more mature. Anyway, because they're not school nights, he can stay up. That's our deal. But that's also the beef with Natalie. Why does C.J. get to stay up and she doesn't? Well, it's easy, kid. He's almost seven. You're not even three. Sounds good to me. But I guess if I was still in my terrible twos, it wouldn't.

It's not *fair,* she kept saying. I used to say that, too, to my dad. Life's not fair, he would say. Kind of self-satisfied, like it pleased him to disappoint me. So I don't say that to her. I don't say that to anybody. It's true enough, but let somebody else rub it in. I never like to be the bearer of bad news.

Anyway, I finally got her down.

Carl came home around midnight and I slipped out right away. Even though I had no work to go to anymore. Every night at just this time I go to work. Have for years, except for that time around when Natalie was born. I always leave just about when Carl gets home. I leave him to look after the kids. Natalie is always sleeping, and five days a week C.J. is, too, but if C.J. is up I leave him with Carl. Because Carl, he just loves C.J., especially right after work. Carl works with the public and when he gets home at night he needs a better opinion of humanity. Or so he says.

Anyway, I've never tested the theory that it would be okay to tell Carl about how I lost my job. And I wasn't brave enough to test it that night.

So for the last nine nights, at least the six of them that would have been my shift nights, I've walked out the door like nothing was wrong. Like nothing was different. I let him assume I'm going to work. But of course I never do. I always ride the subway. Because, really, I don't think I would be welcome there at my old job anymore. Not even for just a little friendly visit. Even though it's a place of business, and it's open to the public. I mean, anybody can go into a grocery store, right? But even so, I think I burned my bridges there, and there is no making it right.

I also think that the longer I put off telling Carl, the harder it's going to be. He'll ask when I got fired. I could lie but he'll look at my pay stubs and see the truth anyway. Every day I tell myself I'm only making it worse. The longer I put off telling him. But then every day I think, Well, I've waited this long and one more day won't make so much of a difference. Since I'm in a world of trouble anyway.

So I just walk out the door and ride the subway. One more night.

What's one more night?

He really only said one thing to me. He put a hand on my chin. Sort of turned my face so he could look at my cheek in a better light.

"You wearing makeup on that?" he asked.

"No. No makeup."

"Oh. That's not that bad, then."

I didn't say how bad I thought it was or wasn't. I didn't say any-thing at all.

Just as I was slipping out the door I looked back and there they were on the couch, watching TV together.

It's really spooky how much that boy is like a clone of Carl. The thin, baby-fine blond hair, and the sort of no-colored eyes. Well, not no color. I mean, they're not just white or anything. It's just that they're not blue and they're not gray and they're not green. They're all of the above and none of the above at the same time. Carl used to be the only one in the world who had them. That I know of. Until C.J. came along. And they both have those thin, narrow shoulders and the skinny chest that looks almost sunken.

Wouldn't you know he would even have to end up with his father's name? And I fought hard against that. Not that Carl is a bad name, but Carl Jr.? That's just plain cruel. Why not name him Jack in the Box or White Castle or something? Jesus. But I guess C.J. will do.

They didn't even notice when I slipped out the door. Those two are in a world of their own. They are a club of two, all right.

All the way down to the subway station I walked in the street, brushing against parked cars. So I wouldn't have to deal with the whole thing about the sidewalk cracks. It's really humiliating to admit it. I mean, I'm a grown woman. I'm not saying I *won't* step on a crack. Just that it's easier for me, in some weird way, if I don't have to. If I don't even have to worry about it. I'm not a complete psycho. But I had a big thing with that when I was younger, and lit-tle bits of that stuff can hang on.

I think it's because my mother died of a broken neck, which is really just a broken back higher up. I mean, if you want to look at it that way.

Not that I think it was my fault or anything. We all knew who did it. Well, all except one. Everybody in the world knew my father did it, except my father. He was weird about stuff like that. It was like he thought he could make history disappear. And he could, in a way. He made it disappear from himself.

I went to see him in jail twice, and both times he just talked nonstop about how much he loved that woman and how he would never do a thing to harm her. But he did a million things to harm her, usually right in front of me and my sister. So then I just didn't go see him anymore.

He died in jail, or so I hear. I didn't think about it all that much. I still don't. I've got no opinion on any of that. Or, at least, none that matters worth a damn when all is said and done.

I don't even know why I'm talking about that. I didn't set out to get into that. I'm just talking about that night because of what happened on the subway.

Not that anything happened. It's very important that I stay clear on that. Nothing happened. I just looked at this kid. And he looked at me. And even Carl can't get upset about that. Right?

Except he would have. He would have hit the ceiling if he'd been there.

I don't guess it's right to call that subway guy a kid. He wasn't a kid. He was probably six feet tall. I just have this thing now where everybody used to be older than I was, and now anybody younger looks like a kid to me.

Probably he was around nineteen.

God, that's young enough. What I was thinking, I don't know.

Except it wasn't really thinking. There was no real thinking to it. It was just one of those moments like when you're trying to change a lightbulb by feel, and you get a jolt. Shock yourself. It's not something you do on purpose and you sure as hell don't see it coming. Sometimes electricity just conducts.

And the funny thing is, I don't even know what it was about him. He's not the sort of guy who would catch my eye for any special reason, and usually I don't even look at guys on the street or in the subway. I mean, I look. But not like that. What I guess I mean is, there was nothing about him I would really even notice, until that power ran along the invisible line between our eyes and zapped me.

I liked his hair, though. Because it was so big. I'm not used to big hair, living with Carl and C.J. Natalie's hair is really fine and thin, too, even though she's dark like me. She got the color of my hair, but not its thickness. But this guy had hair that was really there. Really thick and curly. Some of it came forward onto his forehead, and you just got this sense that however it spilled, it was right. Like, no matter how it decided to fall, or not fall, or lie down, it looked just like it was supposed to. It must be nice to get to relax about something like that.

Other than that, I just looked at him, like I would look at anybody. Not expecting anything at all. But I got something.

That never happened to me before, not once. I swear. Not in the seven years I've been with Carl. Actually maybe closer to eight years. I mean, I see guys. Sometimes I think they look good, but it's just a thought in my head. Like I was seeing them on a page of a magazine. Ever since there's been Carl, which is like forever, since I was fifteen, there hasn't been anything with anybody else.

Sometimes I wonder if that's because of his thoughts on what he would do if there ever was. Which he shares with me. Regularly. But deep down I don't think so. Because I think you can scare somebody out of doing something, but not out of feeling like they want to.

I think it's because my loyalty to Carl is very real.

Where that night fits in, I don't know.

I purposely got off the train while the guy was sleeping. I don't want any trouble.

Atoms

When my father put on one of his opera records, I knew it was going to be a long night. I mean, the minute the needle hit the
record. Yeah, I know what you're thinking: A needle on a phonograph record? What century is this, anyway? But that's my father
for you.

I loathe and despise opera.

But it was worse than just that. My father loves opera; it soothes
him. So he sits in his chair for an extra hour or two, and takes his
sleeping pill late.

I sat in my chair and tried to read, but my assigned reading for
that week was *Finnegans Wake*. Which is like the literary equivalent
of opera, if you ask me. The music was loud, and I guess I felt like I
was being assaulted from every direction. But the main problem
was that I wanted to get out of the house. I wanted him in bed
asleep, so I could go.

"What seems to be your problem tonight, Sebastian?"

I looked up to see my father staring at me. Taking my emotional
temperature.

"I just don't like opera. And you know it, so I don't know why
you keep asking."

"You'll develop an appreciation for good music in time. So I'm doing you a favor to expose you to it."

But he'd been exposing me to it all my life, and nothing was developing. Unless you count even more hatred.

I tried to read again, but when I looked up, he was still staring at me.

"Something you'd rather be doing tonight, Sebastian?"

Anything, I thought. "I'm going to bed," I said.

I lay in my room in the dark for what seemed like forever, until I heard him turn off the music and go into his bathroom and run a glass of water to take his sleeping pill. Then it was only a matter of time.

THE CLOSER WE GOT TO UNION SQUARE STATION, the more nervous I got. And of course I kept telling myself it was silly, because the chances of her getting on again tonight had to be pretty slim. But, see, that was just it. I was nervous about how I would feel if she didn't. Or *when* she didn't, as the case may be.

And I wasn't sure how I would know if she got on some other car. I didn't want to walk up and down the train, one car to the next. That's what people do when they're looking for trouble. And you must know by now that I wasn't one of them.

So when we pulled into the Union Square station, I plastered myself to the glass of one of the doors, scanning the whole platform. And the minute the door opened, I stuck my head out and tried to see everybody who was about to step on, before they did and it was too late to see them. My heart was pounding, and my face felt like it had no blood in it, and my head was going a little dizzy, so I'm thinking, *This can't be normal, right? I mean, normal people don't feel like this at moments like this, do they? Do normal people even* have *moments like this?* I had no frame of reference. I had no way to know.

She wasn't there.

But then I started thinking maybe it wasn't Union Square.

Maybe it was the next stop. Astor Place. So I did the same weird series of things again, all the time knowing in my heart it was Union Square.

Then I looked at my watch and reminded myself it was still early. Only about a quarter after midnight. And there'd be another train coming through Union Square again in the next few minutes, and I could get off and wait for that one.

But I still knew the chances were pretty slim.

And yet every train I got on, my heart and my face and my guts went into their dance, all on fire like it was actually happening, right then and there.

And then, every time I didn't see her, there was a fall involved. I thought about dancing on the fifth-floor window ledge outside our apartment. Every train she wasn't on felt something like hitting the pavement from five floors up. So maybe my father was right about that. Maybe happiness and excitement really are dangerous things.

THE NEXT DAY I VISITED DELILAH in her apartment for the first time. Before I even ran. She caught me in the hall and told me she couldn't go for our walk today because she'd promised to look after James McKinley, her baby grandson, but I was welcome to come by later and have some lemonade if I wanted.

So I did. And then, amazingly, I forgot all about running. But I'm getting out of order.

I sat at the kitchen table and watched this tiny, tiny little baby sleeping in a little soft crib sort of thing near the table. He was only a couple of weeks old, but he had hair. He was a darker black than Delilah, and I watched his lips move like he was sucking on a bottle in his sleep. He looked really peaceful. Delilah was making lemonade from scratch, squeezing lemons in one of those little glass juicers you have to use by hand.

"Never seen a baby before?" she asked.

"Not in person, I don't think." Not close up, anyway.

I got up and started looking around her apartment. She had a big-screen TV, which was something I'd only seen ads for, or seen in store windows. And a DVD player, which was unheard of at our house. My father thought movies were some kind of lower form of entertainment. Something you do to waste your time when you should be reading *Moby-Dick* or listening to opera or something. And she had hundreds of movies on DVD, all arranged on shelves like my father did with his books.

It was hot in the apartment, even though a very tired old air conditioner strained and blew from its spot in the window. I looked out over Lexington Avenue and felt lost for reasons I couldn't entirely sort out.

Then I looked at her CD player, and her stack of CDs. She had stuff like Aretha Franklin and Marvin Gaye. The Spinners. Not an opera in the place.

"You act like you never seen such stuff before in all your life," she said.

I didn't want to tell her that she was almost right. We didn't have a TV. Never had, at least since my mother died. And my father still had his old phonograph. I had a computer, because I convinced my father I needed it for educational research. As an aid to my homeschooling. At first he didn't like the idea, but after I started making so many trips to the library, he backed down. Now I regret losing the trips to the library.

"I had a dog like you once," she said. "No offense. Got him out of the pound. I guess he'd only just been in some backyard before. Had to pick him up and carry him into the house, 'cause I guess he'd been hit or kicked for trying to come in. You shoulda seen him, in a house for the first time. Every time he saw a mirror, or heard a toilet flush, or saw the TV come on, he'd get this look on his face. Like, Where's all this stuff *been* all my life?"

I looked up to see her pouring two glasses of lemonade out of the big jar she'd mixed it in. She set them down on the table and then hobbled over and stood near me, and looked out the window.

The wind from the air conditioner blew her hair back just a little. Delilah had hair that I can only describe as being halfway between braids and dreadlocks. Every piece was kind of heavy, and you could see the wind had trouble lifting it, but it blew back a little all the same.

"Such an ugly, ugly city," she said. "I can't wait to get back to California."

I got a little stitch in my stomach when she said that. Delilah only moved into this sublet in our building because her daughter, who lives ten blocks away, was having a baby. She just came to help out. When her daughter was okay on her own with James McKinley, she'd be going home. But I had no idea when that would be.

I didn't answer.

"What?" she said. "You feeling sad today? You look sad today."

I still felt empty and hollow from the train the night before, but I didn't say so. I said something else that was true. "What will I do without you when you move home?"

"Oh, child," she said, and ruffled a hand through my hair. I loved it when she touched me. My hair or my shoulders, or sometimes she'd rub a hand around on my back for a second when she walked with me. I loved it more than I'd ever be okay admitting. "Is that what's getting you down? Well, you'll write letters to me. Or e-mails. And call me on the phone now and again. And make more friends. Come on, now. Drink your lemonade."

We sat at the table, and I sipped at it, and it was good. Cold and sugary, with a bite that felt good on this hot day. I watched little James McKinley sleeping. There was something sweet and peaceful about his face.

"Do you think I'll ever see that woman again?" I was surprised to hear myself say it. I'd had no idea I was about to bring it up.

"Well, now, child, I can't say as I know. You might or you might not. And here's what I think about that: If God or the Universe or Life or whatever-you-want-to-call-it wants you to meet her again, then you will. If it wasn't meant to be, then you won't."

"And then what would I do?"

"Feel that same way about somebody else." I started to object, but she cut me off before I could even open my mouth. "Now, I know, I know, you think you won't. Every time you feel some way for somebody you think you'll never feel that way for anybody again. But you will. If you have to, you will. Take my word on this one. I been around."

We sat quietly for a while, and drank lemonade, and I just kept getting lower and lower inside, thinking about never seeing that woman again, and losing Delilah back to San Diego.

I know she could tell I felt bad, because she ruffled my hair again.

After a while I said, "Is that really true? About how things happen if they're meant to?"

"Well," she said, "I guess you can think what you want on that score. Everybody always does. But I believe it with every cell of every part of me. I've seen it with my own two eyes."

"My father is an atheist. He thinks the world is just a big accident."

"And what do you think?"

I just looked at her for a minute. I wasn't used to being invited to give my opinion. I wasn't used to being treated like I was allowed to disagree.

"I used to argue with him about it. I'd say, Well, then how did all this get here? You know, people and animals. How could nothing have made us? He'd say, There were these atoms bouncing around and they hit each other just right and then everything else happened."

Delilah raised one eyebrow. "But who made the atoms?"

"I asked him that," I said, getting all excited now. "Those were nearly my exact words. Know what he said?" She just waited. "He said they were just always there."

Delilah laughed low in her throat. A laugh that shook her whole body, but it was soft. I think she would have laughed louder if little

James McKinley hadn't been sleeping. "Did you think that was a good answer?"

"Not really," I said.

Then we both just sat there smiling, and it felt good to smile. Until I actually did it, I could've sworn I had no smile in me. Maybe it was Delilah. Maybe hers was contagious.

I'm not sure how much longer I sat there smiling before it hit me. I had to go running if I was ever going to.

"I have to go," I said. "I have to run."

"You could take one day off if you wanted to, you know."

"Oh, no. I can't. I'll get sick. When I don't run, I get sick."

She looked at me with one eyebrow raised. "I'm not sure I ever heard tell of such a phenomenon," she said. Like she was pretty sure I was full of crap, but too nice to say so.

I tried to convince her. I told her all the stories about when I used to get sick. I'd need to go to the emergency room all the time. For all different things. Or the doctor's office. "And then finally this one doctor who saw me a bunch of times said I needed to get out more. Get out in the fresh air and get some exercise. So that's when my father let me go out running every day. And now I never get sick."

There was something going on in Delilah's face, but I couldn't tell what it was. Something she knew, but I didn't. I felt uncomfortable to hear what she would say next.

"Did you ever stop to think," she said, "that maybe you were getting sick because that was the only way to get out of the house?"

I didn't answer. But the honest answer was no. I had never stopped to think that. I had just never looked at it that way.

We sat quietly for a minute, and then she asked me if I'd like another glass of lemonade.

"I would love another glass," I said. "Thank you."

I never went running that day. And I felt fine.

THE SECOND TIME the train pulled into the Union Square station, I didn't get up. It was hard, but I didn't. The first time had been just like the night before. Only worse. Plus there were three other people in that car, and I felt like I would be making an idiot of myself. So I made myself stay down in that seat.

But then the minute the train pulled away, I couldn't live with the feeling that she might be in some other car. That she might have gotten on, and be somewhere right on this train with me, and I wouldn't know it.

There was only one more car at the front of the train, on my left. I got up and walked to the end of the car and looked through the windows, and there was no one up there except an old Hasidic man with a beard. Then I wandered to the other end of the car and looked through to the next car down and there she was. Sitting right there. I felt like someone had swung a baseball bat and hit me in the guts. She had that same gray hat on, but different shoes with big clunky heels, and a big oversized denim shirt that was almost as big as the shawl. She looked like she wanted to disappear into her clothes.

There was no reason for her to look up. I hadn't made a sound. I was on the other side of two doors separating the cars, and she couldn't possibly have heard me.

But she looked up, and looked right at me. And I was amazed by what I saw.

I'm not sure how to describe why I knew this so clearly. But I saw it in her eyes somehow. She was hit just as hard by seeing me again as I was by seeing her. I could tell. I could see it. Or maybe I could feel it. But whatever it was, I knew she'd just been hit in the guts with a baseball bat.

And I had no idea what to do.

I couldn't go in there. Could I? How could I?

I could hear my own ears ringing and I stood frozen, and I don't think I could have moved if I'd tried. She just kept looking at me and I just kept looking at her, but this time it was more about fear than anything else. That's mostly what it made me feel inside. Fear.

The whole thing felt so frightening and intense that I had to stop it. I had to get out of that moment somehow. I felt like in a minute I wouldn't be able to stand up anymore. So I did the only thing I could think to do. I went back to my seat and sat down.

My head was going so fast I couldn't possibly tell you what I was thinking. My thoughts were racing around in layers, three or four deep, overlapping each other. There was no way to separate anything out.

I kept looking at the door to the next car, and in about a minute it opened, and she came in. She looked at me once, very fast. Then she sat down across the car from me. Not right across, but across and maybe two seats down.

Then she looked up and smiled at me, and I tried to smile back, but I'm not sure what it came out looking like. That's the last time in my life I'd want to be forced to remember how to smile. I noticed that the dark shadow on her cheek had turned into more of a regular bruise. It had a little bit of a greenish-yellowish tinge.

There was not one part of my body or brain that I could work from memory. I couldn't remember where my legs used to go when I sat, or what I was supposed to do with my hands. I didn't know where to look or where not to look. My brain felt like a dog chasing its tail, and I didn't know how to get the cycle unlocked again.

How long we rode like that, I can't say. It felt like hours. No, it felt like days. And I was in pain. I mean, I was genuinely suffering. There's only one actual thought I can remember. I remember it struck me strange that I had looked forward to this and wanted it, because now that I had it, it was so incredibly painful. A big part of me wished I had never left home.

After what felt like another day or two of this torture, the train pulled into Hunts Point Avenue in the Bronx, and by then there was only one other person on the car with us, and he got off. And nobody got on. I think it was after one A.M., but I didn't look at my watch.

She looked up at me again and smiled, and this time I think I smiled something back that would probably do. This time I'd had more time to prepare.

"Hi," she said.

Of course I said, "Hi," but it sounded pathetic. Like my voice was still changing.

After that we just sat there and rode up and down under the city until nearly two o'clock. I had more or less remembered how to breathe by then, but I still had to do it consciously.

At about ten to two we pulled into Union Square again, and she got up, and looked at me one more time and smiled.

"Maybe I'll see you tomorrow," she said, and then she walked off the train. But just before the doors closed, she looked back over her shoulder at me. This time she didn't smile. This time I looked into her eyes and saw in a little deeper. Almost like she took down a curtain and let me see into one of the rooms of her house.

She was sad, and in trouble. That's what I saw.

Trouble

In the morning there was some trouble. Probably not for the reasons Carl said.

He said it was because I didn't wake him up when I got home, and
tell him to go to bed. When I got home that night, Carl was asleep sitting up on the couch, with C.J. sleeping with his head on his pop's
chest. And they just looked so sweet. I hated to even disturb them.

Plus, I never really know with Carl. Usually once he winds
down from work it's okay, but I never like to press my luck.

Then in the morning when I was making coffee, and making
bacon and poached eggs on toast, which is his favorite breakfast,
he came into the kitchen, and he was in a bad mood. He was mad, I
could tell. I can feel it on him. He doesn't have to say a word. It's
pretty unusual for him. Actually. To wake up in a bad mood. Usually if he's rested things go okay.

"Why didn't you wake me up?" he asked right off. "Now I got a
backache."

"I'm sorry," I said. "Just that you looked so comfortable."

"Well, I wasn't comfortable. Obviously. Because now I have a
backache. Now I got to go to work tonight with my back hurting.
How can anyone be comfortable sleeping sitting up on the couch
all night? Why would you even think that?"

"I'm sorry. I don't know. I'm sorry."

He came over and stood really close to me, which is not normally a good sign.

Something weird happened. I thought about that kid from the subway. I have no idea why. I had no intention of ever letting him into my mind at a time like that. I don't know why I did.

It was something that happened without my permission. Like my brain tried to slip back into that moment when the charge was flickering between us on the train. When we were looking at each other, or smiling. Like that would be a safer place to be than this. And just for a second my body remembered. How that felt.

"What's with you this morning?" Carl said.

I said, "I don't know what you mean."

But I did. And I think he knew it.

"Something different about you."

"No there isn't," I said.

And then I made a very bad mistake. I cut my eyes away from him. I looked away like I wanted to be sure he didn't look in and see the wrong thing. Because I was afraid of exactly that.

There's no right thing to do at a moment like that. If I let him see in, that's bad. If I make sure he doesn't see, that's maybe even worse. Maybe what he's imagining is even worse.

I should never have talked to that kid. That was over the line. I don't know what I was thinking. What was I thinking, telling him I would see him again? Or even that maybe I would. I don't know why I do shit like that. Not that I ever did that before. But stuff *like* that. Starting something I know I can't afford to start.

Like I can just buy something and the bill will never come due.

And I can never keep anything secret from Carl. He knows everything.

Now, one thing I will say about Carl. He has never hit me. He has never, in the seven years I've been with him, just hauled off and smacked me.

He gets mad, but all he really does is grab me by my arms. Usually my upper arms. And he digs in too hard, but probably he doesn't know it's too hard, because he's busy being mad and not thinking about how tight he's holding on. My arms bruise really easy, but I guess I can't blame that on him. And it hurts, so I'll tell him to let me go, and then he will, but with a push.

He doesn't hit me, like I say. Just pushes. It's just his way of letting go. Only one time I hurt my back landing on my tailbone, so after that I always try to turn around, like to catch myself. And that's how I got that little bruise on my cheek, bumping into the cabinet. But I guess that's as much my fault as his. I just wasn't looking where I was headed.

Anyway, when I cut my eyes away, he grabbed hold of my arms.

"What happened at work last night?"

"Nothing. Same as always. I just did my shift and then came home."

"You didn't see anybody? Or meet anybody?"

"No. I never do. I would never do that. You know me better than that."

It was hurting the way he was holding my arms but I didn't say he should let me go. I didn't say a word about it.

"Look at me," he said.

But I didn't.

That was when he did something really surprising. He hit me. For the first time in seven years. And I knew why, too. I knew what had changed. For the first time in seven years I was hiding something from him. And he knew it.

It was just a slap. Not like he punched me or anything. Just a backhand slap. It might not have even hurt that much, except for that big class ring he wears on his right hand. I guess at a time like that you don't stop to think that you're wearing a ring. But it caught me on the lower lip and made it bleed.

When he saw I was bleeding he let me go. Without pushing.

I sat down at the kitchen table and there was a dish towel. Sitting there on the table. So I used that, but it was too late, because I got some blood on the collar of my very favorite shirt ever.

He brought me some ice and said he was sorry.

"I know," I said. "I know you didn't mean to. Never mind."

"No, really," he said. "Really. I'm sorry. I don't know why I did that."

But *I* knew. I knew exactly what I had done to deserve it. And I knew if I was smart I would not complain much. Because for seven years he never smacked me, until I went out and felt something for somebody else, and did a little too much about it. So I knew who was at fault here.

By the time I smelled the bacon burning it was way too late to save it.

C.J. was watching some kind of violent cartoon show about the military or superheroes or something. Natalie was sucking her thumb in front of the TV. Holding that fur collar she loves so much. That snap-off fur collar from Carl's leather jacket. They didn't say a word or act like they knew anything was wrong.

Maybe they really don't hear when stuff happens like that. Or maybe they hear but they keep it to themselves. I never know which one.

MOST OF THE REST OF THAT DAY I just sat in front of the TV and watched my DVD of *West Side Story*. I watched it three times.

Normally I wouldn't do that when Carl was home. Because he will complain. He doesn't like repetition. It bugs him. I'm just the opposite. The more I'm upset, the more I like to go with things I know like the back of my hand. Things that are familiar to me.

Anyway, when Carl has gotten mad recently I can do just about anything. Because he's feeling guilty. I get lots of extra slack on days like this.

I had to keep tissues handy. And not because I was crying. I would never cry in front of Carl. Never in a million years. Or the kids, either. It was just the opposite. It was laughing. Some things in that movie are funny. Like a couple of the songs. You would think I would remember not to laugh, because of my lip. But then I would forget, and it would start to bleed again.

Something about that movie. I get lost in it. I forget I'm just sitting on the couch watching it. It gets to be more real than I am.

That's why I like it, I think.

The more bloody tissues I stacked up on the coffee table, the more Carl would probably cut me some slack.

He did say a couple of things.

He said, "I never could understand how you could sit there and just watch the same thing over and over and over like that. Over and over. What gives with that? I don't see how you can stand it."

I didn't answer because I didn't need to. And there was nothing to say, anyway. He has told me that same thing probably fifty times. That he doesn't understand why I like to keep watching the same movie. It's funny how he says he hates repetition, but he will say that over and over. Sometimes I want to say, "God, Carl, do you think I'm deaf, or what? How many times are you going to repeat the same thing?" But of course I never do.

It's a bad habit with him. He likes to share his opinion. A lot.

"And it's so old-fashioned," he said.

"I don't mind that."

"We have movies from this century, you know."

So, that was another one. Another thing he has told me probably fifty times. Maybe more.

Just for a minute I stood outside the whole thing, and I was stunned by how much he says and how much I don't say. It's like everything he thinks comes straight out of his mouth. Just like that. I think things, but they don't go any farther. I just think them, and there they stay. Just for a minute I stood outside both of us and watched it go around and around like that. Like an endless loop. Him talking and me not talking and him talking some more and me not talking some more. Until the end of time, which I guess is how it will be.

I wonder how two people can be so different like that.

I like that movie. That's all there is to it. My mother named me after Maria in *West Side Story*. It has history. And I like it.

And this was the first time I've watched it since that thing with the kid on the subway, so this was the first time I noticed that he reminds me a little bit of Tony. Just a little bit. Not even his face so much, but something about the way his face lights up. Something from the inside.

I don't even know that kid's name. Wouldn't it be funny if it was Tony?

But I guess that's asking too much.

All of a sudden I got this thought that if Carl was feeling guilty enough, maybe I could go out tomorrow night, too. Even though it's not a shift night of mine, tomorrow. I mean, it didn't used to be one. When I had a job.

Then a minute later I realized what a stupid thought it was. I couldn't do that. It would make him totally suspicious.

Why did I even think that?

Why did it suddenly matter whether I got to ride the subway with some tall young guy with a lot of hair? I didn't even know him. I didn't even know his name.

One thing I knew for sure: I had better be careful what I let get started here.

My mother had this thing she used to say. Before she died. "Nearly everything is easier to get into than it is to get out of."

That's a very true thing. And I've always known it. You would think that, since I know it so well, I'd be more careful. More careful of what I let get started. But good advice has always been more or less wasted on me. I can't even say why that is. Just that I can tell you a hundred times which direction is the right way to go, but then damned if I don't go the other way, and half the time I can't even tell you why.

My father said I was always trouble. Born for it, he said. He wasn't right about anything else, but maybe he was right about that.

Dancing on the Wall

The rest of that night was a miserable thing. I never got to sleep, not even for a few minutes. I never even closed my eyes. My body felt like it had been electrocuted and I hadn't had time to recover. I kept replaying the same scenes over and over in my head.

Finally I got up, hoping I could beat my father to the breakfast table. It didn't work. He was there. The minute he put his glasses on and looked up at me, I knew we had trouble.

I tried desperately to look and act normal, but that never works. There's something wrong with the fabric of that system. Normal is when you're not trying, so anytime you try to act normal, you're going to fall on your ass. Pardon my language.

All I wanted was to be left alone until it was night again, and I could go back to that subway. I wanted to wrap myself in cotton or lock myself in a safe, where nothing could hurt me or challenge me until I could see her again. I didn't want to think about anything else. I didn't want to be distracted. And I definitely did not want to be attacked.

I just kept looking away from him, trying to fall back on the most basic animal signals. Trying to say with my body language, *I don't want a fight.* But I could feel his energy crackling in the air between us. He wanted a fight. So we would probably have one.

"You look terrible," he said.

"I didn't sleep."

"What's with you and sleeping all of a sudden?"

"I don't know."

"Well, it's unacceptable."

"I don't know what I'm supposed to do about it. I can either sleep or I can't."

"You'll take one of my sleeping pills."

"No I won't."

"Excuse me?"

A silence fell, a cold, purposeful silence, one intended to give me time to see that I had stepped way over the line. The energy that had crackled before was spitting now. I held very still, the way people are told to lie facedown and play dead during a bear attack. It was that serious. I tried to plot my best way out.

I said, "It's not safe to take somebody else's prescription medication. We don't even weigh the same. You're bigger than I am."

I could see by his face that I had successfully evaded him. I was relieved, and proud. I'd played my hand brilliantly. I'd squeezed away from his rage by saying just the sort of thing he would say. By being exactly the person he taught me to be.

"That's a good point," he said. "We'll have to take you to the doctor and get you your own prescription."

Then I had a choice to make, and I opted for survival. "Okay, fine," I said. It was easier to go get the pills with him and flush one down the toilet every night. The less said, the better.

But the bad energy hung over the house for most of the morning. Every move I made could have been the wrong one. He was just waiting to jump me. But I thought out everything I said or did three or four moves in advance, as if we were playing chess. It was exhausting, and the last thing I wanted to do. I wanted to drift into a dream state where I could replay last night and dream about tonight. But in a war zone you stay focused and watch your step.

I MISSED MY RUN a second day in a row because I was so frazzled and exhausted. But I did take a nice long walk with Delilah. In the park, which is farther than we usually go.

Instead of a fan, she brought an umbrella. A very colorful, fancy umbrella with Paris scenes on it, like cancan dancers and the Eiffel Tower.

"Expecting rain?" I asked, but she explained that it was a sun umbrella.

She spun it around a little in her left hand every now and then, like she was waltzing along with a parasol. And it always made her laugh. All my bad mood from the morning just fell away, and I felt okay. Tired, shell-shocked, but okay.

Of course, she was very excited about my news of the previous night. Wanted to know all the details. "Did she say anything to you?"

"She said, 'Hi.'"

"And what did you say?"

"'Hi.'"

"Well, I guess that's some kind of a start."

"And then, before she got off the train, she said, 'Maybe I'll see you tomorrow.'"

"Oooooooh-weeee. Now we're *gettin'* somewhere."

I could really hear and feel her excitement. It was amazing and wonderful that somebody could be so happy over something that was happening to me.

She stopped walking suddenly, and I stopped, and she looked into my face for a long time. I wasn't sure why, but I said nothing.

"I would think you'd be happier today."

"I'm just tired," I said. But that wasn't entirely true. And I think she knew it. We started walking again. Silently. We passed a woman walking about ten dogs all at once, and a group of old women on roller skates. Well, actually, they passed us. Then I said, "It's my father. He's noticing that I'm not sleeping. And he wants to do something about it. I'm worried I'm not going to be able to keep slipping out much longer."

Then we walked a little more in silence. Down to where you can see Bethesda Fountain. Delilah wasn't twirling her umbrella anymore. She seemed lost in thought.

"I know you don't want me to ask you this," she said, and I braced for the worst. "I know you'd rather I don't, but I got to ask. Can't keep it in another minute. How come that father of yours don't want you to know anybody?"

For reasons hard to explain, I jumped to defend him. "He's only trying to take good care of me." She just raised one eyebrow. "He says people will always let you down."

"Well, now, that's true," she said. And I was surprised. I didn't expect her to agree with my father on anything. "People *will* always let you down. And do you know why? It's because they were put on this earth for a reason. But the reason is not you. They were not put on this earth to take care of you. But that don't mean you shouldn't even *know* 'em."

"He says all I should need is my family."

"Honey, that ain't even hardly a family. It's just one man. Takes more than that to make a family, even if that *was* true. What about your mother? Don't you ever see her?"

"She died when I was seven."

"Oh. I'm sorry to hear that, child. Don't you have grandparents?"

"Not really. My father's parents are dead. And my mother's father died a long time ago. My Grandma Annie is still alive, I think. But my father doesn't want me to talk to her." I knew the minute it came out of my mouth how that would sound. So I jumped to defend him again. Before she could even raise an eyebrow. "It's not what you're thinking. It's because she's crazy. He doesn't let me talk to her because she's crazy."

"Crazy how? How's he know she's crazy? She locked up somewhere?"

"No. She manages a motel out in California. Out in the Mojave Desert. So, no, she's not locked up or anything. But he knows she's crazy because she won't accept the fact that my mother is dead. It's like she doesn't even believe it. He says if she ever tries to contact me I should run for my life. Because she talks about my mother like she isn't even dead."

Another long, unpleasant silence. For the first time ever, I wished my time with Delilah could be over for the day. We walked a little farther. A man slammed into my shoulder in passing and didn't even excuse himself.

"How did your mother die?" she asked. I could feel the weight of something behind the question, but I didn't know what it was yet. But it made me uneasy.

"I'm not sure."

"What do you mean, you're not sure? You were there, right?"

"Not exactly. She'd left by then. She left and took me with her. And then my father found us and took me back. And then she came and visited me for a while. And then she didn't visit for a long time, so I asked where she was. And he told me she'd died."

"But not till you asked."

"Right."

"And he didn't tell you what she died of."

"I don't think so." I could feel my uneasiness like something alive in my stomach. Growing up too fast in too small a space.

By now we had turned the corner and come out of the park and back onto the street, and we stood waiting at the stoplight in silence. Delilah always waited for the light to turn, even if there were no cars coming. That's how you could tell she wasn't a New Yorker.

I looked over at her, and her eyebrows were scrunched down, but we still said nothing.

When our building came into sight, she said, "Let me ask you one more thing about it. You ever go to a funeral for your mother?"

"Funeral?"

"Or a memorial or something? Where family and friends get together? Honor her passing?"

"Um. No. There was nothing like that."

She nodded and said nothing.

When we got to the front steps of our building she turned and looked me right in the face. "Come upstairs with me. We'll have a cup of tea. I know, I know. He'll be expecting you. But this is important."

My stomach tied up into a little knot, but I followed her upstairs.

I'D NEVER HAD TEA BEFORE, and at first I wasn't sure I liked it. But I loaded it up with sugar and milk, and then it tasted okay.

"Please just say whatever you're going to say," I said. "Because this is making me really nervous."

She sat down across the kitchen table from me. "If I was you, I'd talk to this Grandma Annie. See what she got to say."

"Why?"

"Because she might not be so crazy like your father says."

"But she thinks my mother is still alive."

"Well?"

I wasn't following. "Well?"

"Maybe she's right. Maybe your mother *is* still alive."

A wave of tiredness struck me. Like I knew she was wrong, but I just didn't have the energy to explain it. What could I say to prove she was wrong? "My mother is dead," I said. "I know she is."

"You know how? Besides the fact that your father said so?"

I thought about it, but I couldn't think of anything else. The only other relative we had was Grandma Annie, and I didn't know it through her. I'd never seen an obituary in the paper or anything. And yet I had always known it was true. Because my father said it. He wouldn't say it if it wasn't true. Would he?

Something started bending around in my brain. I don't know how to describe it. Like the feeling when you hang backward over your bed and look at the world upside down. That same sense of dizziness, that sense of everything being backward, wrong, distorted.

If what she said was true—but I just couldn't feel it was—then I might actually have a mother and be able to see her again. And yet a big part of me wanted it not to be true, because it would mean that everything I'd believed right up until that minute was wrong.

I thought of that amusement park when I was six, where you walked into a room with a slanted floor, but all the furniture is made to look like you're *not* on a slanted floor, so your body doesn't understand why you can't balance.

I tried to explain it to Delilah, and she nodded her head. "Oh, honey, I know. That's why I wanted you upstairs and sitting down. I knew this would mess up your poor tired brain. It's like that movie, I think it was *Singin' in the Rain,* where he dances from the floor right up onto a wall and then on the ceiling, and your brain just can't get it. Oh, but why am I talking to you about that? I know your daddy won't let you see any movies. But, anyway, don't try to think too much about it right now. Maybe your grandma is crazy. Maybe your daddy is lying to you. You can't sit here and figure out the difference. But maybe if you're strong enough to do it, just find that Grandma Annie and hear what she got to say."

I think I nodded, but I could be wrong. I got up and walked back to my own apartment, but my feet felt weird, like I couldn't tell if they were touching the ground or not.

I remembered that I'd left most of that cup of tea sitting on Delilah's kitchen table.

When I got upstairs, my father started right in on me. "You could not have been running that whole time."

"Please leave me alone," I said. "I don't feel good. I'm going to go lie down."

Amazingly, he said nothing. And I went into my room to lie down.

WHEN I WOKE UP, I shot awake. Sat up fast. I was sitting up in bed on top of the covers, with all my clothes on. I turned on a light and looked at the clock. It was after one A.M.

I didn't change my clothes. I didn't brush my hair. I just got up and ran. I just got out of that apartment as fast as I could.

The night air felt cool as I was running through it. I tried to remember the last time I'd felt cool. I mean, other than the unnatural cool of air-conditioning. When I got to the subway stairs, halfway down I felt that cool disappearing. Felt the air turn stuffy and close.

I didn't care. It was where I wanted to be. I just hoped I wasn't too late.

While I was waiting for the train to come, I tried to comb my hair with my fingers. But I had no mirror, nothing to help me see what I was doing, and I don't think I got very far. When I saw the lights of the train coming, I felt like my knees were going to buckle. I was that scared. Why does something this good have to be scary? Which I guess is a strange question, because everything is scary to me. But I guess I expected something like this to be the exception.

Before the train even stopped, I ran the length of it, looking into the lighted cars.

She was there. I saw the back of her hat. She was sitting faced away from me. The train hadn't even stopped yet, so I had to turn and run the other way with it. Then I stood there feeling my own heart pound. Waiting for the doors to open. The longest three seconds of my life. The slowest that time has ever slowed down for me. Waiting for the conductor to open those doors. When he finally did, the sound made me jump. Even though I heard it almost every night.

I ran inside and stood over her, and she looked up. She looked happy to see me. She patted the seat beside her with one hand, and I sat down.

She had something else going on with her face this time. Something different. Her lower lip on one side was swollen, and had a split in it that was only partly scabbed over. I looked away so she wouldn't think I was staring at it.

Then I realized what a ridiculous position I was in. I couldn't talk. I could barely breathe. I was still all out of breath from running. I was wearing clothes I'd slept in for hours. I hadn't brushed my teeth. My hair must have been a pathetic mess.

I looked over at her and tried to smile. She smiled back, and my insides melted again. It didn't feel exactly like hot water this time. More like molten lava. "I'm sorry," I said. But I was so out of breath. I'm not sure she could understand me. "I fell asleep."

Then I caught myself and wondered what the hell I was doing. Talking like we had an appointment or something. Only we did. And we both knew it. But maybe we weren't supposed to talk about it. I didn't know.

She kept looking at me, and I felt unsure of myself, even though she wasn't looking at me like she thought I was a mess. I tried to comb my hair a little with my fingers again. Get it off my face. A feeble attempt.

"I must look like a car wreck," I said. Partly amazed that I was talking to her at all, partly amazed that it all came out so easily.

"No," she said. "You look fine." And she lifted one hand and touched my hair. Brushed it back off my forehead with one big rake of her long fingers. I couldn't move. I think I stopped breathing. "You look nice."

Then she took her hand back and we sat in a kind of stunned silence. At least, I was stunned. I was looking down at the floor of the car, but really looking at her hands. She had beautiful hands, chiseled and not too small, with long fingers. Strong looking. And beautiful arms, at least the part I could see beyond her rolled-up long sleeves. She always wore long sleeves, even in the heat. Well, I don't know why I say always. I'd only seen her three times. But she seemed to wear a lot of clothes for the weather each time.

We sat back, and the train pulled out of the station. After a minute I looked over at her. "What happened to your lip?"

She held up one finger and put it to my lips to shush me. Gently. "Let's not talk tonight," she said. Then she took off her hat and put her head on my shoulder. I wasn't quite sure what to do. It felt weird to just sit there with my hands in my lap. But I wasn't sure if it was okay to put my arm around her. But I wanted to, because I think she wanted comforting.

A minute later she picked up my arm and put it around her shoulder. Ducked under it and set her head on my chest. I was pretty much just numb with shock. Her hat was sitting half on her leg and half on mine. I felt a jiggling in her shoulder, and I thought she was laughing. That's what it felt like. But then I heard a little sniffle, and then I knew.

Now, there's not a lot I'll thank my father for. But I'll thank him for this: He taught me to carry a handkerchief. An actual cloth handkerchief. Gentlemen do, he says. In case you have to cough or sneeze, or offer it to someone who needs a handkerchief. So I always have one in my back jeans pockets, and I offered it to her. I couldn't see her face, but she took it from me.

"That's so sweet," she said. She had a wonderful soft voice.

She was also the second woman to call me sweet in a very short space of time. So maybe I'm sweet. I'm not sure.

"You can keep it," I said. I liked the idea of her taking something of mine with her.

We rode all the way to the end of the line and back, and she didn't talk much. Just sniffled and wiped her face. Just as we came back into the Union Square station, she spoke again. She said, "I don't even know your name."

"Sebastian."

"What do people call you for short?"

What people? I was thinking. But I didn't say that. "I don't really have a nickname."

She thought that over, and nodded. "You should."

"Okay. Where do I get one of those?"

"I'll give you one. But I need time to think. I'll give you one next time I see you." The doors opened. "Like day after tomorrow.

At the bottom of those stairs." She pointed. "So we don't get on different trains."

It was all I could do to ask her why not tomorrow. But I couldn't do that.

"I should go." She got up to leave. She didn't look back this time. She kept her face turned away and walked off. Like she didn't want me to see her cry.

I froze for a minute, then ran after her. Ran out onto the platform. "Wait. You didn't tell me your name."

"Maria," she said over her shoulder.

I just stood there and watched her walk up the stairs. And then I just kept standing there. Staring at the place I'd last seen her. For the most amazing length of time.

Finally I climbed the stairs myself, and walked home. Block after block. Thinking nothing. Just walking in the cool air, saying her name—Maria—over and over again in my head.

Maria | Three

The Tent on the River

I had a dream that I'm ashamed of.

Is that right? To be ashamed of a dream?

Part of me feels like I shouldn't have to be. After all, it's not like you dream something on purpose. You don't *try* to have a particular dream. *It* just sort of has *you*.

But then on the other hand, I feel like I couldn't dream anything unless it was there in my head somewhere to begin with. I know that's what Carl would say. If I was ever stupid enough to tell him about this dream I had. Which I never would be. Never in a million years.

I dreamed that I was living with Sebastian. That guy from the subway. The kids were there, and he was being like a father to them. And it was a family.

But then I woke up and I was really ashamed, because I already have a family. With Carl.

In some ways it seemed even worse than if I dreamed about sex with him. Because sex, that's just one thing. That's just one part of what it means to be with somebody. But being a family and having a life together, that's everything. So I betrayed Carl real bad in my sleep last night.

And, also, besides the betraying part, that's really stupid. I mean, how can the subway guy be a father? He's only around nineteen. Which makes him only twelve years older than C.J. And you can't be a father starting when you're only twelve.

I guess that sounds like the pot calling the kettle black, because I'm only fifteen years older than C.J. But it still seems like a key difference, because nature says you can have a kid when you're fifteen but not when you're twelve. At least, probably not. Anyway, I never heard of such a thing.

And it's a terrible way to betray C.J., too, because Carl is his father and he worships and adores Carl and vice versa. And I can't just slip in a little substitution. You only get one father, whether you figure you got a good deal or not. And C.J. has his already.

I can't believe I have to stay home tonight.

When did riding the subway with this guy get to be the most important thing I have? It seems wrong that something that big could already be true before you even really give it your full attention. I wonder if other people do stuff like that. Or if it's only me.

JUST BEFORE CARL WENT OFF TO WORK that afternoon, I said this to him: "I'm going to go see my sister today." And then I added, just with the same timing I always do, "Unless you want me to wait till your day off and we'll go together."

He snorted. "Yeah, right," he said.

There's a reason it always goes like this. Carl won't ever go see my sister. He can't stand her. He calls her the Vampire, because she's into stuff like numerology and Tarot cards and crystals. Now, what any of that stuff has to do with vampires I will never know. But it doesn't really pay to question Carl about stuff like that. As long as it makes sense in *his* head, it's not likely he will take the time to explain it to you.

He also doesn't like to go over there because he can't stand cats. Just hates them with a passion. He thinks they're all evil, and out to get him. Even if they rub up against him and purr, he still thinks that's the first step in some kind of fatal cat conspiracy. Anyway, Stella has cats. Nine.

Her husband, Victor, is not so thrilled about that, either. Not that he hates cats; he likes them all right. He just figures nine is way too many. Stella tells him it's okay because he doesn't believe like she does that cats have nine lives. So she says that should be pretty much the equivalent of one cat to him.

I think Victor is just tired of arguing about cats. He owns a TV repair shop uptown. He is very successful, repairing people's TVs. He's not home much anyway, so there are really only a few hours a day he has to put up with nine cats.

Anyway, back to Carl. He doesn't want to go to my sister's, but I have to make sure he never thinks he's not welcome to go. If he ever wanted to. Even though he never will. And he doesn't really care if I go, but he never wants me to go anywhere unless I get his special seal of approval first.

"So, I should just go ahead and go by myself while you're at work today?"

"Go. See the Vampire. Why should I care?"

It works every time. You'd think he'd figure it out after all this time. That I'm playing him. But maybe he doesn't notice. Or maybe he doesn't even care. Just so long as I keep playing him exactly the way he wants to be played.

WHEN STELLA OPENED HER FRONT DOOR, just about the first thing she said to me was "You're in trouble." Actually, technically it was the second thing. Right after she said, "Hurry up, shut the door, you're going to let the cats out." There's really only one cat who will try to get out. This big half-wild tom named Leo. But she always talks about Leo like there were ten of him.

"I'm not in trouble. Why would you even say that?"

"Because I know you," she said. "Because it's written all over your face."

Natalie was snoring on my shoulder, and Stella lifted her down and laid her down on the couch. She even wadded up an afghan so Natalie couldn't accidentally roll off.

Stella had her hair up in those double ponytails. What do they call them? Pigtails, I think. They made her look like she was trying to be ten, but actually Stella is over thirty. She's a lot older than me. We were both accidents, me and Stella, and it just so happened that our parents made their two big mistakes a long way apart.

She was still in her pink baby-doll pajamas and blue terry-cloth robe. She tends to wear them all day because she has gained about seventy pounds and refuses to buy bigger clothes. She says she will never lose the weight again if she gives in like that. I think she still has one big caftan she can wear to the market, but I'm not sure.

"I'm fine."

"There's something going on."

"I'm fine."

"Sit down. I'll do your cards and we'll see what's what. You want coffee? I'll just put on a fresh pot of coffee."

"I'M SURPRISED YOU'RE STILL ALIVE," she said. Shuffling the Tarot cards. "I kept thinking Carl was going to kill you when he found out you got fired and didn't tell him for a week."

"He's not that bad."

"He's plenty bad enough."

"He wouldn't kill me."

"Just because he hasn't yet . . . So what did you say to him? Did you cover up the part about the timing on when it happened? Did he hit the ceiling?"

I pulled the stack of cards over to me and started spreading them out on the table, facedown, the way I know from experience I'm supposed to do. So I can choose ten by feel. Which I began doing.

"Oh, my God," Stella said. She sounded genuinely shocked. And Stella and I, we have both seen and heard quite a lot. "You still haven't told him."

"I'm going to," I said. With my stomach burning like I'd swallowed a bunch of acid or lye or something. But I just kept picking cards.

"Oh, my God," she said again. "Oh, my God. Girl, what are you *thinking?*"

"I'm not sure. I think I'm trying not to think. There's just been a lot going on."

It struck me—I swear, for the first time ever—that I had an extra reason now for not telling Carl about getting fired. The minute he found out I lost my job, I'd have to stay home at night. And then I would never see that subway guy again. Sebastian. I knew his name but I couldn't think of him like that. He didn't feel like a Sebastian to me. He needed a different name. Friendlier. Simpler. Like Tony in *West Side Story*, whose name is really Anton, but Tony is better.

I know it sounds almost unbelievably lame that I wouldn't think about that until this exact moment sitting in front of the cards at Stella's place. But my mind is funny like that. It plays all sorts of tricks on me.

Stella turned over a card. It was the Ace of Cups. A big hand coming out of nowhere, like out of a little puff of cloud, with a cup on the upturned palm of it. Like a Holy Grail sort of cup. Overflowing with these four fountains of water. I guess water.

"Well," Stella said. "That fills in a lot about what you're not telling me. Who is he?"

I'm more or less on the fence about this Tarot stuff. I've lived with Carl so long that part of me almost believes like him. Like it's all a bunch of hooey. But then again, Stella is right on the money nearly all the time. And sometimes, even when she's not, I find out later that she really was. I'm thinking maybe that's more about Stella than it is about the cards. It makes more sense that a human being could know so much. I mean, more than a card could know. Maybe she thinks she sees it in the card but really she just knows me so well. After all, she has known me nearly twenty-three years. Or maybe there's something to this, something I can't find it in myself to understand.

"Nobody, really," I said. Even though I was beginning to think he might be a somebody.

"That's not what this card says."

"Okay, what does the card say?" I said it kind of belligerent. Like as soon as she told me I would argue with it. But really I wanted to know.

"It's a card of emotional beginnings."

"Maybe it means that Carl and I are going to fall in love all over again."

"Oh, my God, girl, don't even put a horrible thought like that in my head. I'll have nightmares all night tonight. No. The Ace of Cups is always talking about somebody new."

I kept my eyes down to the table. I was looking at the other nine cards that hadn't been turned over yet. Wondering what all they had to say. Desdemona, one of Stella's two black cats, was sitting on the table staring at the cards with her big gold eyes. She does that a lot. Stella thinks she was a medium in another life.

I said, "Why would you think I would do something so bad?"

"Bad? Bad?" Stella's voice was coming up to its famous screech level. Desdemona leaped off the table and booked it to someplace out of screech range. "Honey, finding somebody new would be the smartest thing you ever did. I swear I thought you'd have been done with that man five or six years ago. You were just a kid, so I gave you maybe a year to come to your senses. Now I'm beginning to think you got no sense."

My eyes jumped up to meet hers, and I know she could tell I was seriously wounded. "That was mean."

"Well, I'm sorry, honey, but I have to speak the truth as I see it. I'm the closest thing to a mother you got left. You have to admit that."

"I can't leave Carl for this guy."

"Why can't you?"

"He's too young. He can't be a father to two kids. To a seven-year-old. He's too young."

"Well, *you* can be a *mother* to a seven-year-old and you're only twenty-two. How old is this guy?"

"I'm not sure, but I think about twenty." Anything that ended with "teen" would just have been too completely humiliating.

"So? Two years. That's no big deal. Did he say he couldn't be a father to two kids?"

"Um. No. Not exactly."

"What did he say?"

I placed my finger on the next card. Thinking I could turn it over. Even though Stella always turns them over. I thought if I could get that card right side up we could talk about something new.

She slapped her hand down on top of mine. Dashing all hopes of turning the next card. "Oh, my God. You haven't told him you have kids. Did you at least tell him about Carl?" I said nothing. Just looked at the table. "Oh, my God, girl. Oh, my God. You have to tell him. You have to tell him right now."

"He'll never want to see me again."

"Then you need to find that out right now. You think those two kids are going to disappear between now and the time you spit it out? You've got to learn to open your mouth, girl. That's the trouble with you. You never say what you need to say. Even though it's true. Even though you know it'll have to come out sooner or later." I felt Natalie's little hand on my thigh. She was still sleepy from her nap. She put her head down on my knee and just stood there, hugging my leg. "You keep getting yourself in all these impossible situations. Even though you know all the time they're impossible. It's like you're trying to pitch a tent on a river or something. Living in all these temporary lands where you just know you can't ever stay."

"I just thought if I got to know him a little better—"

"That he'd hate you for keeping the truth from him for so long? Tell him. Tell him the truth. Live in the truth, girl. Let the chips fall where they may."

Sebastian | Four

The Fire Hose

First I didn't sleep. Then I slept without meaning to. Right in my clothes. But only for a couple of hours. I woke up and it was a little before five, and the place was quiet. I was pretty sure my father wasn't up yet.

I lay on my back in bed thinking about Maria, but then I got this little catch in my stomach, like there was something else in there. Ever have that happen? Like there's something on the tip of your tongue, and you can't quite remember what it is, but you already know it's bad. Then my mind jumped back to tea with milk and sugar, and then I knew.

I wouldn't have done what I did next at any other time in my life. Not one day before I did it. But this was not any other day or any other time in my life. This was right now.

I booted up my computer and opened the Web browser. And then I did a search for Tehachapi, California. That's the little town in the Mojave Desert where Grandma Annie worked. But she lived in a little town that was actually called Mojave, on the other side of the Tehachapi Pass. Of course, I had no way of knowing if she still did. Either one. And I didn't even know the name of the motel, but I hoped I'd remember it if I saw it. So if I could just act like a tourist and look up lodging in that town, maybe something would strike me.

I hit the first link to come up, and what I saw moved through me like a rush, like a flash flood. Like the fire hoses they used to use to knock down protesters on the street.

It was a picture of the windmills on Tehachapi Pass. Hundreds and hundreds and hundreds of windmills. Spilling up and down the sides of these mountains. All exactly alike, but staggered by their placement on each slope. They're not like the old-fashioned windmills you see in books about Holland. They're very modern, streamlined and grayish-white. Three long, clean blades each. And whole sections of them would spin at once while other sections held still.

Now, of course, the picture on the Internet didn't tell me that some spin while some hold still. I knew that on my own. Because I had seen them with my own eyes.

It came back in a big rush, like I said.

I guess I must've been five or six, and I was riding in the back seat of the car, and my mother was up front in the passenger seat, and she said, "Sebastian, see the windmills?"

I had been looking at her face, but when she said that, I looked out the window. But I couldn't see them. So she took off my seat belt and pulled me up front with her, and sat me down on her lap, and put her seat belt around both of us. And then I looked up, and there they were. Hundreds and hundreds of windmills.

"They make electricity," she said.

"How?" I wanted to know.

"They make it out of the wind. They take the wind on this mountain pass and turn it into electricity. What do you think of the windmills, Sebastian?"

"I like them." Which, as I recall, was a huge understatement. But I was only five or six.

"When we see Grandma Annie, tell her what you thought of the windmills, okay?"

And while she said that, she was running a hand through my hair. And then, a minute later, rubbing my back a little bit.

I started to cry.

No, not there in the car when I was little. I was happy then. I started to cry right there in front of my computer. I couldn't even see the link that said, "A helpful guide to hotels, motels, inns" until I'd gotten a few tears out of my system, and out of my eyes. I had to get up and get a fresh handkerchief out of my drawer, because I'd given the one in my pocket to Maria.

After a while I hit the helpful guide link, right through the tears. There were only seven listings. I ran my eye down the list, and when I saw the Tehachapi Mountain View Inn, I knew right away. I didn't have to wonder. I remembered it as surely as I remembered the windmills, and my mother rubbing my back. And then when I thought about my mother rubbing my back, I started to cry all over again.

I WROTE MY LETTER to her in pen, on stationery. Not on the computer. It's one of those things like carrying a cloth handkerchief. My father taught me that's what gentlemen do.

Here's what I said, because I was feeling emotional, and there was a lot I just wasn't prepared to go into right then.

Dear Grandma Annie,

I know it's been a long time since I've written to you or you've written to me. But I just want you to know that I forgive you for not writing. It's been a long time, and I can understand how you could forget all about me. In case you don't forgive me for not keeping in touch, I have to tell you that my father strictly forbids it. So I'm doing this behind his back. So please don't do anything to get me in trouble. Not to sound wimpy, but I have to live with him. If you want to write to me, please write to me at the same address as always, the one on this envelope, only

instead of our apartment number, 5J, please send it care of Ms.
Delilah Green in apartment 3B. She's my friend and she'll make
sure I get your letter, and then he'll never have to know. I want
to ask you some questions, mostly about my mother.

Very Truly Yours,
Your Grandson,
Sebastian Mundt

Then I sealed it into an envelope and addressed it to her care of
the Tehachapi Mountain View Inn, where I hoped she still worked,
and then I sat alone in my room until I heard my father get up.

MY LESSONS THAT DAY were a disaster. Right from the start. I couldn't
concentrate. My head felt hollow, and sore inside, like too many
things had been banging around in there. Like the jumble of
thoughts from the last few days had all been sharp, dangerous
objects. Maybe they were.

My father wanted me to behave just the way I always did. No
way to have an off day. That's him in a nutshell, actually. No toler-
ance for any kind of change.

He finally broke down and called me stupid. Well, he said I was
stupid today. He said, "I can't stand this another minute. You're
just stupid today. With all I invest in making you smarter and more
educated, all of a sudden you're just falling down a well of stu-
pidity."

I was pretty deeply insulted, but I didn't yell at him, because all
hell breaks loose when I do. I didn't want to have to live with the
fallout. I felt like I couldn't take it. Not today.

So I just said, "I'm sorry."

"Sorry isn't good enough," he said.

That's when I lost it. I actually shouted at him. Shouted. I said,
"I need a break. I need a goddamn break. Kids who go to school
get breaks. Easter, Christmas, summer. They get to rest. I need to

rest. You work me too hard. You're killing me with this, don't you see it?"

I almost never swore in front of him, because I was not allowed to. And I expected to get leveled for that. But he seemed to let it go by. Instead he shouted back and said don't put this off on him when he was sacrificing everything for me and I was the one screwing up.

And I shouted that anybody would screw up under this kind of pressure.

And he shouted, What pressure? What did I have to do that was so hard? And why was I always able to do it until just now, all of a sudden? And why was I refusing to admit that something was different with me? And what was going on, anyway?

I shouted, "I just have a lot on my mind, is all."

And then the room went deadly silent and I thought, Oh, crap. Now I've done it. I really stuck my foot in it now.

His voice went weirdly calm. Artificially calm. "So, tell me what's on your mind."

"No."

More deadly silence. I thought I could see something throbbing in his temples. "Why not?"

"Because it's *my* mind. Not yours."

Yeah, I know. What was I thinking? But I just couldn't take it anymore. Besides, I felt like I had nothing to lose. Usually I avoided saying things like that to keep the peace. Today there was no peace to keep.

I waited for him to say something. But it was almost as though he was too upset to form words.

I said, "What are you going to do when I'm eighteen? When I turn eighteen, I can walk out that door and never come back, and there's nothing you can do about it."

"And go where?" he shouted. "And do what? You have no idea how to function in that world out there. You have no idea what it's like."

I shook my head. Under my breath I said, "And whose fault is that?"

"What did you say?"

I just shook my head again, and headed for the door.

"What did you say to me, Sebastian?"

My hand on the knob.

"Sebastian! I forbid you to walk out that door!"

I walked out the door. Slammed it behind me. I guess I'd finally had enough.

Then, about ten steps down the hall, I turned around and went back in.

"Ah," I heard him say. "I knew you'd see the light."

I didn't answer. I walked into my room, got the letter to Grandma Annie out from its hiding place under my computer keyboard. Stuck it in my pocket. Then I walked out again. Never looked at him or said a word. This time, I slammed the door even louder.

DELILAH SWUNG HER DOOR OPEN, took one look at my face, and threw her arms around me.

"Child, child," she said. I could feel her hands on my back. Why hadn't anybody ever touched me until now? Up until a few days ago, I couldn't remember the last time anybody had touched me. "Come tell me all about it. You want to go for a walk? Or you want to sit here?"

"Let's walk," I said.

And she hobbled off to get her cane from beside the refrigerator.

"I don't know what he wants from me," I said. Trying not to cry. I'd be humiliated to cry in front of Delilah.

"Whatever he's not getting from his own life," she said. "Whatever big hole people got in their heart, they want something to fill it up. That's what he wants from you. But he'll never get it. Because you can't ever fill a hole in you with somebody else. But everybody keeps trying, though, even though it never brings nothing but heartache to both parties." She came hobbling back with her cane in one hand, her geisha fan in the other. "Now let's go walk it off," she said. "You'll feel better."

I took the letter out of my pocket and showed it to her. I said, "We'll have to get a stamp while we're out, and mail this. But I wanted to get your permission first. To use your address." She read the envelope and seemed to get the message.

"Oh, child!" she said, breathless with pleasure. "There's hope for you yet. I got you a stamp, right here."

"I WANT TO SEE A MOVIE," I said.

She said, "Well, that shouldn't be hard. What one you wanta see?"

We had just turned the corner onto Lexington Avenue. I could see the mailbox on the next block. It looked more important and more dangerous and more frightening and more attractive than anything else on the street. Anything else in the world.

"I want to see the one where the guy dances on the walls."

"Oh, yeah. I think it was *Singin' in the Rain*. Unless it was *Anchors Aweigh*. Or *Royal Wedding*. But no, I don't think Donald O'Connor was in *Royal Wedding*. And I'm pretty sure it was Donald O'Connor dancing on the walls. Unless it was Fred Astaire. Or Gene Kelly. No, it was Donald O'Connor. In *Singin' in the Rain*."

"Do you have that one?" I could see the mailbox getting closer. It looked even more dangerous close up.

"No, but we could stop at that video store and rent it."

"Let's do that."

"But, you know, child, I'm not sure that's really the movie you want to see. It's an old musical, with dancing, from the fifties, before you was even born. Don't you want to see something from this century?"

"What's it about?"

"Oh, it's a love story."

"I want to see that one, then," I said.

"Okay. Whatever you say."

"Her name is Maria."

"Well, that's some kinda progress. You gonna see her again?"

"Not tonight. Tomorrow night." We stopped in front of the mailbox. I just stood there, staring at it. Like we were about to face off in a duel. "I think she's in some kind of trouble. She was crying. And twice she's had a bruise or something on her face."

Delilah leaned on the mailbox, fanned herself, and sighed. "Well, child, I'd tell you to be careful, except for two things. One, it wouldn't do any good anyhow. And two, I think we tell each other that too much. Be careful. Don't get hurt. Don't take chances. Don't try anything. Don't feel. Might as well be telling each other not to be alive at all. Boils down to the same thing." She waited, but I didn't say anything. Just stared at the mailbox. "You okay?"

"Never been better," I said. I opened the box and dropped it in. Gone forever. Too late to take back. Done, and could never be un-done. I had done it now. "Now let's go rent that movie," I said.

IT WAS FUNNY. The movie. I knew it was going to be about love, but I didn't know it was funny. It was about this big famous Hollywood actor, played by Gene Kelly, who met the love of his life when he jumped into her car to get away from this mob of his fans. They were tearing at his clothes, and he yelled for help to his friend, the Donald O'Connor guy. He said, "Call me a cab," and Donald O'Connor said, "Okay, you're a cab."

I just cracked up laughing. Not just once either. Every time I thought about it again, it cracked me up.

Delilah was giving me this look.

"What?" I said.

"That is the oldest joke in the world."

"Not if you've never heard it before."

"Well, that's true. Besides, it's nice to hear you laugh. I'm not sure I ever heard you laugh before."

"I'm not sure *I* ever heard me laugh before, either." If so, I'd forgotten it now.

Then Donald O'Connor did this wonderful, funny dance. He was singing a song called "Make 'Em Laugh," and the dance part was funny. He was in a movie studio, with guys carrying boards around, and he kept banging his head into them as he danced. And dancing circles lying on the floor, and over couches, and running into brick walls, and I just kept laughing. Then he danced right up a wall about three steps and flipped all the way over and landed on his feet and then did the same thing on the other wall.

"Is that the part you were telling me about?"

"Oh, no, this is the wrong movie. It just hit me. That wasn't Donald O'Connor who did that, it was Fred Astaire. And he actually danced up there, a long time, not just three steps. I'll have to figure out what movie that was again."

"How'd they do it?"

"Tell you later, after you've seen it. Want to turn this off?"

"No! I want to see the end of this. I like this."

So Delilah made microwave popcorn while I watched Gene Kelly close up his umbrella and do a song and dance in the pouring rain, after kissing the girl he loved for the first time.

"You sure you like this?" Delilah asked. "It's awful old."

"I love it."

And I really did. It was silly. I wasn't allowed silly. It was about love, and it made you laugh. Two more things you don't get at my house. It had absolutely no educational value. No real purpose, except entertainment. So it was the perfect entertainment. It was unlike anything I had ever seen in my life.

It was my first vacation I could remember, all in itself.

WHEN I GOT HOME, my father was sitting in his chair. Staring straight ahead. Not reading, not listening to music. Just sitting.

"I'm not even going to ask you where you've been," he said.

"Good."

"But I was thinking, you *do* work awfully hard on your studies. Maybe a little spring break would do you a world of good. Maybe you'd even make better progress in the long run."

I stopped and looked right at him, but he wouldn't meet my eyes. "Thank you, Father, that was thoughtful of you to decide that."

Putting the day to rest once and for all.

It had never occurred to me—before that exact moment—that if *I* refused to give an inch, *he* would have to.

Maria | Four

Surprises

Carl surprised me by coming home from work early. About seven-thirty. I'd been home from Stella's for a couple of hours. But it really hit me hard.

First of all, any surprise from Carl is hard. The more things go just according to plan in this house, the better. Second of all, he had this big smile on his face. Like this was some big happy surprise. But I couldn't help wondering if this was his way of reminding me that he could show up anywhere, anytime. Carl has this way of delivering a couple of different messages—or more—all at one time.

"What are you doing home?" I asked. Trying to sound like it was a good thing.

"It's a surprise. I got a half day off work. Just for you. I'm taking you out on a date. Just like the old days. Like we used to do before the kids. Just the two of us. It'll be very romantic. I thought we'd go to that steak house we went to on our anniversary."

"Just the two of us?"

"Yup. Just the two of us."

"We can't just leave the kids alone."

"And that's another surprise. I got us a babysitter."

This was one of those moments when my stomach starts doing

acrobatics. Somersaults and loop-the-loops and some kind of aerial spins but I have to try to hide it. When Carl says he has a happy surprise, you do not want to rain on that parade. Things can take a bad turn real fast. But Natalie and a babysitter was just not going to work out.

"What babysitter?"

"The girl the McCrimmons use."

The McCrimmons were our neighbors two doors down the hall.

"But we don't even know her."

"But *they* know her. They've been using her for years."

"But Natalie doesn't know her."

"Natalie will be fine."

But it was clear by the way he said it that he knew perfectly well she wouldn't be.

He knew it just as well as I did. But he had made up his mind that she *should* be fine. So he was going to twist the world around to be what he wanted. He was going to insist that she be exactly what he thought she ought to be.

"I've never left her." She needs me.

"My point exactly. It's time."

So, it was time. If Carl said it was time, it was time. But, oh my God. This was going to be bad. This was going to be fifteen different kinds of bad. Maybe more.

CARL ORDERED US a bottle of wine.

I was trying not to fidget.

I said, "First a cab, now a bottle of wine. What'd you do, rob a bank or something?"

It made me kind of sick to see so much money fly away. In a couple of weeks I'd have to break it to Carl that C.J. was outgrowing his shoes. And Carl would say he'd have to wear them a little longer, because he isn't made of money. It made me sick to see all this money go for something I didn't even want.

"Just relax and enjoy it," he said.

But I wasn't relaxed. I wasn't enjoying it. And he knew that. And it was starting to tick him off. I was supposed to be having a good time. So I tried to pretend like I was. But I was just about to jump out of my skin, thinking of poor Natalie at home, wailing. She'd wailed and hung on to my leg until I was all the way out the door. Carl had to peel her off me. The girl he got to babysit wasn't strong enough. Or brave enough. I could hear her all the way down the hall. Until we were in the elevator and starting to go down. Carl kept looking at my face, like a reminder that I wasn't allowed to feel what I was feeling.

In fact, he was still doing that as we drank our wine.

If I knew Natalie like I figured I did, she would be losing her voice right about now, or at least very soon.

It was all I could do to just hold still. I have never had a harder time staying in a place, in a moment, in as long as I can remember. I think even life with my father was better than this.

Natalie should have had more practice before I left her alone.

Meanwhile Carl took my hand and was looking into my eyes. Or trying, anyway. I wanted to take my hand back. I felt like it was on a hot stove. I let him keep it, but it was torture. I was trying not to think about the subway guy. So of course, whatever you try not to think about, that's all you can think about. Everything else disappears, except for that one thing you don't want.

"Look," Carl said, "I'm not spending all this money so you can sit there and be a million miles away. That's not why we're doing this."

"Why are we doing this?" That was a brave question. So I followed up real quick by saying, "Not that it's not nice. It's really nice. I just wondered."

He still had my hand. It still took every ounce of everything I had to not fidget. I tried not to think about Sebastian. I tried not to think about Natalie wailing. I wondered if Sebastian was the kind of guy who would go get takeout as a surprise. Because he would know it would be too hard on me—and on her—to leave her alone.

Ho. There's a stupid thought. If he even knew there was such a thing as Natalie he would run like the wind. What an imagination I have.

Carl said, "Lately I feel like we're not close. Not like we used to be."

"We're close," I said. Trying to hold still. Trying not to take my hand back.

"Not like we used to be."

"We're fine," I said.

"Look," he said, "I know it's hard for you. Don't think I don't know that. Working a job and then taking care of two little kids while you're off. It's a lot of work. I know that. That's why I wanted to give you this little vacation."

"Thank you," I said. Gearing up to lie big. "It's very nice."

A long silence, during which I mostly willed him to let go of my hand. He didn't.

Then he said, "I'd be nothing without you. I couldn't live without you. I need you. You know that, right?"

I didn't answer. I didn't know how to answer a thing like that. What do you say to a thing like that? I didn't know.

"Well? Do you know that or don't you?"

I was looking down at the table. Not into his face. Which I know is wrong. Bad. But looking up would not have been a good plan either. "I know I'm important to you," I said.

"I don't want to have to be afraid of losing you," he said. "It has to be like it was before."

"It is. It is like it was before."

"Okay. Okay, good."

He let go of my hand, thank God.

We said very little else for the rest of the meal. Every now and then, I looked up at him and smiled a little. That seemed to be enough for him. I guess because he really wanted it to be.

He insisted on having dessert, which nearly killed me.

WE ENDED UP WALKING the twelve blocks home. After getting a look at the check, Carl decided that the weather was nice and we needed more exercise anyway.

He was also finding more and more reasons to slow us down. The more he could see how bad I wanted to get home to Natalie, the more he came up with new ideas.

"The market is only two blocks out of our way," he said. "Want to stop in and say hi to the gang?"

Now, that is a very many-layered question.

By the market, he meant my work. The market where I used to work. And where he thought I still did. But he didn't like the people I used to work with, and he never, ever called them "the gang." There was just no real reason for him to make a suggestion like that one. Except for the hidden ones.

First off, he was challenging me not to rush home to Natalie. That's just an obvious one off the top.

Secondly, he might have had some kind of suspicion regarding something around my work. I don't think he'd guessed that I got fired. If he had even suspected I was having experiences on the subway at night instead of going to the market, believe me, I'd know it. That would hit the fan very big. But I do think he might have thought I was having something going on at work, like a customer or some new employee I was getting overly close with. He was reading me to some degree.

All this happened in my head very fast, just in a split second before I said, "No! God, no!"

"Why not?"

"Because it's my night off. Why would I want to go to work on my night off? Would you want to go to work on your night off?"

"I guess not," he said. And I started breathing again. Then he said, "What's with your paycheck?"

I knew this was my moment. Either tell him now or go into bald-faced-lie mode. So far I hadn't exactly lied to him. I'm pretty sure. I just hadn't volunteered the truth. Beyond this moment I'd be lying to his face.

I opened my mouth to speak and thought about Sebastian. Pictured him. What he looked like and how he felt. Not how he felt physically, but more like how I knew he was. Like the kind of guy who would go out and get takeout for a surprise.

"It's just delayed."

"They're always good about paying you on time."

"That's why I thought I should be patient this one time."

"What's the delay?"

"I forget. Danny explained it but I forgot just what he said."

"A few more days and I'm going to call them. Get the story."

"No. Please don't do that."

"Why not?"

"It's embarrassing. You should let me take care of it myself."

"But you don't. I know you. You don't take care of things. You're always afraid to speak up."

"I will if I need to."

"A couple of days and it will be time."

"Okay. Okay, already. Let's just walk home."

"SEE?" CARL SAID as we stood outside our door. "She stopped fussing."

Fussing was a bit of an understatement to describe what she'd been doing.

"I guess," I said.

When we opened the door, the babysitter was already halfway there, rushing to greet us. She looked like she'd been though a couple of car accidents and maybe a small war. And as soon as the door was open, I could hear Natalie. She was still wailing, but now it was just coming out as a hoarse little croak. She had wailed herself into full-on laryngitis. She had not been about to stop until I came home. If I had stayed away two hours longer, she would have wailed her near-silent wail for another two hours, easy.

I went in to her and held her and lay on her little youth bed with her, where I don't really fit. And told her I was sorry. Very quietly. So that Carl, who was out paying the poor frazzled babysitter, couldn't possibly hear.

She went silent, her thumb in her mouth and her other tiny hand holding a piece of my shirt sleeve with surprising strength. I listened to the wet sounds of her thumb-sucking, and to the easy breathing of C.J., asleep in his bed on the other side of the room.

A few minutes later, Carl stuck his head in the door.

"You spoil her too much," he said.

I said nothing.

"We're going to stop spoiling her so much," he said.

"Look, I'm trying to get her down, okay?"

He stepped out, closing the door behind him. I breathed deeply, knowing our date night was finally over.

Natalie fell asleep in a matter of a couple of minutes. But I stayed with her, on that tiny uncomfortable bed, until I was sure Carl must be asleep.

The Anvil

For some reason I got it into my head that we'd fly into each other's arms. You know, see each other across a crowded platform and run in seeming slow motion. I guess I'd been watching too many old movies. Well, one. But my father would've called that one too many, I guess.

The real scene was a little less dramatic. I was sitting on a bench, my back snug up against the slats. Just for a minute I'd looked away from the direction of the stairs. Then I looked up, and she was standing over me. Smiling, but shyly.

She said, "Hi, Tony."

My heart just fell. I thought, She doesn't even remember my name. Here I've been thinking I actually meant something to her, and she doesn't even know my name.

I think she saw my face fall. I thought I saw my own disappointment reflected back to me in the mirror of her face.

"It's Sebastian," I said.

She just kept smiling. "No, silly. I said I'd give you a nickname. Remember?" She sat down next to me, purposely bumping her shoulder against mine. "I know it's not exactly short for Sebastian. Then again, what is? But it's still the right one for you. And I'll tell you why. Because of that movie, *West Side Story.* My mother named me Maria because of the Natalie Wood character in that movie. And Tony was the name of the boy. So, that's us. Tony and Maria."

I just sat there, looking at her eyes. They were so dark I was wondering if they were actually black. Or just really dark brown. And underneath that I was thinking how handicapped I was, not knowing about all these movies that everyone else seemed to know. So I just nodded, like it was all very fascinating. Which it was. While another part of me was wondering how old she was, and if she thought I was older than I actually was. Because I'm tall. And whether she would lose interest altogether if I told her the truth.

"So, is that okay?" she asked.

"What?"

"If I call you Tony?"

"Oh. Yeah. That's great." It sounded like a compliment. I couldn't wait to find out.

Then she said, "Walk with me, okay?"

She got up and held out her hand and I took it. I could feel a jolt of current run up my arm, like she was plugged into a high-voltage wall socket. I wondered if she felt the same thing the same way. I got up, and we walked up the exit stairs and out into the cool Manhattan night. Holding hands.

The city at night is actually more comforting than the subway at night. It's anything but deserted. At least, in that neighborhood. There are so many people out on the street, it's almost like broad daylight. Just darker. Everything is open. Everything functions pretty much the same.

I watched people walk by us. Pass us going the other way, or overtake us and pass in the same direction. We weren't walking very fast. They looked at us the way people look at each other on the street: not for long. Just looked, then looked away. It struck me that they accepted what they saw. They looked at Sebastian and Maria—Tony and Maria, I mean—and saw us as a couple, walking down the street holding hands.

I noticed that she glanced a lot at the ground in front of her, and stepped carefully, like she was worried about tripping over something. But I didn't ask and I couldn't find it in myself to care.

I got this feeling in my chest like my heart was getting bigger and bigger, until it almost hurt. I kept thinking in a minute it wasn't going to fit. That my chest would rupture or explode.

I looked up at the sky, and it was clouded over. It had been cloudy all day. All of a sudden I wished it would rain. All of a sudden I felt like Gene Kelly. I wanted to get soaked in the pouring rain like an idiot, and break into a song and dance instead of running for cover. I actually wanted to dance in the rain. I felt that good. And I don't even dance.

"I'm hungry," she said. "The vendors are still out. Not sure why, but I thought maybe we could get a hot dog."

She indicated the hot dog vendor on the next corner with a flip of her chin.

My stomach turned to ice.

I had never, not once, not in my entire life, eaten food sold on the street. My father had convinced me that you would pretty much clutch your stomach and die on the spot. To him it was about the equivalent of jumping in front of the cross-town bus. Somewhere in my head I knew people must eat hot dogs and survive. Then again, I figured they were sick for days with food poisoning, off in a place where I couldn't see them.

I said, "Have you eaten hot dogs from a vendor before?" Trying not to sound too unsure.

"Yeah, lots of times. Why?"

"No reason."

If Maria wanted a hot dog, Tony was going to get her one.

We walked right up to that cart like we owned the world. On the outside. On the inside, I hated to even have to tell a stranger what I wanted. And I sure didn't want to die young.

Maria said, "Two with everything."

I paid for two. Praying that meant she was hungry enough to eat two. The guy spoke very little English, but he seemed to understand "Two with everything." I guess you'd have to, in his business. He heaped two hot dogs with mustard and ketchup and relish and onions, and handed one to each of us.

We started walking again, but of course we needed both hands to hold the hot dogs, which seemed like losing ground. And she was looking over at me, waiting for me to take a bite. So I took a deep breath, and I did. It was good! It was really, really good. Not like the soups and stews my father made, night after night. Organic vegetables and free-range chicken. You are what you eat. He actually says that. Often.

I thought, *Okay. So I'm a New York all-beef frank with everything. Named Tony. And I have no regrets. Because it's so entirely better than what I was before.*

I ate the whole thing in about six bites. I didn't feel sick. I felt wonderful.

And even though in my head I knew it takes a while for food poisoning to strike, I somehow instinctively knew it wouldn't. Once again, my father was just wrong.

I vowed to try even more forbidden experiences.

She finished her hot dog a little slower than I did. We threw the papers and the napkins into a trash can as we walked by. Then we walked on and I felt her hand slip back into mine.

I felt another electric shock, but this time it was different. Deeper and mellower. Not something that would make you jump. More just something you'd feel and then smile.

"I know I don't really know you," she said. "But I feel like I can trust you."

"You can."

"I should have answered your question. I know you asked out of caring. I should've answered. I'm sorry. I was afraid if I told you, you'd never want to see me again. I still am. Afraid. That you'll never want to see me again."

I could feel the shift in the energy of the conversation. I searched my brain trying to remember what question I had asked her that she hadn't answered. I could feel her looking over at the side of my face, so I looked back. She still had a little line of scab on her lower lip.

Oh. Right. That question.

"There's nothing you could tell me that would make me not want to see you again."

"Nothing? Promise?"

"Well, unless you savagely murder people for fun or something."

"No. I never killed anybody."

"Then whatever it is, I'd still want to see you."

"Promise?"

That actually caught in my stomach for a split second. Because it could be anything. It could be something awful. But of course I said, "Promise."

"Okay. But remember, you promised. The reason I had some bruises on my face . . . and that I wear long sleeves . . . and that I ride up and down the Lexington line at night . . ."

There was a long pause. I was thinking, Long sleeves? It was a disjointed thought, I guess. But I'd never dreamed that the long sleeves were part of the picture. I waited in agony for her to go on. I felt like there was an anvil teetering over my head. Just in the process of being dropped out a window.

". . . is because of Carl."

Bang. The anvil landed. On me. Direct, painful hit. Good shot.

"Carl?"

"Yeah. The guy that I . . . you know . . ." I didn't want to know. I wanted to beg her not to tell me, but it was too late. ". . . live with."

I stopped walking. She stopped walking. I looked at her face but she wouldn't look at me. She was looking down at the sidewalk. I was vaguely aware of people spilling around the obstacle of us. But only vaguely.

I can't tell you what I was thinking here. Nothing, I guess. The anvil had knocked out every thought on its way through. Now it was lodged firmly in my stomach. Where I figured it would sit for the rest of my life.

"He kind of loses his temper. But it's partly my fault. You know, if I could just stay out of his way. If I wouldn't always say the wrong thing at the wrong time. He comes home from work at eleven. And he hates his job. So until he settles down . . . you know . . . unwinds . . . that's a good time to be somewhere else. So usually I'm on the subway. And then things are okay. Pretty much. Usually. Pretty much okay."

I looked at her face again. She still wouldn't look at me. But I saw a last little trace of the bruise on her cheek, and the line of scab on her lip. And then for the first time I noticed a couple of old scars. One near her eyebrow and one on her chin.

It seemed like a weird definition of pretty much okay. But I didn't say so. I didn't say anything. I'm not sure I could have. Even if I'd tried.

She looked up at me suddenly, and it surprised me. "So what about you?"

"What *about* me?"

"Why do *you* ride the Lexington line at night? Who are *you* running away from?"

I had trouble getting my head to take the sudden turn. The news that she lived with some guy named Carl was like an eclipse of the brain, blocking out everything else. When I finally hauled my mind around to her question, I realized I didn't want her to know the answer. I was afraid to tell her *my* secret, too. That I was under the thumb of my father because I was only seventeen. Just a minor, a kid. Not even in control of my own life. It seemed almost as horrible as her secret. I thought, *If I tell her, she'll never want anything to do with me ever again.*

"Oh, come on," she said. "After what I told you, how bad could it be?"

"Why don't you leave him?" I asked. The words came out too

strong. Too angry. I wanted to grab them back again. Pull them back in and erase that history.

"And go where? And do what? I've been with him since I was fifteen. I don't know where else I would go."

I wanted to have an answer for that. Wanted it badly. And I wanted to be part of the answer. But nothing came. I couldn't exactly sneak her into my room and hope my father wouldn't notice. And I didn't know anyplace else *I* could go, either.

She said, "You didn't answer my question. Who are you trying to stay away from?"

"My father."

"Oh. Couldn't you move out?"

"Well. Yeah. I guess." But the truth had to come out. Sooner or later. She'd told me her truth. Because she trusted me. And now I had to trust her in return. "When I'm eighteen."

If she was shocked, she didn't let on. "How long will that be?"

"Almost four months."

"Well, that's not so bad. You can sit on the Lexington line for four months, I guess."

Then we started back up walking, and she took my hand again. I thought I saw her glance over, to see what my face was doing. But I'm not positive. I didn't look back.

Out of all the dark clouds in the sky, I felt like the darkest one was sitting about six inches over my head. My own personal disaster, raining on me everywhere I went.

We walked for a long time like that, in silence. I didn't know what she was thinking and I didn't ask. I don't even know what *I* was thinking. But my earlier thought about the anvil in my stomach was correct. It wasn't going away. Maybe not ever. And it wasn't the hot dog, either. It was definitely not the hot dog. It was definitely Carl.

After a while I saw the subway sign, and the stairs, and I realized she had walked me back so I could catch the train home.

I said, "You've been with this guy for seven years . . ."

"Almost eight."

"How come you never got married? If you've been together so long, why did you not get married?" I was hoping, I guess, that there might somehow be good news hidden in the answer.

"Carl thinks marriage is a crock."

"And what do you think?"

I could tell by her silence, and by the look on her face, that she wasn't used to being asked to share her opinion.

"I'm not sure. I guess I'll have to think about that. So . . . day after tomorrow?" I noticed a little unsteadiness in her voice. We both knew it was a very important question.

I reached for an answer but my brain just felt blank. Black. Just all black.

"Yes," I heard myself say. "Day after tomorrow."

She stretched up onto her toes and kissed me on the cheek and I closed my eyes. I was hoping there would be more, I think. But then I opened my eyes and she had gone.

I WANTED TO STOP at Delilah's apartment, even though it was the middle of the night. Well, it was two-thirty. That's the middle of the night to most people. I'd never asked Delilah what time she goes to bed. But I knew she must have by now.

I didn't take the elevator. I climbed the stairs, three floors. Got to her floor and walked down the hall to 3B and stood there in front of the door, not knowing what to do. I would've given anything to talk to her. Anything. Twenty years off my life. My computer. My time outside the house running. Just for an hour of her time.

I would have given anything to be the kind of person who could rap on her door at this hour, and when she answered say, "I'm sorry. It's late, I know. I know I woke you, and I'd never do that lightly. But this is just really important."

I'm not that guy, and we all know it.

I walked up to her door and pressed my whole body up against it. Pressed my ear to it. It felt cool and hard against my face. I prayed to hear something. The quiet drone of the TV. A toilet flushing.

All was silent.

I let go of the door and walked two more flights up to my own apartment.

I never even bothered going to bed, because I knew I wouldn't sleep. I just sat by the window, looking out at my tiny piece of world. No thoughts ran patterns in my head. I had no thoughts. Just a kind of blank heaviness. A patch of black that filled up my whole brain.

It was a long night.

"I DON'T KNOW WHAT TO DO," I said. Probably more than once.

I was sitting slumped over on Delilah's couch. Having already said everything about the situation I knew how to say. Knowing in advance I would sacrifice my whole running time. My whole outdoors time. Not that it was much of a sacrifice right now. Just walking down two flights to her apartment had been something like climbing Mount Everest.

"Well, I could tell you what *I* would do," she said.

"Okay. Yeah." That's really what I needed from Delilah. She'd obviously gotten a look at the rule book on life. The one my father had carefully kept from me.

"No, never you mind," she said. "You'd think I was nuts."

I looked up at her. Maybe for the first time this visit. She was bustling around in the kitchen. I mean, as much as Delilah bustles. Making iced tea. From scratch, of course. Unwrapping tea bags while she waited for the kettle to boil. It was just too muggy and hot to drink hot tea out of a cup. More than either one of us could manage. After a moment of silence, she looked back at me. Saw I'd been watching her.

"I would never think that," I said. She just smiled. "You're the least crazy person I know." She shot me a sarcastic look. "Okay, granted, I don't know a lot of people. But you're saner than my father."

"Honey, he don't set the bar all that high."

"But you're happy. You don't have to know lots of people really well to know that most of them aren't happy. You're happy. So I want to hear your advice."

She hobbled over and sat on the couch next to me. Patted my knee hard. We could hear rustling from the kettle, like it was about to whistle any minute. But she just ignored that.

"If I was unhappy like you are now, here's what I'd do. Now just listen and try to take this in. Might not make much sense when it first hits your ears. When life just cuts me to ribbons and bloodies me and knocks me down, I go out of doors into nature. Now that's gonna be hard for you, where you live. If you could get to the ocean, that would be great. But I don't guess you can. But, you know, even the stars are good enough. Except, I suppose you don't see many stars in the city, because the city lights wash 'em out. But I guess you see some, don't you? And even if you don't, there's the moon. The moon'll do. See, you're looking for something that's not man-made. And you won't get it indoors. Everything indoors we invented. No bigger powers involved. But we didn't make the stars nor the moon. Or trees or oceans or rivers, and we never could. Never will. That's how come you know something bigger's at work. So, look at that proof of something big. Breathe it in. And then here's what you say. You say, 'Thank you for my life.'"

I just sat there, slumped on the couch. Confused. The kettle started to whistle, and she got up to tend to it.

"Why? Why would you say that if you're so miserable?"

"That's exactly why. Because you're miserable. It's like, if you love somebody. When they hurt you or let you down, you let 'em know you still love them. That's called unconditional love. Anybody can love somebody when they're making you happy. That requires no special talent. That's also how most people do it. But when you get a little wiser, you know you got to love somebody with all their faults. So, if you can do that with a person, what about your own life? This is like unconditional love for your own life."

I could hear the ice cracking and popping as she poured hot tea over it.

"And then, after I say thank you for my life, then what?"

"Then you keep going. Keep living. You wake up every day and get dressed and brush your teeth and see what life has in mind for you next."

I wondered if, when I looked at Maria tomorrow night, I could love her in spite of Carl. Which, let's face it, was a pretty big fault.

I guess the better question was, could I *stop* loving her because of it?

In other words, did I really have any options?

THAT NIGHT I WENT OUT into the street after dark. After my father had gone to bed.

I looked up at the sky, hoping to see the moon. Not that I knew what I would have said to it. I just wanted to at least do the first part. See and feel something bigger.

But it was still all clouded over.

I had another rush of memory. I remembered the stars in the desert, from my grandma's front yard. Billions of them. Like, you just never dreamed there were so many stars. You could hold up your hands and make a circle with them and there would be hundreds, just in the tiny round window you created. A whole sky thick with stars.

I stood there for a long time, staring at the cloudy city sky. I was vaguely aware of people passing me on both sides. I could feel my neck start to ache under the strain.

Then the sky opened up and it rained on me. Buckets, all at once. It just came down and hit me in the face. I finally got that rain I'd been hoping for.

But, ironically, I did not feel like dancing.

Off to See the Whizzer

I showed up at my sister Stella's house less than twenty minutes after Carl left for work. This time I had not asked for special permission. Because I'm not supposed to go so often. Only when it's been too long. That much even Carl can understand, Stella being blood family and all, and also the only blood family I've got left. But not just a couple of days apart. That would have been a big red flag, or a red cape with Carl playing the part of the bull. So I just packed up Natalie while C.J. was in school, and I went.

She opened the door about an inch so Leo couldn't bolt. "Oh, God," she said. "You must be in even more trouble."

"Can I at least come in?"

"Hurry quick," she said.

I slipped in with Natalie, who was unfortunately not asleep this time. She was just hanging on one of my hands with her left hand. Sucking her thumb with her right.

"Do I even want to know?" Stella asked. She was wearing her hair up. Piled up on top of her head like the kind of hairstyle a woman will wear if she's going out for the evening. Which, I gotta say, looked really bizarre with pajamas and a robe. Not that I ever want to judge or criticize Stella, but it's hard not to comment on the fact that her life is full of a lot of very odd combinations.

I guess I'm a fine one to talk.

I said, "I have a very important issue on my mind. I was hoping for some information from your expertness in Tarot." I was purposely trying to use words that Natalie wouldn't understand.

Meanwhile Natalie pulled out of my hand and ran to greet Ferdy. Ferdy was her favorite of Stella's cats, which was not a hard choice to make, because he was the only one patient enough and friendly enough to be mauled by a two-year-old. She was trying to pick him up, but he was this huge fat orange tabby, maybe close to twenty pounds, and she could only get his front end off the carpet.

"Come," Stella said. "Sit."

"Well . . . Only thing is . . ." I gestured with my head in the direction of the cat-carrying kid. "Little pitchers have big ears."

"She barely talks."

"She's starting to talk."

"Okay. Okay." She swept over to her entertainment center and picked a VHS tape out of potentially hundreds. Stella had no system of organization, as far as I know, so how she found it so fast was beyond me. "Natalie," she said. With that kid-bright voice people use. "Do you want to watch your favorite movie ever?"

Natalie's head popped up. She still squeezed the ever-patient Ferdy. Holding him half off the ground. Her eyes lit up. It looked like excitement with something else thrown in, something more like eagerness and also fear. "*Whizzer da Boz?*"

"That's right," Stella said. "Come sit down on the couch. Bring Ferdy." Natalie hauled Ferdy over to the couch, still with only his front end off the floor, his back legs walking on the rug to keep up. "Now you sit right here and watch Dorothy and Toto and the Witch while your mommy and your auntie talk about boring grown-up stuff."

Natalie climbed onto the couch and pulled Ferdy up after her. She looked once over her shoulder to make sure I was still close. I sat at Stella's card table, so she'd know where I would be. Then she stuck her thumb in her mouth and put her head down to rest on the cat pillow of Ferdy as Stella pressed Play.

"Thanks," I said, when Stella joined me at the table.

Desdemona appeared from nowhere to join us, leaping up and sitting on the corner of the table. I think she knows what Tarot cards smell like or something.

"What's this big issue? What do you want the cards to tell you?"

"Well . . . You know this guy . . ." I lowered my voice to a hiss of a whisper. "This guy you think I ought to leave Carl for?"

She shuffled and spread out the cards as we whispered. "Honey, that would be just about any and every guy on the planet."

"The one I already know."

"What about him?"

"He's a little bit younger than I thought."

"How much younger?"

"Okay, a lot younger than I thought."

"How young?"

"Very young."

"How long do you want to keep going around like this? How young?"

"Kind of shockingly young."

"Well, he's legal, right? I mean, he's over eighteen?" I didn't answer. Just looked at the table. Just me and Desdemona, silently staring at a spread-out deck of cards. "Oh. Oh, dear. How far short of eighteen?"

"Only four months."

"And you want to know what the right thing is to do."

Desdemona jumped off the table and sulked away. A split second later, Stella gathered up the cards with one long, expert sweep of her hand. She tucked them away in their lavender velvet drawstring bag.

"Why are you putting the cards away?"

"Honey, for this we don't need them. You call on the Great Spirit when faced with something hard. This is easy."

"It is?"

"Oh, yes. Very. You have a choice between a guy who's young

and a guy who hits you and controls every move you make. Take the young one. Wait four months, just to be decent. And then take the life that doesn't hurt."

I sat quietly for a moment, listening to Judy Garland singing "Somewhere over the Rainbow." I'd thought Stella would tell me seventeen was too young. Out of the question. I'd thought I would lose my Tony dream in one sitting. But I didn't. And I was so relieved. In fact, I think I was kind of shocked by how relieved I was.

"But I wanted to ask the cards something else."

"What's that?"

"I wanted to know if he's going to be there tonight. 'Cause last time I saw him, I kind of dropped this bomb on him. And then I said, 'Day after tomorrow, right?' And he said yeah. But like he wasn't too sure. And I figure once he gets off by himself to really think about it, maybe he won't show."

"And you want the cards to tell you the future."

"Right."

"But they won't."

"They won't?"

"I've told you that about a dozen times."

"You have?"

"I keep telling you the future isn't set in stone. It's not all decided yet. The future is just what's down the road we decided to walk on today. You can change roads anytime. And that changes where you end up."

"Oh. I guess that does sound familiar. Yeah. So how do I change roads?"

"Well, you have to start early. It's a little late to change your outcome now. But just focus on him being there. Don't get into doubts. Don't picture him standing you up. Picture him showing up. You usually get what you think most about."

I looked over at Natalie, lying on the couch. Sucking her thumb. Dorothy and Toto were swirling around and around in the house, spinning in a tornado.

"Well, that leaves us with some time to kill," I said. "You know we'll never pry her away from *Whizzer da Boz.*"

"I'll just put on a fresh pot of coffee," Stella said.

IT WAS POURING RAIN when I went to meet him. The kind of rain that doesn't even feel like it could be made up of drops. It feels more like somebody just turned the biggest bucket in the world upside down. Dumped a whole ocean on New York City all at once.

I was wearing my long raincoat and my big gray hat, but I could feel my hair frizzing up anyway, in the humidity, and the bottoms of my jeans were getting soaked.

This much rain seemed like maybe a bad omen somehow. Not that I could really explain how exactly. Just sort of seemed like God would have to be pissed to dump an ocean on me. But that's extra stupid when you consider that I don't even believe in God.

That's one of the very few things Carl and I have in common. We met in the Atheists Club at school. I was a sophomore and he was a senior. But I'm getting off track.

No talk of bad omens, anyway. Stella said don't think about him standing me up. Think about him being there. So no more of this bad-omen crap. I would just force myself to think about something else.

I thought, I'll have to give him some way to get in touch with me. Just in case. Because maybe I'd get myself painted into some kind of corner, and have to tell Carl about getting fired. But I couldn't give him my address or phone number. Maybe I could just get his. Or maybe also I could give him Stella's address, just in case of an absolute emergency. I tried to really burn it into my brain. Don't forget to do that. If he shows up.

When he shows up. When.

I waited in our special spot for a long time.

I paced.

I didn't have a watch with me. In fact, I didn't have a watch, period. But it seemed like maybe it had already been too long.

Stella said keep thinking he will come.

I decided he probably just fell asleep. That happened once. But he woke up just in time and came running. Yeah. That could happen again.

But this voice in the back of my head was just too big. It said, *You're a liar and you know it. He's gone forever. You knew he would be. As soon as you told him the truth. Why would he be interested after what you told him? Why* should *he be?*

After a little more pacing I gave up and took the stairs up to the street. He was never going to show. And the sad part was, I didn't even blame him.

. . . And Dancing . . .

The next day, instead of running, I went down to the video store and rented *West Side Story,* with Delilah's blessing and on her account.

Of course, I took it to Delilah's. How else would I see it?

Delilah said that was really good, my new nickname. The whole Tony-and-Maria thing. Because it was basically just *Romeo and Juliet.* "Only told modern," she said. "Except this was a movie from the early sixties. So it's not so modern now. Not anymore. One of these days you got to see a movie that was made after you were born. With no singing and dancing."

"I like the singing and dancing. What's *Romeo and Juliet*?"

"You're kidding me. Right? *Romeo and Juliet*? William Shakespeare?"

"I know Shakespeare. My father just had me reading *Julius Caesar.* But he never gave me *Romeo and Juliet.* Is it a love story?" That's what I'd been hoping for *West Side Story.*

"Child, it ain't *a* love story, it's *the* love story."

So, that explained why I'd read *Julius Caesar* instead. My father didn't give me love stories. He didn't believe in them. According to him, that drivel about romantic love was just a big waste of time.

"I forgot to tell you," I said as she turned on her TV. "I had my first hot dog ever."

She stopped what she was doing and turned her face to me, staring at me like I'd just said something that wasn't in English. "You never had a hot dog before?"

"Never."

"What do you two eat over there?"

"Stuff that's good for you. Only. And nothing you buy on the street. You know. No hot pretzels, no pizza. He thinks people die of that stuff. But I had a hot dog, and I feel fine."

She still had that same look on her face. "You never had a slice of pizza."

"No. Is it good?"

She looked up at the ceiling like she was praying. Seeking guidance. Then she shook her head and hobbled over to get her purse, which was on a little table by the door. She rummaged around in there and pulled out her wallet and held a twenty out to me.

"I demand you walk out that door," she said, "and you may not come back until you have two slices with pepperoni and a hot pretzel for each of us. And get plenty of mustard for the pretzels. And if they have slices with extra cheese, get that. God help us all. Somebody got to teach this poor boy how to *live*."

THE MOVIE WAS REALLY DIFFERENT from *Singin' in the Rain*. It wasn't about all these pretty, happy people living well-scripted lives. It was about these two tough street gangs in a really rough section of New York. Only it was funny, because here the white gang was menacing the streets, fighting this tough Puerto Rican gang, but they snapped their fingers and danced. Even when they were running or fighting, they danced every step. And for a long time it was just about being a Jet, which was the white gang, but no Tony and Maria. I was getting really impatient.

But there was one thing that made me less impatient, and made it all livable. Well, okay, two things. Pizza. And a hot pretzel. The pizza was all greasy with cheese, and the pepperoni was hot and made my mouth tingle, and the pretzel was soft and had all these big rocks of salt on it. I could actually hear and feel the salt crunching between my teeth. I wasn't supposed to eat too much salt, because I guess it isn't good for you. According to you-know-who. But I ate that greasy slice and that salty pretzel with tons of hot mustard, and I've never tasted anything better in my life. It was almost enough to make me forget my troubles.

Almost. Not quite.

Then the leader of this white gang, Riff, went to see Tony to try to talk him into going to the dance. And there he was. Tony. He was tall, and better looking than any of the other white guys. The rest of them were kind of goofy looking.

I said to Delilah, "Tony is the best-looking guy."

"Well, of course he is," she said. "He's the romantic lead."

So then I missed a lot of the dialogue of the film wondering if I was Maria's romantic lead, and how I possibly could be, if there was such a thing as a Carl. How could she love me if she was living with him? Did that even count? And what did it mean?

But in spite of all those questions, I knew it was love. A weird version of love, maybe. But also the only love I had. Weird or not.

Only then I had to stop thinking about it, because there was Maria. The movie Maria, not the real one. "Oh," I said. "She's pretty."

"She sure is, child. That's Miss Natalie Wood."

"Oh, yeah. She said her mother named her for the Natalie Wood character."

"Is she Puerto Rican?"

"No. I don't think so."

"Her mother just liked this movie, I guess."

Then they met. Tony and Maria. They were at this dance, and when they saw each other, everything around them got all blurry. It was like they could see each other and not anybody else. It went on for a long time like that, and they just kept looking at each other.

Delilah said, "See? What did I tell you? Across a crowded room. If two people have that chemistry, they just have it. Right from the minute they set eyes on each other."

But I only half-heard her, because I was watching them look at each other. And then they came together.

And then Maria's brother pulled them apart.

From that part on, I got really caught up in the plot of this movie, because I didn't know if it would have a happy ending or not. Because they were from two different ethnic groups, Puerto Rican and white, and there was practically a war on between them. And nobody wanted them to be together. Except them.

But I figured they would be, because of that song. There's a place for us. There would be a place for them. They said so. They sang it. And I believed it. I believed there was a place for them. I wanted that to be true.

But I didn't dare ask any questions, all the way through the part where Tony's going to go meet Maria, and they're going to run away together, and Tony is talking to this nice old guy he works for, and the guy says something like, "Are you scared?" And Tony says, "No. Should I be?"

Then I got a funny feeling that I wasn't going to like how this came out.

I asked Delilah, "Does this movie have a happy ending?"

At first she didn't say anything at all, so I looked over at her face.

"Oh, child," she said. "I keep forgetting you don't know the whole *Romeo and Juliet* thing. It's a story about star-crossed lovers."

"What does that mean?"

"It means it's a tragedy."

"Oh, great."

I just sat there, my heart getting heavier and heavier, and watched as the cop showed up, and then Maria couldn't go meet Tony.

And the cop said something to her. Something about something that happened at the dance last night.

I looked over at Delilah. "This all happened in one day?"

"Yep. Just like *Romeo and Juliet.* Just all at once like that."

"Is that really love? When it happens so fast?"

She sighed. Paused the movie. Sighed again. "Some would say it's only love after you've been together long enough to work out who takes out the trash. And there's something to that. That part of love where you have to work at it. Learn to live together. But when you set eyes on that person, it's something. Call it what you want. If it turns into love, then maybe it's just love in all its stages. It's still real."

"Really? Is it?"

"Does it feel real?"

"Yeah. Very real."

"Then if I was you, I'd start learning to trust what you feel."

She put the movie back on Play.

Maria sent her brother's girlfriend, Anita, with a message for Tony, but the white gang got on her and abused her, so that went wrong and she got so mad she left a message that Maria was dead. And when Tony heard it, he ran out in the street and yelled for Chino, the guy he thought killed her, to come kill him too. Which Chino had been wanting to do anyway.

All this time I could feel this hard dead lump of pizza and pretzel in my stomach, but I really don't blame the pizza and the pretzel. I think I was just too upset about this love story to do a good job digesting anything.

Then all of a sudden he saw Maria, and he knew she wasn't dead, and they ran to each other. And I thought, Delilah was wrong. She remembered wrong. It does have a happy ending. Of course it does. It's a love story. It has to have a happy ending. What good is a love story without a happy ending? Right?

And then Chino caught up with them and shot Tony.

Maria held him in her arms and cried and sang that there was a place for them, but there wasn't. Because he was dying. Right there in her arms, he died.

I just sat there numb while they carried Tony away, and then the credits rolled.

Delilah got up to turn it off, and I felt like I couldn't even move.

When I talked, the words sounded like I'd said them in my sleep. They felt startling. "Shouldn't a love story have a happy ending?"

"Well, child, I don't know from should or shouldn't. Some do and some don't. I'd like to tell you every two people who love each other live happy ever after. But even *you* know better than that. It's the whole star-crossed-lovers thing. Two people that love each other but can't ever really be together because something keeps them apart. Right from the start. So don't get too wrapped up in that. Because that's not the story with you and this girl, right? You don't have something like two warring families keeping you apart."

"We have Carl," I said. "And my father."

"Well," she said. "That *is* a point."

WHEN I CAME BACK IN, my father was waiting for me. And I felt too numb and too raw and too sore to be attacked by him. But I had to go home sometime. And the longer I'd waited to come home, the worse it would have been.

"Yesterday I purposely did not ask you where you'd been," he said. "I hope you didn't think that would be the case every day. Today you'll tell me where you went."

"I was out walking," I said. Which was true. To a point. I did go out walking, to get the video, and the pizza, and the pretzels. It wasn't the whole truth and nothing but the truth. But I had to try it. See if it would fly.

"I don't believe you walked for a solid three and a half hours," he said. "Tell me the truth. Now."

"Okay, fine. I saw a movie. You said I could take a little vacation. So I saw a movie."

"What movie did you see?"

"*West Side Story.*"

"*West Side Story*? That movie is about forty years old. Why did you want to see that?"

"I don't know. I just wanted to see a movie."

He looked really confused. I guess in a way the truth worked on my behalf. By just throwing him completely off his stride.

"Well, I suppose if you're going to defy me and see a movie, I should be thankful it was an old classic. Instead of some profane trash like they make these days."

"No kidding," I said. "They didn't even swear in this film. They said things like 'buggin'' and 'everlovin',' so they didn't have to use the F word." I wanted him to know I was telling the truth. That I really had seen the movie I said I'd seen.

"Don't confuse the issue," he said. "You still disobeyed me, and you will still need to be punished."

"So, what are you going to do? Ground me? I've been grounded since I was seven."

Maybe this was not the world's best example of playing my cards right. But sometimes he just made me so mad.

He didn't really answer directly. Just told me to go to my room. Which I did. Which I was happy to do. But when I came out for dinner, there was no mention of any punishment. So I guess he couldn't think of anything, either.

What do you take away from the guy who has nothing?

MY FATHER PUT ON OPERA that night. And he wouldn't go to bed. And he wouldn't go to bed. And he wouldn't go to bed.

I thought I was going to explode.

I was smart enough to stay in my room with my door closed and my light off. Because I knew there was no way I could have covered up all that anxiety. Part of me even wondered if he could feel it anyway. Maybe it was pouring under the door. Or right through it.

It was after midnight, and I could still hear the music. All my nervousness and impatience turned into hatred of the music. I thought if I had to listen to one more minute of it I was going to scream. Or hurt somebody.

And tonight of all nights. After what she told me last time, if I didn't show up tonight, she'd think I never wanted to see her again. And then maybe I never would. Maybe she'd never ride the same subway line again. Never be where I could meet her.

I thought of a possibility, but it was risky. But I had to try.

I threw my door open and yelled at him. I yelled, "Will you please turn off that music and go to bed? Don't you know I've been having trouble sleeping lately? Do you think that racket helps? It's after midnight!"

I couldn't see him from my spot in the bedroom doorway. So I just froze, and waited. A moment later I heard blessed silence. I breathed for the first time in a long time.

"I'm sorry," he said. "That was thoughtless. I didn't know it was so late."

"Thank you," I said, and closed the door. And held my breath. If he sat down quietly with a book, I was dead. But the living room light clicked off, and I heard him running his glass of water in the bathroom.

I didn't even wait for him to go to sleep. He'd vacated the living room, so I slipped out. Even if he found out I was gone, I didn't care. Just so long as he was too late to stop me, or see which way I'd gone.

I couldn't bother to wait for the elevator. I ran down the steps two at a time and out into the pouring rain. It was raining in buckets. Sheets. I had no raincoat or hat, not even a jacket, but I didn't care. I was soaked to the skin in an instant, but I was free.

I sprinted all the way to the subway station, ran down the stairs. Bruised my thigh badly on the turnstile. Paced until the train came.

When we got to the Union Square station, I strained to see the bench under the stairs, before the train even stopped. She wasn't there. She had left already. Or had never showed up.

I shot out when the doors opened, and ran up the exit stairs and out onto the rainy street. I looked both ways and thought I saw her gray hat turning the corner. But it was hard to tell, because she—or whoever it was—had a long raincoat on. I screamed her name, but she disappeared around the corner. Maybe she didn't hear me. Or maybe it wasn't even her.

I ran all the way to the corner, screaming her name. I ran harder than I ever have in my life. I could feel myself splashing through deep puddles, but I just kept running. My chest felt like it was about to explode. When I got around the corner, I saw her. It was her! It was really her! And she was running back toward me, almost as hard and as fast as I was running. I thought she was going to run into my arms. For real this time. Instead she grabbed me by the arm and turned me around and told me to run with her and not ask any questions. She looked over her shoulder twice before we blasted around the corner. Then she pulled me down into a basement doorway, and we huddled in the shadows, breathing together. I wanted to ask what we were running from, but I didn't have enough breath to speak. I was panting too hard.

"Oh, God," she said. Out of breath, but not like me. "I'm afraid Carl heard you."

After a moment to catch my breath, I said, "You live that close?"

She didn't answer. We just went quiet. Huddled there together. Nothing happened.

I could feel her up against my chest, and I felt this pounding that I thought was my heart, but then I realized it was hers. It was such an amazing moment. It's like all my life I'd wanted to be close enough to someone to confuse her heartbeat with mine. I just didn't know it until now. I wondered how much of her heartbeat was the running, how much was her fear of Carl.

When I thought about her heart beating in fear of him, I wanted to kill him. Follow her home and kill him. Or die trying. But it was a stupid thought. I could never kill anybody. Besides, you don't kill guys like Carl. You just leave them. That's more like real justice.

"Want me to look out?" I whispered. She put a finger to my lips to shush me. I did something I wouldn't have imagined I could do. I kissed her. She didn't try to pull away. She went soft in my arms and kissed me back. "Run away with me," I whispered.

"Where?"

"I don't know yet. But I have four months to figure it out. Will you go with me?"

A long silence. "I still don't really know you very well."

I took her gently by both upper arms and looked right into her face. Close up in the dark. "I would never hurt you," I said. "Physically, or any other way. I would never lay a hand on you. Doesn't that make me a better bet than him right there? No matter what else you might find out about me?"

"It's just that I've been with him so long. Seven years."

Seven years. I did the math in my head. She was at least five years older than me. But I shook the thought away again. If she could live with the difference in our ages, so could I.

"We could have a real life. A good life. Just the two of us. I love you, Maria. Come away with me." A long silence. "Will you think about it?"

"Yes."

"You'll think about it?"

"I'll do it."

I almost couldn't believe what I'd just heard. I kissed her again. Then I poked my head out onto the street. No Carl. "I don't think he heard me," I said. "I'm sorry. I didn't know you lived so close. I was afraid you'd think I changed my mind about coming."

"I did. I did think that." An awkward moment. I didn't want her to go, but I could tell she was about to. She had to go home now. Make sure everything was okay. As if she heard me think that, she said, "I hope when I get home he doesn't ask who was calling my name."

That set up a knot in my stomach. How could I send her back there knowing she could be in trouble and it was all my fault? I could feel my brow scrunch up while I thought about it. "Could have been another Maria entirely."

"Right! It could have been!" The tension had drained suddenly from her voice. "Tomorrow night," she said. Then she kissed me and ran.

I WALKED RIGHT PAST THE SUBWAY. Set off for home on foot in the rain, smiling, when I could have gone underground. I could feel that I was smiling. I felt like an idiot. But I couldn't stop. Then I did something even sillier. It was still pouring hard. Raining in sheets. And the puddles were getting deeper. I started splashing in them on purpose. And the splashing got more rhythmic. And then it turned into a sort of dancing.

Now, I'll be the first to admit that I don't dance. And yet I was dancing. Not well. But there was no other word for what I was doing. I held my arms out, did a little spin after each step or two. Tried out a few new moves, each more awkward than the one before.

I sang out, "I'm singing . . . and dancing . . . in the rain."

Then I heard a voice. It came from over my head. "I give you a D-minus for dancing and an A-plus for enthusiasm."

I looked up to see an old woman leaning out her window. Looking down at me through the grating of the fire escape. She was smoking a cigarette, and a saw I big cloud of smoke flow out into the rain to be dampened down and erased.

"Thank you!" I said. Called, really. No, I guess I sang it. Really sang it out. "I'll take it!" Then I blew her a big, expansive kiss and danced my way home.

My father was asleep, and apparently had never missed me.

Life was good.

Downstream

I sat drinking coffee at a little all-night coffee place until what would have been the end of my shift. Watched it rain buckets, and watched the few people who were still out walking at that hour try to deal with it. There were these really deep puddles at the corners, and they were hard to get around. The women mostly tried to chart a path around them, which involved going almost half a block out of their way. The men mostly tried to jump, but they all failed. They all landed smack in about six inches of water, soaking their pant legs and ruining their shoes.

Speaking of soaked pant legs, my jeans were still soaking wet at the bottom, where my raincoat didn't cover. They felt cold against my legs. But it had been so hot lately. I hadn't been even a little bit cold for so long. It felt good. Like something I'd been missing without even knowing it.

Right before it was time to walk home, the rain stopped on a dime. So, that was convenient. Or so I thought.

But when I got home, Carl was wide awake and in a very bad mood.

"Who was that calling your name?" he asked. Right off the bat. No hello or anything. He had been waiting a long time to ask. That much was obvious.

"I don't know what you mean." My guts were all frozen, and it took every ounce of everything I had to try to keep my face soft. Like I wasn't scared. Like I really didn't know what he was talking about. Not like I was just pretending I didn't.

"Someone was on the street outside yelling your name."

"When?"

"Couple hours ago."

"Well, I was at work a couple hours ago."

"Were you?"

"What's that supposed to mean?"

"Was it raining when you walked home?"

"No. It stopped just before I left the store."

"Then how come your pants are still wet? You were on shift for hours. You would think they'd have started to dry out by now."

I had one of those moments. One of those weird things where I click out of something. Or into it, as the case may be. I can never figure out which is which. I looked at him and remembered the reason I fell in love with him in the first place. But I don't really mean that in a good way. It's like, I got a flash of that love he held out to me. He really did. At one time. But now what I saw was the lack of that same thing. All this time I guess I've been thinking it's still in there somewhere. But what I clicked into is this: It doesn't matter if it's in there somewhere. He still isn't giving it to me.

I've had these little clicks before. They always click right back again.

"Oh," I said. "That. I tried to jump a puddle coming home. But I missed and landed right in it."

"Then your shoes will be wet on the inside. And your socks will be soaked."

This was getting worse. This was only getting worse. Stella would say this was my consequence. Sooner or later he was going to catch me in this lie. She would tell me to hold still and face my music. But this might be too much music. This might be more music than anybody could be expected to hold still and face.

Even me.

I decided I would talk my way around it. And then run away with Tony early. Just get through tonight and then run to Tony and say, "I need help. I can't go home anymore. You have to help me."

Now I look back and think that was something of a half-baked plan. But at the time it was the only plan I could find.

"I just splashed. That's all. I didn't soak my shoes and socks. I don't know what you're getting all suspicious about."

"There was somebody on the street calling your name."

"Did he say my last name? Or did he just say Maria? Because, you know, there are other girls in New York named Maria. So why would you assume this guy was calling me, when it could have been any Maria? Why do you have such a suspicious mind?"

He said something I didn't expect. Calmly, too. Which is not a good sign. He said, "How did you know it was a guy?"

My stomach went dead cold again. In between I'd somehow been managing to live in this land where everything in my body was all quiet, like it really believed I wasn't in a world of shit. But now I definitely was. And every part of me knew it.

"You *said* it was a guy."

Oh, thank God. I'm smarter than I thought I was. I was actually washed up on the beach by a wave of gratitude for myself. For being so smart so fast.

"I did?"

"Yeah."

"I did not. I said someone."

"Not just now. When I first came in. You said some guy was calling my name."

"I did?"

"Yeah."

"I didn't think I did."

"Well, you did. Now if you don't mind, I'm tired from my shift. I'm going to bed."

He didn't say anything more about it that night.

My body went back to pretending that meant we were all okay.

JUST AS I WAS LYING IN BED trying to go to sleep, it hit me. I couldn't go anywhere with Tony. Not now. Not in four months. Not ever.

Because, even if he was okay with two kids—and, let's face it, that is just about one of the biggest ifs on the planet—there was no way I could take C.J. away from Carl. C.J. is really more Carl's son than he is mine. He made that choice based on who he is. And on who they are to each other.

And even for Carl's sake, too. I remembered him at that steak house, telling me he couldn't live without me. In a lot of ways, that's really just bullshit. People say that all the time, but then they do. If I leave Carl, he'll learn to live without me. But C.J. Without me and C.J. That would be too much.

No. I wasn't going anywhere.

And I had made my home into a place where I couldn't afford to live any longer. I had made a bed that no one could lie in.

Not even me.

I thought about Stella. How she said I was pitching a tent on a river. I think, lying there in bed, still feeling the imprint of the cold where my wet jeans legs had been, I really got it for the first time. Really understood why I frustrate people so much with what I create.

I had only two choices, that I could see. And they were both completely impossible.

I never got to sleep that night. Just lay there and felt the current of the river. Sweeping my tent downstream.

A Place for Us

I slept. It was amazing. I slept like the dead. Like I hadn't slept in weeks. Which was more or less true.

It was after one-thirty in the afternoon when I finally stumbled into the kitchen. My father wasn't there. I mean, not in the kitchen. But of course he joined me soon enough.

"Well," he said. "If it isn't Rip van Winkle."

I wasn't in the mood for a fight. I was happy. Blissfully happy. I just had to be careful not to show it. "I needed it, though."

"I guess it's partly my fault. I'm sorry I had music on so late."

"That's okay. I'm sorry I yelled at you."

He gave me a funny look. Wondering why I was being so nice, I think. So calm. I held my breath briefly, but the moment seemed to blow by. Close call. I'd almost let on that I was feeling good.

Just before he left the kitchen he said, "We have a doctor's appointment for you. Today at four."

"Today? That's awfully fast."

"Well, I was on his list for a cancelation. Just be grateful I got one."

"Okay, well, I better run right after breakfast then."

In a funny sort of way I almost liked the idea. I'd be out running around all day. Sebastian's busy day, I said to myself, like a children's story. I should have more busy days.

I made up my mind about something. Suddenly and completely. I was going to insist that my father stay out in the waiting room while I saw the doctor. And then I was going to tell the doctor the truth. And let the chips fall where they may.

I WENT FOR A FULL, LONG RUN, even though I knew it would cut way into my time with Delilah. Because I'd missed too many runs lately. And I missed my running when I missed it. I really wanted it back.

I ran past the video store and stopped in my tracks. I walked inside, puffing. There was a different clerk that day, a girl no older than me and the place smelled like smoke. She looked up at me. Like she'd been bored before I got there, and I hadn't really solved that problem.

I said, "Do you know which movie has the scene with Fred Astaire dancing on the walls and the ceiling?"

She just blinked at me. I thought, *Why did I even ask?*

Then she called out, "Hey. Fred." An older guy came out from behind a curtain. "This guy wants—"

"I heard 'im."

But he just walked up and down a couple of aisles, like he didn't care much about what he'd heard. So I turned to leave. Figured I'd poke around online and see if I could locate it.

Then I heard Fred say, "Hey. Don't ya want this?"

I turned around. He was holding a copy of *Royal Wedding* on DVD.

"Yeah," I said. "Thanks. Can I get a two- or three-day rental?" Because I had a doctor's appointment. But I didn't tell him that, because I was smart enough to know he didn't care.

"All our rentals are five days."

So I rented *Royal Wedding,* and ran it home to Delilah. To tell her two pieces of good news. The little news, that I'd found the movie where Fred Astaire dances on the wall. And the big news. That Maria and I were going to run away together. I hoped she'd be happy for me.

SHE WAS, for the most part.

At first she seemed a little . . . like she had a doubt she wasn't sharing with me.

"When?" she asked. "Right away?"

"No, in four months. When I'm eighteen. That way I have time to make a plan."

Then she took a big deep breath and seemed happier with the news.

"I should've known you'd use your head," she said. "I shouldn't've doubted you. I think you're smart to get out of that house the split second you can do it without him being able to call you a run-away. And to think you're going off with that girl you love by your side. Oh, honey, I'm just so happy for you! And so proud of you for being so brave."

"Don't call me brave yet," I said. "I haven't done it yet. I think I'll have to get braver between now and then."

"It was brave just to ask her."

I thought about that for a minute, and it was true. I was brave to ask.

"I brought you something," I said, and handed her the rented copy of the movie. "I found the one where Fred Astaire dances on the walls and the ceiling."

"You're amazing," she said. "And I got something for you, too. A little present." She hobbled off into her bedroom and came back out with a small paperback book. "Maybe your father doesn't think you ought to read about love, but I think you should. So there."

It was *Romeo and Juliet*.

"What a nice present," I said.

"Oh, child, that ain't nothing. Want to put that movie on?"

"I can't today. My father is taking me to the doctor today."

She raised one eyebrow. "You sick?"

"No, I feel fine."

"Whew. For a minute there I thought you really might get sick missing a few days running. So . . . do I even want to ask?"

"He's worried because I'm not sleeping. So he wants the doctor to prescribe sleeping pills for me." I could see Delilah chew that over for a minute. "But don't worry. I'm going to tell the doctor the truth."

"You think he'll help you? Or you think he'll tell your father everything and get you in a world of hot water?"

"I don't know," I said. "I'm not even sure I care at this point. I'm just tired of making up lies to get to do what everybody else has been doing all their lives. I'm just going to tell the truth and let the chips fall where they may."

I heard a long rush of air come out of her. *"Vaya con Dios, mi hijo,"* she said.

"I didn't know you spoke Spanish."

"Yeah, and now you heard just about all the Spanish I speak."

"What does it mean?"

"It means, Go with God, child."

"In other words, I need all the blessing I can get."

"El correcto," she said.

I WAS SO HAPPY, and so relaxed, and so set on dropping all the deception and living my life that I made a weird mistake. I walked into the apartment with the book in my hand. It never even occurred to me to hide it under my shirt.

My father homed in on it immediately. "What is that?" he asked.

I had been caught red-handed. We could both tell by the way I looked down at it. I was almost tempted to shuffle it away under my shirt. A weird response under the circumstances. Like he hadn't totally seen it already. "It's a book," I said.

"It's obviously not a book I want you to read. Or I would have assigned it. You will give it to me."

"No," I said. "I won't."

Lately I had learned something new about my father. And yet it wasn't until now, this third time I openly defied him, that I consciously realized what I had learned. All my life I'd backed down to him, because he was so much bigger and stronger. Because he held all the cards, and because he could make my life hell. And I'd always assumed if I stood up to him, he'd flatten me. But now I was standing up to him, and he wasn't flattening me. I thought about the awful previous night, yelling at him to turn off the music. He did what I asked, and apologized. Twice. I read in a book once that all bullies are really cowards. I hoped it was true, and that I could depend on what I'd just discovered.

"I'll *show* it to you," I said. "So you can see what I'm reading. And that it isn't something I should have to hide. But it belongs to me. And I won't let you take it away."

I walked up to him, as tall and calm as I could be, and held out the book. But, truthfully, I felt a little shaky inside.

"*Romeo and Juliet*," he said. "I didn't figure you'd read Shakespeare on your own."

"Maybe you should have more faith in me."

And then I closed myself in my room with the book. I opened the front cover, and discovered that Delilah had written a little inscription to me. It said, "For Romeo. Don't be afraid to love. Or, if you have to, be afraid but do it anyway. Your friend, Delilah."

Only then did I realize the bullet I had dodged by not letting him confiscate my present. I felt like something had shifted between us. All these years I'd been afraid of my father. And I'm not going to say I suddenly wasn't. Of course I still was. How could I not be after all this time? But now my father was also a little bit afraid of me.

I WALKED TO THE SUBWAY with my father, watching him every step of the way. Well, maybe *with* him is the wrong word. I was a couple of steps behind and maybe an arm's length away. I was thinking about how long it had been since I'd gone out on the street with him. A long time. Not since I'd started going out on my own at night. Not since a different time, when I was somebody else. And it seemed as though he'd been somebody else then, too. But maybe not. Maybe he wasn't changing at all. Maybe it was only the way I was seeing him that changed.

"Sebastian," he said. "Don't walk behind me."

I caught up about one step. "Why not?"

"You're not a second-class citizen, you know."

"I never thought I was."

"Well, just stay close to me."

"Why?"

"I don't want anything to happen to you."

"It's not a war zone, Father."

"That's what you think," he said.

But suddenly it hit me that I knew this city, this world, better than he did. At least, I had more recent experience with it. I caught all the way up to him, and walked by his side. I glanced over at his face. He had his brow furrowed, and the frown lines made him look older. And scared. He looked scared. I wondered if he was really scared for me, or really more for himself. Or, worst of all, if he barely knew the difference anymore. If he had lost track of where he ended and I began. He walked fast, and I had to readjust my pace, because I was used to walking slowly for Delilah. He kept his gaze trained down, toward the sidewalk, at all times.

I looked up at all the people going by. Into the faces of the businessmen on their cell phones, the young, fashionably dressed women. I smelled the sewer as we walked over the grates, and the puffs of cigarette smoke that drifted back to us on the wind.

"Filthy habit," my father said. "Stop looking at people."

"Why?"

"They'll think you're looking for trouble."

"So how come I'm not getting any?"

He never answered. But the whole rest of the way to the doctor's, he didn't tell me again that I was moving through the world incorrectly. So I guess that's progress.

I DIDN'T TELL HIM not to come in with me, because I was hoping the nurse would. And she did. She came out with my chart and called my name, and he got up, too.

She said, "You can just wait here in the waiting room, Mr. Mundt."

"No. I'm going in with Sebastian. I have to tell the doctor what the problem is."

She put her hands on her hips. She was pretty young. Under thirty, I think. And she couldn't have weighed much more than ninety pounds. But she didn't look like she was about to take any crap from my father. "I thought it was Sebastian who had the sleeping problem."

"It is, but—Sebastian, don't you want me to go in with you?"

"No. Please just go sit down, Father. You're embarrassing me." It even embarrassed me to have to call him "Father" in front of people. It sounded like I was in some old British play from the nineteenth century.

He looked truly perturbed. Betrayed, even. But he did not come in.

The nurse led me down the hall and had me step on the scale.

"I'm sorry about my father," I said.

"Don't worry," she said. "I can handle him. I've had worse."

She led me into an examination room, and took my temperature and my blood pressure. She didn't seem to like the blood pressure reading. Not surprising. I could feel my own heart pound. She said, "Do you have a history of high blood pressure?"

"No. Low-normal, actually. Maybe you could take it again after I tell you what I'm about to tell you. Then maybe I won't be so scared." She didn't react quite the way I thought she would. She just leaned back and waited for me to go on. "My father doesn't want me going out of the apartment. The only time I ever get to go out is when I'm running. Which I only get to do because some other nice doctor stood up for me and told him I needed fresh air."

"What about school?"

"He homeschools me. Anyway, I've been going out at night after he's asleep. Not getting into any trouble or anything. Just going out. Walking, or riding the subway. So I've been sleeping later, so he thinks I have a sleeping problem. I'm sorry to waste your time like this, but if I'd told him the truth, he would have put a stop to it. So I just couldn't bring myself to do that. So, I don't know what the doctor wants to do. If he wants to give me sleeping pills, I could just not take them. But I made up my mind that when I came here, I wouldn't lie."

"How long has it been since you had activities outside the house?"

"Since I was seven," I said. She looked shocked. I think she'd thought I meant I'd been grounded for a month.

I watched her sit with that for a long time. Then she said, "You know, if he really isolates you to the degree you say, it might be considered a form of abuse. Do you need help? I don't want to make your situation worse. I want to do what's best for you."

"I'm almost eighteen," I said. "Four more months. Then I'm leaving. So, thanks. But I think the best plan is just to ride it out from here."

Then I realized, sitting there watching her think, why I'd chosen to do this. I wanted some kind of perspective. I wanted to get a third opinion on my own weird reality. My father said it was right. Delilah said it was not. I wanted to know what someone else would think. And now I knew. I also realized something else I hadn't known before: That doctor who got me out running—who told my father I needed fresh air—saw exactly what was going on and wanted to help me. And he did help me. And now I wanted someone to help me again.

I said, "You know, before that doctor got my father to let me go running, I used to get sick all the time. And my friend Delilah— who my father doesn't even know about, by the way, so don't rat me out—said maybe I was just getting sick to get out of the house. And when she said it, it sounded strange to me. Like something I'd never thought of before. But today, on the way over here, I had this funny feeling. Like part of me had known that all along."

She sat thinking another minute, then leaned forward and patted my arm.

"Okay. I'm going to go talk to the doctor. He'll probably want to ask you some questions, too. And I'm guessing he'll want to talk to your father. But I'll tell him what you told me. And we'll see what he wants to do."

I SAT IN THE WAITING ROOM while my father went in. He looked defensive. And he looked small. He looked so small and so afraid that I wondered why I'd ever been scared of him.

Just before the nurse disappeared with him, she smiled at me, which made me feel good. Actually, it made me feel like I was about to cry. I had this feeling in my chest and at the back of my throat like I could cry at any minute. But I don't even know why.

After about twenty nervous minutes, my father came back out. He looked and sounded bristly. "Come on, Sebastian," he said. "We're going home."

HALFWAY HOME ON THE SUBWAY I got up the nerve to ask him what the doctor said.

At first he didn't answer. For so long that I thought he never would. Then he said, "He thinks you need more activity. That you can't sleep because you spend too much time cooped up in the house. I told him you run every day. He said he has nothing against homeschooling, but he wants you to have social opportunities with people your own age."

"Well, that's close to what the other doctor said. And look how much healthier I got after I started running."

He made a sound like a snort. "Seems no matter what I allow it's not enough."

"So, are you going to do it?" No reply. I waited. Still nothing. "Father. I said, are you going to do it?"

"Sebastian. Please be quiet and let me think."

All the way home, no more word from my father. We ate dinner, he went to bed. Not a word. But he looked intimidated to me. And I took that to be a good sign.

I SAT ON THE SUBWAY SEAT with Maria beside me. Holding her hand.

"I've been thinking how it's going to be," I said.

"Oh. You mean if we go away together?"

My stomach turned to ice. Heavy, tingling ice. *"If?"*

"When. When, I mean."

"You didn't change your mind, did you?"

"No. It's just scary to think about it."

"But you still want to do it."

"Yeah. I think so."

By now I was full-on scared. And I couldn't think what to do to fix it. I had to get us back to that place where we definitely knew what we would definitely do.

I reached deeper into myself than I ever have before. And this is what I found.

I said, "When I was little, I spent some time in the desert. The Mojave Desert, in California. Have you ever been to the desert?" She shook her head no, and I went on. "It's hot. But then, so is the city. But it's a different kind of hot. I guess it's hotter, but it's dry. A baking kind of heat. It doesn't make you feel like you're going to faint. And at night, the stars are so clear. There are hundreds of thousands of them. Maybe more. Maybe millions. And they're so bright. It's like every little square inch of sky has a thousand bright stars. And it's not flat, either. There are mountains. A whole range of mountains on the horizon. And on the mountains are windmills."

"Windmills?" she asked. I felt as though she had clicked out of her worry and into my story for the first time.

"Windmills. Thousands of identical windmills. They sit up there on Tehachapi Pass and turn the wind into power. And there are layers after layers of them. So you could just watch them spin forever. It's like watching water flow. I don't really know how to describe it."

"I'd like to go somewhere where there are windmills," she said. "Is that why you told me that story?"

"Yes. It is. I wanted you to know there's a place for us."

Her eyes lit up and she squeezed my hand tighter. "Oh, Tony! You *do* know that movie! I thought you didn't, when I first brought it up. I know it's old. But I love that movie."

"Me, too," I said. "Except it didn't have a happy ending. But *we* will. Right?"

"I wish I could picture those windmills," she said. "But I can't see them in my head."

"I'll bring you a picture of them." I figured I could print one off the Web.

"Will you, Tony? I'd love to see."

She put her head on my shoulder all the way back to Union Square. It seemed like, if that really had been a rough spot, it was smoothed over now.

When the doors opened, she kissed me, short and fast on the mouth. "Windmills? Really?"

"Really."

"I can't wait to see that," she said. "Day after tomorrow?"

"Yes. Day after tomorrow."

"Good."

Then she was gone.

Tuck In

On my way up the stairs that night, I had a Knowing Moment.

I guess in some ways I'm like my sister, Stella. She just pays more attention to stuff like that than I do. I can do a lot of the same things as Stella can, but most of the time I just ignore it.

Stella says that the past and the future aren't really so different, like we think they are. I mean, in metaphysical terms. I don't quite get this part, but I think it has something to do with quantum mechanics, which I guess nobody exactly gets anyway. Stella says there's no reason why we shouldn't be able to remember the future exactly the way we remember the past. Well, I guess *remember* is the wrong word, but there isn't exactly a right one. Because we don't do it, so we never made up a name for it. But Stella says we only use some really small percent of what our brains can do, and maybe that's one of the unused parts.

I'm taking a very long way around to say this. On the way up the stairs, I knew something. Very plainly. I still had not gotten Tony's address. Or phone number. Or last name. And as I was walking up the stairs, I knew it was too late.

If I had really thought about it, I could have gone a little further in my head and put together that lots of big trouble was waiting for me upstairs. But all I thought about was Tony. Losing Tony.

It was almost like my life flashed before my eyes and all I saw was Tony.

When I opened the door, I didn't even see Carl. I swear. I felt his fist hit my cheekbone, slamming me back against the door, slamming it closed as I hit it. I hadn't even seen him coming. I think I saw a flash of the fist, but it seemed unreal. Like something you would dream.

I felt the wood floorboards under my knees.

"I went by your work today," he said.

And part of me thought, Good. Good. It's over. It was ridiculous, it needed to be over. Now it is. My whole head was throbbing. I could feel a trickle of blood run down my cheek where Carl had caught me with his class ring.

He said, "I was going to stand right with you and be some support for you while you asked Danny about your paycheck."

I thought, *You liar. You are such a liar. You didn't go there to support me.* But it didn't matter. Nothing mattered.

I pulled up to my feet and walked into the kitchen. A little dizzy, but I was going. I was going to get some ice to put on my face.

"Don't you walk away from me!" he screamed. Loud enough for the neighbors on both sides to hear. But I didn't care about the neighbors. I only cared about my kids. I knew they could hear, but there was nothing I could do about that. I just hoped they stayed in their rooms. I was pretty sure they would. They always did before.

"Don't you dare walk away from me! I want to know where you've been."

"Nowhere," I said. And I opened the freezer door to get the ice. "I just rode around on the subway."

"Bullshit!" he screamed. "You look me in the eye and tell me there isn't somebody else."

I looked down at the kitchen linoleum. I had to. There was nothing else I could do.

Stella says when we were kids and things got bad she would go outside herself. She said she would be in a spot near the ceiling in the corner of the room. Watching. Like everything was happening to somebody else. Like you watch a movie on a screen.

Not me. I tuck in. I go into an even deeper place in myself. And I pull the covers in over me. And then I dare you to find me. You have to find me to touch me or hurt me. At least, the part of me that really counts. I go inside and just hold very still. And part of me feels dead. Like it doesn't matter. Whatever it is. It just doesn't matter.

I think I had my eyes closed when I got hit with Carl's flying tackle. I just remember falling with him on top of me. And, of course, hitting the kitchen table is one of those things you don't ever forget. We have a big glass kitchen table with a border of metal all around it. Like a frame. I hit it with the side of my body, and then we hit the ground, and I just lay there on the floor feeling like someone had stuck burning hot knives into my side.

I'm not sure where Carl went, but he wasn't on top of me. And I didn't really care. I kept trying to take a breath. But I couldn't get any air in. I was used to getting the wind knocked out of me, so I guess I was just waiting. It would hurt too bad to breathe anyway, so I wasn't going to try too hard.

The door to the freezer was still standing open. I could see steam pouring out of it, the way fog pours over the top of a mountain. Or, at least, the way it poured in a photo my mother used to have over her bed.

My breath wasn't coming back. You'd think I'd be all panicky around that. But not so much. It was strange.

That thought came into my head one more time. You didn't get his address, and now it's too late.

I don't remember anything else after that.

Sebastian | Eight

The Shredder

I can only describe my father's mood the following morning as sullen.

He looked almost like a little boy to me. An old child with gray hair. Sulking.

I got it in my head that I was just going to open my mouth and ask a brave question. But I froze. I opened my mouth and nothing happened. After that it just got harder.

It's like if someone had a loaded gun in your face. I don't know how else to describe how it felt to try to talk to my father. Even on a good day. If someone always has a loaded gun in your face, you weigh every word before you say it. You only dare say it if it might save you. But you're never sure, so there's this tendency to freeze. Say nothing at all.

This went on for nearly a whole bowl of granola.

Then I decided to say "Father." Put it out there really fast. Then I'd have no choice but to finish the thought.

"Father."

He looked up. Suddenly he looked more angry than sullen. It was something like looking right down the barrel and seeing a live round. I couldn't go on.

"What?"

"Nothing. Never mind."

"What is it, Sebastian? Spit it out."

"I just wondered . . . if you'd thought any more about what the doctor said."

The minute it came out of my mouth, I knew it was a stupid question. He'd thought about nothing else since. I had interrupted his thinking about it to ask if he was thinking about it.

"We're getting a second opinion," he said. I dropped my spoon. On purpose. The clanking sound startled him, set him off as if I'd yelled at him or challenged him. "Not even an *opinion*," he said. "I don't pay a doctor for his *opinion*. I wanted him to prescribe sleeping pills for you and instead he tells me I'm raising my son wrong. Where he gets off, I don't know. He barely knows you. He hasn't sacrificed his life for you, like I have."

Now, mind you, my father said this a lot. That he sacrificed his own life to raise me right. He quit his job as a college professor when his mother died, and has managed to live on the money she left him. And, yes, it's been all about me. Even I have to admit that. And I'd heard that same song about sacrifice a hundred times. And this was the first time I didn't believe it. And I can't even explain what changed.

All of a sudden it was just written all over his face. He didn't sacrifice anything for me. He didn't want his life anymore, so I was a convenient excuse not to have it. Letting me have friends, that would have been a sacrifice. Keeping me all to himself was purely selfish.

"I'm going running," I said, and stood up rather abruptly. My legs hit the underneath of the table so hard that I knocked over his glass of orange juice. He scrambled for a dishcloth to clean it up. I didn't. I headed for the door.

"What about the rest of your cereal?" I heard him ask.

I didn't answer.

I think I finally got it. It doesn't pay to try to communicate with my father.

I DIDN'T GO STRAIGHT TO DELILAH'S. I was going to run first. I wanted to run some of the bad thoughts and bad energy out of my system. I wanted to outrun my bad morning.

But as I passed by under her window, I heard a big voice yell, "Hey!" But I didn't catch that it was *her* voice. That one little word wasn't enough for me to recognize it. A second later I heard, "Hey! Tony!"

Amazingly, I looked around. Isn't that amazing, that I would answer to Tony? I thought that was amazing.

"Up here." That was when I recognized that it was Delilah.

I looked up. She was waving her arms frantically. Yet somehow happily, too.

Of course, I went back upstairs. She was waiting for me in her open doorway.

"Isn't that amazing, that I answer to the name Tony?" I asked her that from halfway down the hall.

"I didn't want to get you in trouble with your father. You know, if he heard."

It struck me that this was the second time in a couple of days that just yelling someone's name on the street could have spelled disaster. Then it struck me how wrong that was. To have to keep your life sectioned off like that. A signal that you'd fallen into a bad way to live.

"Hurry up," she said. "Hurry up. Get your skinny little butt in here." Her face seemed happy, lighted up—but scared, too. And I got a little scared myself. Started thinking Maria was standing in her apartment or something. Not that she ever would be. I just couldn't think what else would be so exciting and scary. "I got something for you."

As I walked through the door, she set it in my hands. A big nine-by-twelve cardboard Express Mail envelope. I looked at it for a minute without comprehension. I really didn't know, at first, what it was.

Even when I looked at the name on the return address. Anne

Vicente. I knew I knew that name. It was so familiar. It's not that I couldn't place the name, exactly. It just all happened so fast. Or maybe in a weird way it almost happened in slow motion. So I could almost feel the bits of information drop into my brain and find a spot. Before I could even process the name, click with why I knew the name, my eyes fell on the last line of the return address. Mojave, California. My stomach went cold, my knees almost buckled, and I got so dizzy that Delilah had to step in and lead me over to the couch to sit down.

"It just came in the morning mail," she said. Like the words had been ready to explode from her mouth for a long time. "Just about an hour ago. I didn't know how to let you know. I was going nuts."

The words sounded hollow coming into my brain. Like I was half asleep, and someone was talking to me. Dull and far away. The envelope was sitting on my lap. I just kept looking at it. I looked up at Delilah. I expected her to tell me to just open it. But I underestimated Delilah. She was smarter than that. She knew it wasn't all so easy. My answer might be in this envelope. My whole life might be about to change. Retroactively. That was the weird part. I might be about to have to go back and rewrite—or at least reframe—the last decade of my own history. Or maybe I'd read this letter and still wouldn't know what to believe. Suddenly that seemed a thousand times worse.

I picked up the envelope. Held it in both hands. "I didn't think this could possibly get here so fast," I said. It sounded like somebody else. In a way. "Three days?"

"Might have been four," she said. "Pretty sure it was four."

The envelope had one of those tear strips on the back. Lift the little tab and pull off a whole long strip of the cardboard and then you're in.

I held it out to Delilah. Closed my eyes. "Pull that, okay?" Might've sounded stupid. But I needed help. I felt the tug of it, and heard the quiet rip of the cardboard letting go.

I looked inside. There was an envelope, but something more, too. What looked like separate small papers or pictures.

I turned it upside down and spilled the whole thing out onto my lap. The envelope said, "To our darling Sebastian." It caught in my chest like something solid I'd breathed into my lungs, something I'd meant to swallow. I picked up one of the pictures. They were pictures. I could see that now. They were lying facedown on my lap. I picked one up and turned it over.

It was a picture of my mother.

I want to put something to how I was feeling just here, but there's nothing to say. Part of me knew it. Part of me was expecting it. That part had already given up and stepped out of the way. It just fell into this perfect blankness, like a fresh fall of untouched snow. Nothing moved, and it never made a sound. For that moment, I mean.

It was a moment when something became so inevitable that I just surrendered to it.

She was standing in front of a big jeep sort of vehicle. Very new. The car couldn't have been more than a couple of years old. Her hair was partly the honey brown I remembered and partly gray. She looked about the same age as my father. Which she was, almost exactly. But, I mean, my father *now*. I mean, she wasn't the age I remember her. But it was her, and I knew it.

I picked up another photo. I'm not sure how much later, though. It was my Grandma Annie, sitting on the porch swing of her little house in Mojave. It was the same house. I recognized it immediately. And, ten years aside, the same Grandma Annie. The same tanned, leathery skin and cheery gray eyes.

I turned over the third picture, and it made my stomach buzz and tingle. She had sent me a picture of the windmills the way they look from her backyard.

I looked up at Delilah. It's hard to describe what I saw in her face.

I handed her the picture of my mother.

"Is this your Grandma Annie?"

I shook my head. I couldn't talk.

"Didn't think so. She looks too young. This is your mother."

I nodded.

Then I started to cry. And you know what? I wasn't even humiliated to cry in front of Delilah. You tell me, do you know anyone who wouldn't at a time like that? Because, well, if you do, I don't want to know them. You'd have to be made of stone. You'd have to be dead.

I wasn't dead. Not anymore.

Delilah brought me about three big handfuls of tissues and piled them in my lap. She even hobbled over and got me a little wastebasket. I was going though them pretty fast. I needed a system. I never bothered to take out my handkerchief. Wouldn't have been enough.

I'm not sure how long that went on before she said, "Don't forget you got a letter under there. Not to rush you now, child. Take your time."

But I could tell she was curious. And truthfully, I'd more or less forgotten. I was so busy processing the information that I had a mother. The letter from my grandmother, who I'd always known was out there somewhere, had fallen to the back of my mind. Besides, it was obliterated by a sea of tissues.

I plowed through and found it. And opened it up. I read it once through quietly to myself. Then I read it out loud to Delilah. Because I knew she wanted to know. Not out of nosiness. Just caring. She wanted to be part of this. And she was. How could she not be? She'd started it. This whole moment was courtesy of Delilah. I owed her.

"Our dearest, darling Sebastian,

"Your mother, Celia, and I were so excited to get your letter, we hardly knew what to do with ourselves. I called her at work, even though I usually never would. I got a call from the folks at the motel. I retired from there years ago, but I still know all of them, and they called me up right away. And I called your mother as soon as I got home. She works as a hairdresser in Port Hueneme. That's near Ventura. Even though she can't really take calls at work, because she has a client waiting right there in a chair with their hair all wet and everything. But we talked and talked and she danced around and around right there in the salon and I danced around and around on my front porch. We were so happy, we hardly knew what to do.

"But your letter broke my heart, too. It just broke my heart when you said you forgive me for forgetting all about you. Honey, we never forgot you. Not for one day. The biggest regret of Celia's life is that she let that awful man bully her out of seeing you again. But she was afraid of him, and she thought things could get worse for you if she didn't do what he said. But over the past ten years, between the two of us, we probably wrote you a hundred letters. We sent them to the right address, too, we know that now. Same place you still live. And they never came back returned. So we didn't know if your father didn't let you see them or maybe you were mad about her leaving and didn't want to write back. Now we know. He never showed them to you. Honestly, I didn't think he would sink that low. Even with all I know about him.

"Ask me anything you want about your mom. Anything. You'll hear from her, too, in about a day. Now that we know how to write you. She missed the last mail pickup the day you wrote, having to finish work. But you'll be hearing from her.

"We love you, Sebastian. We always did. We never stopped. We always dreamed we'd see you again. Maybe when you were eighteen, and he had no say. Won't be long now.

"With all the love in the world, Your Grandma Annie.

"P.S.: I'm sending a photo of both of us, and of the wind farm the way it looks from my house. Do you remember how you used to love those windmills, Sebastian? You'd sit on the porch and watch them for hours. I never saw anything like it. It's like you were hypnotized. Oh, but you were so little. You probably don't remember.

"P.S.S.: Thank Delilah for us. She is a lifesaver."

I put down the letter and looked up at Delilah.

She said, "Do you remember the windmills?"

"I was telling Maria about them last night. I told her I'd show her a picture of them tomorrow night."

We both just pondered the wonder of that in absolute silence.

After a while I said, "They wrote me a hundred letters. And he never let me see them."

"How does that make you feel?"

The minute she asked, it happened. It came up out of me like a bad meal that had been making me sick. Like a storm suddenly built up pressure inside my gut and then let go. I was so angry, I couldn't even talk. I couldn't even answer the question. I couldn't even make myself say the word.

I SLAMMED BACK into the apartment. I'm sure my eyes were still red and swollen from crying, but I didn't care. I slammed the door shut again at my back.

I could hear him in the kitchen. He called in, "Your vacation is over, Sebastian. You have lost your privileges because you abused them. You will no longer take off, and not tell me where you're going, and come back as you please. Is that understood?"

I just stood there. My back to the door. Hoping nobody was about to actually get hurt. And that if anybody did, it was me. Because the last thing I could accept right now was suddenly becoming my father. He stuck his head out from the kitchen. I saw the alarm on his face when he looked at me.

"You son of a bitch," I said. The look of alarm turned to genuine fear. He was afraid of me. Good. "You lying bastard."

He said nothing. It was a horrible yet satisfying moment. Terrible and beautiful all at the same time. There was nothing he dared say to me. He looked down at the carpet. And he didn't even know what I'd busted him for yet. But he looked down in shame.

"What did you do with them?" I was not shouting. My voice was measured. Carefully measured. As if I didn't dare shout. As if I couldn't afford to. "The letters from my mother. The ones that were my property. That belonged to me. What did you do with them? I want to know. Did you throw them down the garbage chute? Burn them? Flush them down the toilet?"

"Sebastian—"

"Answer me!" Now I was shouting.

"What difference does that make?" Quietly. As though he was talking to someone who held a loaded gun in his face.

"Answer my goddamn question. What did you do with them?"

Long pause. I could feel something in my temples throb, and my ears rang.

"I put them through the paper shredder."

"You said that was for credit card statements. Oh. Never mind. That's right. You also said my mother was dead. I forgot. You just lie."

"Sebastian, I—"

"How could you tell a seven-year-old boy that his mother is dead? What kind of monster could do a thing like that?"

"I'm not a monster, Sebastian."

"Are you sure? Have you looked at yourself lately?"

"I did it for you, Sebastian. Someday you'll understand. Maybe even forgive me."

I shook my head so hard I almost unbalanced myself. And at nearly the same time I flew across the room in his direction. He stumbled back about four steps. Hit his own chair and fell back and caught himself halfway into a sit. I managed to stop myself just a few inches short. I could have hurt him. It would have been easy. But I didn't. That's what my father would have done—the easiest thing. The easiest thing is not always the best. Usually not, in fact.

"No. Don't say that. I will never forgive that. Never. It was un-forgivable. Don't ever say that again. In fact, you know what? Don't talk to me again. Just don't talk. Don't say a word to me anymore."

I turned and paced back to the middle of the room, then got

stuck there. Totally lost. I didn't know where to go or what to do. I couldn't think or remember what might come next.

"For how long?" I heard him say.

"Forever. Never talk to me again."

"Sebastian. We'll get through this. If you'll hear my side."

"No. No. I won't. I'm not interested in anything you have to say."

"But I want you to hear my side."

I whirled back to face him, and he dropped into his chair. He had been hanging like that, half up, half sitting. And he just fell back. "I don't give a goddamn what you want! All my life you've had what you wanted! You know what I wanted? I wanted friends. I wanted a mother. I wanted to get a letter from my grandmother. I wanted to go outside and play. You didn't care. So don't expect me to care about what you want. I'm leaving."

Just as my hand touched the knob I heard him say, "When are you coming back?"

"When I damn well please." I looked over my shoulder at him. "You want to stop me? Go ahead." I faced him and leaned my back on the door. Just to be clear I wasn't running away. I wasn't sneaking out. "You want to enforce your rules? Feel free. Come stop me."

I could tell by his face that he knew what I meant. To stop me he'd have to physically overpower me. If he thought he could do it, if he wanted to take control again, this was his chance to try.

Thing is, I wasn't a little kid anymore. Any coward can bully a little kid. I was six feet tall and pumped full of adrenaline. I waited. But he never even looked me in the eye.

"Yeah, that's what I thought," I said.

Then I went back downstairs to Delilah's for the rest of the day.

Maria | Eight

The Taking of Hostages

I think I was in the hospital for around two or three days. Stella told me how long, but I forgot. You would think I'd know for myself, since I was there. But I wasn't there. Not really. Not most of that time.

I was on a lot of morphine, and time became a whole new theory.

If it had only been the broken ribs, I don't think they'd have kept me. Even though there were four broken. But even so. You break four ribs, they tape you up and send you home. Especially when you don't have insurance. But they had to keep me, because of the punctured lung.

Stella says Carl came to the hospital the very first day, and was all bent out of shape about how we were supposed to pay for this. She also said she brought me a paper to sign because she got a restraining order against him. She says I signed it. She also says he was in jail for a couple of days after that, but unfortunately his mother made bail. You couldn't prove any of this by me. I don't remember any of the above.

I just remember that about four days later I started to get my head up a little, and I was at Stella's, in their spare bedroom. I wasn't on morphine anymore, but Stella brought me two pills with a glass of water every four hours. I don't know what they were, but they helped some.

Most of the time I couldn't move my legs at all, because of the cats and Natalie. When I first woke up at Stella's, I thought I was paralyzed. Seriously. Then when I could finally pick my head up and look I figured out that Ferdy and Alexa and Rahema and that new cat with only one eye whose name I forget and Natalie were sleeping all piled onto my legs. Well, Natalie was mostly just lying there sucking her thumb. But I'm always happy for company, so I never moved them. They seemed comfortable and I didn't want to put them out. Natalie had latched onto an old feather boa of Stella's, as a substitute for the fur collar of Carl's leather jacket. Sometimes she almost disappeared inside it.

Once I remember saying to Stella, when she brought my pills, "I have to go meet Tony tonight. I was supposed to meet him days ago."

"Who?"

"Tony."

"I thought the guy's name was Sebastian."

"I call him Tony, though. I have to go meet him."

And she laughed. "Honey, you couldn't get to the *bathroom* without my help."

"But he'll give up. He'll think I'm never coming. He'll go away."

"So? You'll call him."

"I don't have his phone number."

"Maybe he's listed."

"I don't know his last name."

I closed my eyes so I wouldn't have to watch her shake her head or roll her eyes or whatever she was going to do. With my eyes squeezed shut I realized two things. One, she was right. I couldn't get down to the subway if I tried. Two, he probably gave up days ago. It was probably already way too late.

TWO DAYS AFTER I LANDED AT STELLA'S, Carl came to see me. I could hear him by the door in the living room, fighting with Stella. She was saying that he was violating his restraining order and she was going to call the cops on him. And he was saying that he was going to at least talk to me and if I said he should get out then he would.

He came into my room with this bouquet of flowers in colored plastic wrap, like the kind you get at the supermarket. He hadn't shaved for about three days. He didn't look like he had ever slept or eaten in his life.

Stella ran in after him with the cordless phone. "I'm calling the cops right now," she said.

Carl took the phone out of her hand and smashed it through the closed bedroom window. Stella lives three floors up, so I never heard it hit the ground.

I'm not sure where Stella was after that. Probably calling the cops on the kitchen phone. I was hoping so, anyway.

Carl said, "You don't want me to leave, do you?"

"Yes," I said. "I do."

He handed me the flowers. "For you," he said.

"You know I'm allergic to flowers."

"Oh. I brought you your DVD of *West Side Story*. In case you want to watch it while you're here." He set the flowers on my bedside table, like he hadn't heard a word I said. Then he took the DVD out of his pocket and handed it to me.

"That was very thoughtful," I said. And I meant it sincerely. "Now please get out."

"Let me take the kids," he said. "You're in no position to take care of them."

Stella screeched in from the kitchen. "I'm taking care of the kids."

"Besides," I said, "how can you watch them? You have to work."

"I'm taking a few days off," he said. "And my mother said she'd help with them."

Stella. From the kitchen. "You touch those kids I'll have you arrested so fast it'll make your head spin."

"You can take C.J.," I said. "Natalie stays with me. You can pick C.J. up from school today and take him home."

The whole apartment got very quiet.

"Okay," Carl said.

I saw Stella stick her head back into the room. At first she just stood there with her mouth open. She looked at me, but I just looked down at the blankets.

Then she said to Carl, "I called the police. So, if I were you, I'd be going now."

He did.

After he left, she came and sat on the bed with me.

"Please take those flowers away," I said. "I'm allergic to flowers."

"Why did you let him take C.J.?"

"C.J. will be fine with Carl. Carl loves C.J. He would never hurt him."

"But don't you see what he's doing? He's taking a kid like a hostage. So you have to see him again. So you have to come home."

"I know."

"Then why did you let him take C.J.?"

"It's kind of hard to explain."

I could tell Stella was very upset. I think she thought it meant I was planning to go back to Carl. And I hated for her to think that, but there was nothing I could do. I couldn't tell her the real reason. It was the sort of thing you just didn't tell anybody. At least, until it was way too late for them to talk you out of it. The kind of thing you can't even say to your own sister.

She stomped out of the room. And forgot to take the flowers.

I was a little scared to see her again right then, so I just lay there, feeling the edges of my eyelids start to burn. Feeling the breeze through the broken window. Dreading the moment when I would learn what it felt like to sneeze with four broken ribs.

What We Break

I stood at the bottom of those stairs in the Union Square station. For close to two hours. After the first hour, I took to pacing.

I had the photo of the windmills in a file folder in my hand. Because it was too big for my pocket. And I didn't want to get fingerprints on it, or to get it all dog-eared.

The worst part was, I didn't know whether to be worried or scared or pissed.

Part of me pictured her sitting at home laughing at me. Like, *Imagine that little idiot, thinking I was going to go away with him. He's just a kid.* But my heart and my gut said she'd never do that to me. But then again, my father was always telling me that people will hurt you and let you down in ways you never could have imagined. As long as I can remember he had taught me to expect the worst from everybody.

And now it seemed like the worst had arrived.

Then I started thinking something had happened to her. What if she was hurt? What if he was holding her prisoner and she couldn't come? Or he'd put her in the hospital? Or . . . I couldn't go down that road any further.

I walked up the stairs and onto the street. Walked to the corner, and turned it. Was this her block? Must be. This or the next. I looked up into every lighted window. Saw nothing, of course. Except the flickering of people's TV sets. Dim light behind curtains.

I wanted to call out Carl's name. Challenge him to come down here. Because she might be hurt, and she might need me.

Or she might be fine. And she might get hurt because I called Carl out.

I paced up and down the block I was pretty sure was hers. About another hour, I guess. It was after three.

The anticipation of seeing her had been so huge, so overwhelming, that I couldn't make the adjustment to giving up and going home. Couldn't accept that it wasn't going to happen. It felt like the whole world was crumbling away under my feet. Like the place I'd been standing in the world had suddenly turned to shifting sand. Then it struck me that if it didn't happen tonight, she wouldn't be able to tell me, "Tomorrow." Or "Day after tomorrow." And I'd walk away without knowing when it would happen again.

I opened the file folder and looked at the photo again. Stood under the streetlight and looked at it. And thought, *What if I never see her again? Until I see her again, I can't run away to Mojave. I have to stay here until I know.*

Then I thought, *Get ahold of yourself, Sebastian.* Then I corrected it to Tony. *She just couldn't make it tonight. You'll see her tomorrow. Or the next day.*

I checked the subway station again, in case we'd missed each other.

Then I paced around on that corner some more, the one I'd watched her turn that night in the pouring rain. It was nearly four o'clock.

I finally gave up and walked home.

I MADE A STOP at my own apartment first. I mean, my father's apartment. It had never been mine. And it wasn't my home anymore. But I needed my toothbrush, and a pair of pajamas. And I needed clean clothes for the next day, and my *Romeo and Juliet* book, and a couple of other little things. And I was pretty sure he'd be asleep, anyway. But I was also braced for what would happen if he wasn't. I could feel it coiled up in my muscles. Like the way you walk through a room if you think there's a ghost or a robber afoot.

I opened the door quietly. Heard only silence. The living room was dark.

I turned on the overhead light. No father.

I took a deep breath and walked into my room.

On my pillow was a note. My heart fell down into my stomach. Even though I had no idea what to expect. I turned on the light and picked it up.

"Sebastian," it said. "Someday you will have to let me explain. Your mother leaving was the worst thing that ever happened to me. It's as if my life ended that day. And she took you with, so I had nothing. I got you back, but I couldn't take a chance on her having you. And I couldn't be forced to see her again. It would have killed me. I had to cut it off clean. Please hear my side, Sebastian. I'm your father. I think you owe me that much."

I crumpled the note into a ball in my fist.

"I owe you nothing," I said. Out loud. To no one.

I gathered up my things, and wrapped the book and the toothbrush into a little bundle with my pajamas and my change of clothes. I took a sheet of writing paper out of my desk.

Here's what I wrote on it: "So, you admit it. You did it for yourself, not for me."

I carried it out of my room with me, trying to decide where best to leave it.

On my way back out through the living room, the light was still on, and my eye fell on his shelf of opera records. I'd say there were probably about thirty. Somewhere between two dozen and thirty. All carefully stored upright in their own oak cabinet with the phonograph.

I set my bundle down by the door.

I walked over to the phonograph, and grabbed the needle arm in both hands, and bent in until it snapped. Unfortunately, it snapped right where my left hand was holding it, and the sharp edge of the plastic sliced my palm. But I kept going.

I took each record out of the cabinet, one by one, broke it consciously and carefully against my knee, then left it on top of the growing pile of broken records in the middle of the living room floor. I left them in their cardboard jackets as I did this, so the jackets wouldn't survive the assault, either. It was deeply satisfying to feel the snap of each of his vinyl treasures inside its cardboard sleeve. The fact that I was bleeding onto the cardboard seemed like a fitting punctuation. But I guess that's a tricky one to explain.

The rest, I hope, goes without saying. There was very little I could take away from my father, because there's really nothing he loves. But he loves his records. And we're still on the fence about whether he loves me.

I knew it would be quite a loss for him. Then again, records are just things. They can potentially be replaced. They're not on the level of a really important loss. Like, say, your mother.

When I had broken the last one, I wrapped my handkerchief around my left hand to stop the bleeding. Or slow it down, anyway.

I left my reply to his note on top of the pile I'd created.

Then I went back to Delilah's.

AFTER I'D READ GRANDMA ANNIE'S LETTER for the fifth time, I looked up at Delilah, sitting in her big recliner, fanning herself with her geisha fan in spite of the best efforts of the noisy air conditioner.

"They love me," I said. It was the dearest darling Sebastians that gave her away, and the image of her dancing on the porch, on the phone with my mother, who was dancing at work.

"Of course they do. You're their flesh and blood."

"I'm my father's flesh and blood. But he never called me dearest, darling anything."

Neither one of us said anything for a time.

I felt completely drained inside. Like someone had hollowed me out. And then gone in and sandpapered the empty walls of the shell they'd left behind. Even the inside of my head felt sanded. I'm not sure I could've gotten up and walked across the room. I felt like my bones had turned to rubber. Or been stolen entirely.

"Do you think my father loves me?" It seemed like a reasonable question. He did terrible things to me. He never touched me. He never said anything about love.

She didn't answer off the top of her head. She just sat there and fanned for a minute. Nodding her head as if to stimulate more thoughts.

"Give you two answers," she said. "One, yes. He loves you more than anybody or anything. You're the only one he loves. The only one he's got. So you're everything to him. Two, no. He doesn't love you because he doesn't know how. Because he doesn't love himself. Because he wouldn't know love if it stood up in his soup."

I laughed. It was just a funny way to say a thing, so I laughed. I would have bet you cash money nobody could make me laugh at a moment like that. Not even Delilah. But Delilah made me laugh.

"Which is the true one?"

"They both are," she said.

"How can two things be true at the same time?"

"Oh, child. Lots of things can be true at the same time. You'll see."

We were quiet for a while, and then I said, "I can't stay with him. Not even for four months. I can't. I have to get out of there."

Delilah just nodded. Like she'd been thinking the same thing at the same moment. Like she wasn't even surprised to hear it again, outside her own head.

SOMETIME AROUND SIX she showed me the scene in *Royal Wedding* where Fred Astaire dances on the walls. She got up to put the DVD in the player, but then she sat in her recliner and fanned and held on to the remote control.

"Now let me set this up for you," she said. "So's you don't need to see the whole thing. He's in love with this woman. Only she thinks she's in love with somebody else. But we can see that's going nowhere. But right now she can't see. You know how people are. Or . . . no, maybe you don't. Anyway, she'll see later. So, she's a dancer, and she told him once that she was so in love with this boy when she was young, she thought she could dance right up onto the walls and the ceiling."

Then she hit Play.

Fred Astaire had a picture of this woman he loved. He was in his hotel room in some foreign country. England, I think. Looking at it while he danced. He had it propped up so he could see it while he danced. And sure enough, he danced sideways on the wall. First a testing step. Then for a long time.

I started to ask Delilah to tell me how it was done, but then I realized I didn't want to know. I wanted to believe it was love. I know that sounds stupid. I don't mean I *did* believe it. I'm not saying I did. I'm saying I wanted to.

When the scene was over she clicked the movie off by remote control.

"So it was love," I said. "That's what makes you dance on the walls. Love."

She shot me a serious look. Leaned in closer toward me, like she was about to share a gravely important secret. "Kids, don't try this at home," she said.

I burst out laughing.

I got up and walked over to where she was sitting. Which felt like quite a production, because I was still feeling shaky and drained. Scraped out inside. I leaned over and gave her a big hug, right there in her chair, and kissed her on the cheek.

"Well now," she said. "What was that all about?"

"Because I love you. Because you're my best friend."

"Well, aren't you just the sweetest. I will accept that as the compliment you intended it to be. Even though I happen to know I don't have much in the way of what you'd call competition."

I WOKE UP ON DELILAH'S COUCH, and she was gone. It was still light outside, but going a little dusky.

I sat up slowly, and looked around. Stood up, testing my legs. I felt a little better. A little more rested. I poked my head into the bedroom, but she wasn't there. The bathroom door was open. I called her name. No Delilah.

I had no idea where she would keep something like writing paper. Stationery. If she even did. I think most people just e-mail anymore. Or call.

But she had a little desk in the corner of the living room, and it had a computer and printer on it. And the printer was loaded with paper. So I pulled out one sheet. And I folded it crosswise and made a very sharp crease and then tore it neatly into two little sheets of writing paper. I couldn't find a pen but I borrowed the pencil Delilah had sitting next to her book of crossword puzzles.

I read Grandma Annie's letter one more time, even though I could almost have closed my eyes and recited it by heart.

Then I wrote back.

Dear Grandma Annie,

Thank you for never forgetting me, all these years. And thank you for sending me a picture of my mother, and for loving me.

I can't stay here. I can't stay with my father anymore. I was going to stay four more months, until I was eighteen. And then leave. But I can't wait that long, and I'll tell you why not.

He told me my mother was dead.

I wasn't even going to tell you that. Because it's so awful I didn't even want you to know. I didn't want you to feel the way I knew you would feel when you heard that. But now I feel I have to tell you so you'll understand when I say I can't wait. I have to get out of here, and it has to be now.

I want to come back to Mojave. I remember Mojave really well, even though I was little. I loved it there. I loved the windmills, and the stars at night. I loved the mountains on the horizon. I even loved the heat. The way it felt dry like an oven. I remember the way the heat would shimmer in the air between my eyes and the mountain on a hot day. I'm sure Port Hueneme is nice, but I really loved Mojave. If I can think of a way to get out there, can I come? I won't sponge off you. I'll get a job. I'll get my own place as soon as I can. I just need a way to get started.

I know it's a big favor, and now I'm about to make it bigger. I wouldn't be coming alone. I have a friend. A girl. Well, a woman. She's older than me. Please don't judge about that, okay? Her name is Maria, and she's quiet and sweet.

I know you don't know her, but you'll love her. I know you will. And she'll love you. Please say yes. I don't know what I'll do if you say no.

Your Grandson,
Sebastian

PS: Thank you for the picture of the windmills. I promised Maria I would show her a picture. You've already helped me more than you know.

DELILAH CAME BACK about twenty minutes after I'd finished my letter. It was nearly dark out, and I hadn't turned on any lights. Just let the whole world get dimmer and dimmer. Inside and out.

She clucked her tongue and turned on the overhead light and I blinked like I'd only just been born.

"Sittin' here in the dark," she said. "What were you thinking?" But it was a rhetorical question. Unlike my father, she didn't really insist on knowing my innermost thoughts. "Here," she said. And handed me a little bag.

I turned it upside down and slid a small object out into my hand. A key.

"In case you need to be here when I'm not home. Or if it's late."

I wanted to tell her I could have a hundred friends and she'd still be the best one. But I couldn't bring myself to say all that. Instead I just held it up and held it tightly. And said thanks.

I WENT BACK TO THE SUBWAY and waited for hours, but Maria never showed.

Anita i'm Not

When Stella's husband, Victor, came home from work that night, he taped cardboard over the broken window. I figured that would make it kind of weirdly dark when the morning came. But then again, it made my room a better movie theater.

I asked Victor to bring in the DVD player, and he did.

The first time I watched *West Side Story,* it didn't even hit me. Maybe because I'd seen it all so many times before.

IN THE MORNING, Stella came into my bedroom and threw open the cardboard broken window. She cupped her hands to her mouth and screeched down to the street.

"I'm calling the goddamn cops on you! You're violating your re-straining order just by pacing so close to the door! You have to keep . . . oh, I forget, but a bunch of feet away at all times!"

I couldn't hear what he said in return.

Natalie stuck her head under the covers, like an ostrich.

"And where's C.J.? Huh? Who's taking care of him?"

A pause while I couldn't hear him. Probably just as well.

"And when he gets out of school? You're going to be there to get him? You have to be at work by then."

"He said he was gonna take a few days off," I said.

Stella stormed away from the window and out of the room. The window was still open, and it was too light to watch my movie properly, and I could hear the city noise from the street too well.

I wanted to tell Natalie to go get Stella and bring her back in here so she could close the window. But Natalie still had her head under the covers and I couldn't bring myself to bother her. I could hear water running in the tub. I thought Stella was taking a bath or something.

A few minutes later Stella was back, with a big soup pot. It looked almost too heavy for her to carry. She set it down on the edge of the windowsill and just waited for a few seconds. Looking out, but not leaning out. Not attracting attention.

Then she turned it upside down and dumped it.

This time I could hear Carl.

"Shit!" he yelled.

"Ooooh," Stella said. "I'm a good shot."

Then Stella went and called the cops on the kitchen phone, but by the time they showed up, Carl was dripping dry on the bus bench on the other side of the street, and there was nothing they could—or at least cared enough to—do about it.

WHEN IT WAS AFTER THREE, and Carl had to go pick up C.J. from school, I got out of bed by myself for the first time in a long time.

Natalie said, "Mommy?" But it was the *way* she said it.

"It's okay, honey. Mommy's just going to go look out the window."

But I couldn't get the window open. There was no way. I was in too much pain to grab the thing and pull up on it.

Now, Stella and I had talked about a bell, for when I needed something. But she didn't have one and neither of us was really sure where you go to buy a bell. So this was the bell system we figured out.

"Natalie. Go get your auntie."

"Okay," she said.

STELLA OPENED THE WINDOW FOR ME, and we looked out. There was Carl. Sitting on the bus bench across the street. Looking right back at us. With a binoculars.

Stella gave him the finger.

"I'm going to go find out where C.J. is," she said.

I sat and watched while she went over there and talked to him. I was trying to think how fast I could get to the kitchen phone if things took a bad turn. Which they sometimes do with Carl.

But after a minute she just turned away from him and came back upstairs.

When she got back in my room, she closed the window again.

"His mother's taking care of C.J."

"So he can watch my window night and day."

"Looks like."

"So he can see if I go out to meet anybody. Or if anybody comes to see me."

"That would be my guess."

"I wonder how long he can keep that up."

"It's Carl," she said. "You tell me."

IT WAS THE NEXT TIME I watched the movie. Later that night. That's when it hit me. Right at the part where Movie Maria sends her brother's girlfriend, Anita, with a message for Tony.

I hit Pause.

"Natalie," I said. "Get me that pad of paper off the dresser, okay?"

She did, and I wrote a note to Tony. My Tony.

I told him I was at my sister's but I couldn't tell him where that was, because if he came here, Carl would kill him. And that I had no idea when I could get away. But sometime I would. If he would just keep coming to our place. Only earlier, like before eleven. Because sooner or later Carl would get tired of this and go back to work. Only I had no idea when.

"Please don't give up on me." That's the last thing I said.

"Natalie. Go get your auntie."

"Okay."

A couple of minutes later she came back in, dragging Stella by the hand. Stella was in her pajamas and had on an avocado-colored face mask. With anybody else that would mean she was ready for bed. With Stella it was hard to say.

"What?" she said.

"You need to take him a note. Just like in the movie."

"No freaking way."

"Stella, please. You have to do this for me."

"I don't even know what he looks like."

"He's over six feet tall and has tons of curly hair. And he's young. That weeds out nine guys out of ten right there."

"And there are how many guys that cross that platform every night? And I'm supposed to ask one in ten of them what their names are? In the subway? After midnight?"

"But you're so good at knowing things. Maybe you'll just know by instinct that it's him. Oh, please, Stella. Please? You just gotta do it. It'll be just like in the movie."

"First of all," she said, "stop saying that."

"Saying what?"

"How it'll be just like it was in the movie. Because, as you may recall, in the movie Anita gets herself into quite a bit of trouble doing that little favor. No good deed goes unpunished, as they say. And I'm the one who has to ask a bunch of very tall young men to identify themselves in the subway late at night. So stop comparing it to the damn movie."

"Does that mean you'll do it?"

She sighed very dramatically. And I knew I had won.

Sebastian | Ten

Swirling

After that night, life took on a circular motion. Sometimes it reminded me of a dog chasing its own tail. Other times it was more like water—and other things I'm too polite to mention—circling the toilet bowl when you flush. Either way it was hardly a pretty picture.

When I woke up, Delilah made me pancakes with berry syrup, and then I took the subway to Maria's neighborhood, where I mailed my second letter to Grandma Annie and waited.

And waited.

And waited.

I knew it probably wasn't near the time Carl would have to go to work, but whenever a man walked down the street past me, I looked into his face and wondered. Silently. Carl?

I saw older men who looked civilized and younger men who looked tough. I saw scared-looking guys and nondescript-looking guys, and I realized I really had no idea of what kind of guy could do the things Carl did. I guess I had this image in my head of some big, macho bruiser. But then I'd see a guy go by with neatly combed hair and a suit, and I'd look into his eyes to see if he could do that. Be that. And it seemed like the potential was there.

Maybe all of us could. Maybe it's not that most of us *couldn't*. Maybe it's more that most of us *don't*.

The spiraling was something that happened in my head.

I would think, She's in trouble. She's hurt, she's scared. She can't get to me. She's thinking of me and worrying I'll give up, and then she'll never see me again. And then I'd vow to never give up. To be there whenever she came out to find me again. And for a few minutes I would be this brave Romeo who could swim the widest, deepest ocean to be there for her in her time of need.

Then the doubts would set in. I'd remember her voice and her face when she said, *If* we go away. And, I *think* so. And, *It just feels so scary.* And then this voice in my head would say, Wake up. Grow up. She changed her mind. She doesn't want to see you again.

Then I'd get angry because she didn't even have the decency to come look me in the eye and tell me the truth. And I'd vow to stand here on this corner forever, because sooner or later she had to come by. Sooner or later she had to go to the market or something, and then I'd get to look her in the eye and say, How could you do that to me? Not even have the heart to tell me the truth?

But hours went by, and she didn't come out and walk to the market, and I'd start thinking, She's not coming out because she can't come out. She's hurt, or in trouble. And the cycle would swirl all over again.

It was making me dizzy. It was actually making me sick.

I tried checking all the names on all the buzzers on all the apartment buildings on that block. Maybe they would have first and last names on their buzzers. But they didn't. Last names only.

I was in love with this woman, had offered to share my new life with this woman, and I didn't even know her last name.

And if I didn't know her last name or where she lived, I couldn't call the hospitals to see if she was hurt. And I couldn't call her or see her at home. So there was this very real chance I might never see her again.

That's when it hit me that she *was* my new life, and I could never go back to the old one.

Until I met her, I'd had no life. Nothing had ever happened. Suddenly things had been happening, and now I couldn't go back to the old nothingness. I couldn't.

The rest of my time on that street, I was too tired to pace. I sat on a fire hydrant, feeling the sun burn the back of my neck. I thought about animals in a zoo. About the importance of being born in captivity. I could believe that the animals were happy enough in their cages, if they were born in captivity. Because they knew nothing else. How can you want something if you don't even know it exists? But if one of them got out. Spent a few weeks running free. How would it feel to be caught and caged again?

I was pretty sure I knew.

In time I went back to Delilah's to wait out the midday sun.

THE LETTER FROM MY MOTHER was waiting for me.

Delilah handed it to me without a word.

This time I found my own way over to the couch and sat down. Turned it over in my hands. Read the return address. Celia Vicente. A Spanish-sounding street name I couldn't pronounce. Port Hueneme, CA.

I opened it all by myself.

I could feel Delilah watching me, but not in a bad way. Never the way my father watched me. I can't explain the difference but on a feeling level it was very clear.

I read it out loud to her. On the first time through. That's how much I trusted Delilah. Whatever my mother had to say to me after all these years, she could hear it, too. Funny how when someone insists on knowing everything about me, like my father, I want them to know nothing at all. When someone lets me have as much privacy as I want, like Delilah, sharing everything starts to sound like a good idea.

My dear son Sebastian,

I can't tell you how scared I am, writing this back to you. I keep thinking about what you said in your letter to Grandma. That

*you wanted to ask some questions about me. I keep wondering
what questions you wanted to ask. In my mind you're asking
things like, How could you? Where were you? How am I
supposed to forgive you now?*

*I don't know, Sebastian, but I hope you'll try. I hope you can
understand that I was afraid of him. Of what he'd do. Afraid
not just for myself, but for you. I guess I thought it would be best
for you, too. To just grow up with him and not be torn apart by
the fighting. But maybe I wasn't being completely honest with
myself. I hope you'll believe what I'm about to tell you, because
I've never said a truer thing in my life: Not a day has gone by
that I haven't wished I could have that decision to do over
again. I thought we'd at least be in touch the whole time you
were growing up. I thought we'd write to each other and talk on
the phone. When you didn't answer my letters, I thought you
hated me.*

Maybe you do.

Can we still start over, Sebastian?

*You're almost a man now. That's a hard thing for me to
accept. What's even harder is that you're a man I barely know.
I'm not going to try to say much more for right now. I'll just say
that I want to know you. I want you to be part of my life again.
If you want to know me, just say so. We'll start from there.*

I love you, Sebastian. Always have, always will.

Your mother,
Celia Vicente

I looked up at Delilah and saw the softness in her eyes. She
didn't ask me any questions, but I could hear the one she wasn't
asking.

"I don't know," I said.

"She's your mother."

"She could have fought for me."

"You never really know why people do or don't do what they do or don't do. Until you hear their side of the story. At least hear her side."

"She just told me her side. What does it change? She could have stood up to him."

"Maybe," she said. "Maybe she could have. Or should have. I don't know. I don't like to render judgment, 'specially when I don't know. I'm just saying this to you: Think long and hard before you turn your back on your own mother."

A long silence, during which I said nothing. Because there was really nothing to say.

Then she said, "Ever had Chinese food?"

I shook my head.

She sighed. "Why do I even ask? Come on, child. We're ordering in."

I DON'T WANT TO TALK TOO MUCH about my time at the subway station that night. Just that I got there not too long after dinner and sat right there—in our special spot near the stairs—until four A.M. I guess I don't mind telling you the part where I saw people get on the train, ride away, and then hours later look surprised to see me still sitting there waiting when they got back. From wherever.

What I can't tell you, don't want to, couldn't explain properly even if I tried, was the inside of me. The way my thoughts swirled, the huge leaps from blackness to hope, back to blackness. I'd be ashamed to say I started to bite my own lip out of sheer nerves. Until I made it bleed. But I guess I just did say that, didn't I? Shame and all.

There were too many thoughts to try to recall, and nothing I want to relive anyway. And they didn't make a lot of sense. It was like raw emotion, running around in my head where clear thoughts should be. It colored everything.

I couldn't remember a time when my life hadn't felt exactly like this. I thought of holding her hand on the street, kissing her in a doorway, but it felt like something I dreamed. Like something from a previous life. Maybe none of it had ever happened at all. Maybe my brain invented her to keep from going crazy.

At four, I gave up. Got on a train and rode home.

When I came up the stairs to Lexington Avenue, there was the moon. Floating up there in the sky, looking unusually low and bright. A crescent moon, about a quarter of the way to full. I stopped dead and looked at it. Remembered what Delilah said. About something bigger.

"Thanks for nothing," I said.

Then I walked back to Delilah's place.

THE SUN WAS JUST COMING UP, and I hadn't slept at all. The pillow and blanket Delilah had left out for me were still all neat and folded on the couch. I hadn't even bothered to lie on the couch and try.

I was sitting in her window, looking out. She had one of those windows with a sort of bench. You know, a window seat. We had that in our apartment, too, in the living room. But no way I would sit staring out the window in front of my father.

My eyes felt grainy, like they were full of sand, and my stomach was a little unsettled. I wished I could sleep, to feel better, but I knew it was pointless.

I watched people bustle out of their apartments to go to work in the morning. Watched cabs bunch up and honk and scrape too close to pedestrians. Watched all these people go about their lives.

They had lives.

They went places, and did things, and never thought twice about it.

I wondered how that would feel.

After a while I felt Delilah's hand on my shoulder. I hadn't heard her get up. She was in her bright pink robe with the big many-colored flowers embroidered around the bottom, and on the collar.

"Still no Maria, huh?"

I shook my head.

She looked out on the street with me for a minute. Like she was seeing the world through my eyes. But Delilah had a life. Always had, as best I could figure. So I couldn't imagine we could see things the same.

I said, "What if I never see her again?" But then, even as the words were coming out of my mouth, I realized I had asked Delilah that question already. A long time ago. Or, at least, it sure seemed like a long time ago now. And she had answered me. The answer had seemed impossible even then. Even back when I didn't know Maria's name. Had never touched her. So imagine how impossible it seemed now. "Never mind," I said. "I guess we've been through all that already."

I felt her hand ruffling through my hair.

Next thing I knew, I heard her in the kitchen making breakfast.

IT ONLY TOOK ME about two more days to completely lose hope.

Well, maybe I shouldn't say completely. Maybe I should say *almost* completely. Because I still walked up and down her street all day. And I still sat by the stairs at the Union Square station at night. But all the time I was doing that, I was sure I'd never see her.

It's funny how fast these things flip over. That first night when I was supposed to meet her and she didn't show up, I was just positive she would show. She always had, so I knew she would again. And when she didn't, it was so hard to wrench my brain around to that truth. I almost couldn't believe it.

Now it was just the opposite. I sat for hours by the stairs, never believing for a second that I would actually see her.

I guess that makes it hard to explain why I was even there. Well, where else would I be? I couldn't just sit at Delilah's all day, doing nothing, while she was trying to have a life. I couldn't go home. I couldn't move to Mojave without Maria. The only solution was to find her. So I sat there, trying to squeeze something impossible out of thin air.

But she didn't show.

IT WAS BEFORE BREAKFAST one morning. About eight o'clock. Delilah was sleeping in, later than usual. I was scrubbing the kitchen floor. Not that it was all that dirty. But I thought it would look really nice if I could strip off the old wax and put down one fresh new coat. I thought I could make it look better than she even knew it could look.

I heard the phone ring.

I figured it was Delilah's daughter. And that she would answer it in the bedroom.

A minute later she came out in her big flowery robe, with the phone pressed to her shoulder. As if to keep what she was about to say from the person on the line. She had a surprised, almost startled look on her face.

"It's for you," she said. My stomach went cold. The blood in my veins went cold. I thought, It's my father. He found me. Or it's the police. He called them. They found me. "It's your grandma."

But the icy feeling didn't move off right away, and my head was still spinning when she handed me the phone. I said, "Hello?" Kind of stupidly, like I didn't already know who it was.

"Sebastian? It's me. It's your Grandma Annie."

The words got stuck in my throat. I was trying to think if her voice sounded familiar, but I couldn't honestly claim to remember after so many years.

She went on. Somebody had to. "I got Delilah's number from information. I hope it's okay. She said she didn't mind. But oh, I hope I didn't wake her up. I think I might've woke her up. I wanted to talk about you coming out here."

That woke *me* up. "Can I? Is it okay?"

"Well, of course you can. We'd be thrilled. I told Celia you asked. She comes out to visit every other weekend. But she says it'd be every weekend if you were here. Thing is, right off the bat I don't have a real private space I could offer. You know, for you and your friend. I got that little guesthouse—I don't suppose you even remember that. But it's been so long since anybody used it. It's really fallen into disrepair. It'd need to be cleaned and probably painted and new carpet put down or at least the old carpet tore out. That'd take you a couple weeks at least and meantime I got nothing to offer but a fold-out couch in the living room. But if you're willing, you're welcome to what I got."

My thoughts were spinning so fast, I could hardly think what to say. She said yes. She said yes. To me and Maria both. Then my heart fell down into my shoes, remembering. How could I leave for Mojave without Maria? "I'll get a job," I said. "I won't live off you."

"If you're not too picky," she said, "they're always looking for young people to clean rooms at the motel. It's something to start you off, anyway. Maybe you could do better later on. So, when do you want to come?"

Her voice sounded too cheery. Eager. Almost to the point of being scared. It struck me that this was hard for her, too. That she was scared about how it would work out. Just like me.

I swallowed hard. "Well, I'll have to talk to Maria. See how soon we could leave."

I caught Delilah's glance and watched her cut her eyes away. And felt ashamed. But what could I say? I can't find my girlfriend because I don't even know her last name or where she lives? I wanted badly to change the subject, so I said, "You know I'm still not eighteen. He could make trouble."

"I know. But I talked to a lawyer friend last night. Well, friend of a friend. She says if he never went to court to get legal custody, which he never did, then he'd have to fight through the courts to get you back. And that'd take longer than four months, probably."

"He won't," I said. It hit me as clearly and suddenly as watching the sun come up in the morning, and I knew it was true. He wouldn't go to court to get me back. Because he knew I would tell the truth. Tell everybody he lied to me and told me my mother was dead. He was ashamed of that truth. And his shame would be the best weapon in my own defense. Especially since he knew I'd be gone in just a few months anyway. There wasn't much to gain. "He'll just let me go at this point. I really think."

"Well, we'll see," she said. "Got a pen? I want to give you my number. Call me as soon as you know when you're coming."

I ran the phone over to Delilah's work desk and wrote the number down.

"Okay," I said. "I'll let you know." Then, realizing how much I was leaving off, I said, "Thank you. Really. Thank you. You don't know how much this means to me. I don't know what I would have done if you'd said no."

A brief silence on the line. Then, simply, "We love you, Sebastian."

I wanted to say something back but it stuck. Froze. Did I love Grandma Annie? Did I even remember her well enough to love her? I sure appreciated her right then. But all I could say was "Thank you."

And then we said good-bye.

I stood there with the phone limply hanging off one hand, her number in the other.

I looked up at Delilah. "Sorry it woke you up," I said.

"It didn't," she said. "I was awake almost an hour ago. Sometimes I don't get up right off the bat. Sometimes I just like to lie there and think my own thoughts for a bit. What were you doing down on your knees on my kitchen floor?"

Though, frankly, it was obvious what I had been doing, just to look.

"Stripping off the old wax."

"How come? Who said you had to clean?"

"Well, I have to do something to pull my weight. I don't pay for food. I've been sleeping on your couch for days. I have to do something to make myself worth having around."

She hobbled up to me, took the phone out of my hand. "We're friends," she said. "You and me. You don't have to be my maid. Just my friend."

"Well, I have to finish now. I can't just leave it half-stripped like that."

We both looked at the mess of her kitchen floor in progress.

"Yeah, I'll go along with that," she said.

So I got back to work on the area around the refrigerator, and she moved the coffee machine over to the stove and made coffee in an area that was already stripped. I worked hard and fast because I knew she'd want to make breakfast soon. I knew we were both hungry. I figured I could put down the fresh wax after breakfast.

I looked up to see her watching me. She seemed lost in thought.

"What?" I said. Because she looked like she needed permission to say it.

"How long you gonna wait on her before you give up and go?"

Something heavy twisted back into my stomach. Amazingly, I'd been stripping wax and managing to have an empty head. I'd been forcing myself not to think. Probably because I knew my thinking would lead me here.

"I don't know. How long can I stay on your couch?"

"Well, long as I have this couch for you to stay on, I suppose. But I should warn you, I was fixing to move back to San Diego in about three more weeks. Maybe four, tops."

I sighed. And went back to my work. About a minute later, I said it. Something very hard, but very true. Something we were both thinking anyway. I had to be brave enough to spit it out. "Well, if she hasn't turned up by then, I guess she's not coming."

"Sounds about right to me," Delilah said. "Sounds like you're using your head."

And we spoke no more about it, all the way through breakfast.

I didn't go stand on her street that day. It just didn't feel like any use. I stayed home on Delilah's couch and read *Romeo and Juliet* straight through. I know she must have wondered. It was unlike me. But she didn't comment, or ask any questions.

I was so out of hope that, after dinner, I nearly chose not to go to the subway station at all. It seemed safe and friendly at Delilah's. We could watch a movie. Make popcorn. I could try to be happy. I was never happy sitting by the stairs in the station all night. Because she never showed.

I was just about to open my mouth and tell Delilah my decision. But I didn't. Because I remembered something. Something Delilah had said to me. While we were watching *West Side Story*. She said, "If I was you, I'd start learning to trust what you feel." Or words to that effect.

I thought, What do I feel about this? What do I believe is true? And the answer came back right away. If she could come meet me, she would. That's what I felt. That's what I believed. She'd meet me if she could.

So I showered, and changed my clothes. Walked to the subway and took the train to Union Square. And sat under the stairs.

I THINK I'D PROBABLY BEEN THERE for about an hour when I heard a strange voice say my name.

"Sebastian?"

I jumped up and spun around.

In front of me was this strange woman. Maybe in her mid-thirties, wearing a huge muumuu sort of dress in wild colors. Her hair all piled up on top of her head.

"Yes, I'm Sebastian," I said.

She handed me a letter. I looked down at it. On the front of the sealed envelope, where the address would be if you were going to mail it, was written "Sebastian/Tony." So there was only one person it could be from. My heart leaped up to where I thought I could taste it.

When I looked up, the strange woman was halfway up the stairs.

"Wait," I called, and she stopped and turned around. "Who are you?"

She gave me a funny look. A quizzical sort of look. Like she was surprised I would even ask. "I'm Stella," she said.

Then she walked on. Like that explained everything.

Maria's Choice

I woke up the next morning to find Stella sitting on my bed. Staring at me.

"I gave him your letter," she said.

"Oh, my God. You're an angel. I could kiss you. I mean, if I could move."

I had six cats sleeping on me. Six. Good thing I'm only allergic to flowers.

"I'm going to ask you a point-blank question. And I want an honest answer. Because, honestly, kid. I'm busting my ass to help you here. Which I do not care to do any longer if you're not at least going to help yourself. So you tell me right now. Are you going right back to Carl when this is over?"

"No," I said. And I looked her right in the eye so she would know it was true.

"Then why did you let him take C.J.?"

"I can't separate Carl from C.J. They're too important to each other."

"Ever?"

"I wasn't planning on it, no."

"So every time you want to see C.J. you'll have to see Carl."

By this time I was looking down at the sheets. So she couldn't see into my eyes. So I wouldn't give myself away. "I did what I did for a reason," I said. "Is it fair to ask you to just trust me for now?"

"Not really, no. Do I have a choice?"

"Not really, no."

"Well, then. What will you be wanting for breakfast?"

CARL STALKED STELLA'S BUILDING for about three more days before the building super knocked on the door and wanted to talk to Stella.

The bedroom door was open, and I could hear most of what they said.

"He's following guys into the building. Every time a man comes in the door he follows him to see which apartment he's going to. It's starting to make some of our tenants a little edgy."

Stella said, "Call the goddamn cops and have him arrested."

The super said, "I'm not sure if following somebody up in the elevator is illegal."

Stella said, "It is when it's in violation of his restraining order."

The super said, "We were hoping you could just talk to him."

Stella said, "Sure. Sure I can talk to him. I can talk to him till I'm blue in the face but the stupid bastard won't listen. Believe me. If you want it to stop, you better call the police."

"Well, okay, then," he said. "If that's what you want. If you really think that's best."

"Can I say something?" I yelled out as loud as I could. It hurt.

Natalie did her ostrich routine with the covers. I could see half of Stella's feather boa sticking out.

Silence. Then a minute later Stella and the super stuck their heads through the open bedroom door. Stella had her hair up in curlers. The super was a weirdly short guy with a bad comb-over.

Stella said, "This is his wife, my sister, who he put in the hospital, the son of a bitch."

I wondered why she said we were married when she knew we weren't. Maybe she was trying to make me sound more respectable than I was. Maybe Stella was embarrassed that I wasn't married to the father of my kids. Ashamed, even. I didn't know. I had never asked her before, so I didn't know.

"Pleased to meet you, ma'am," the super said with a little wave. "What did you want, Maria? Why were you yelling for us?"

"I'd like to ask a favor of you," I said. "I would like to ask that you wait a few hours and have him arrested later this evening."

Silence.

Then the super said, "Why this evening?"

"Because it would help me. If he was under arrest this evening I could go out of the house without him following me. I wonder how long it would take for his mother to bail him out again. How long did it take last time, Stella?"

Stella was looking a little confused. "I don't know. A few hours, I guess."

"Yeah, I guess I could wait a bit," the super said. "Probably take them a long time to show up, anyway."

Stella said, "By the way, Mr. Parseghian, I hope you understand that it's only because of this dreadful family emergency that I have my sister here with her six cats. It's only for a few more days. Then we'll be back to three cats, like always. You can overlook our breaking the three-cat rule for just a few days, right?"

"I never saw the extra six cats," he said. "I didn't happen to see them. I'll call the police on that wife-beating son of a bitch when it gets dark tonight."

I PUT NATALIE DOWN TO SLEEP in Stella's bed. And I got dressed real carefully. And then I watched out a two-inch opening in the window for the police to come and take Carl away.

As soon as they did, I was out the door. Slowly. Gingerly. But with plenty of enthusiasm.

I was praying Tony hadn't given up on me already.

No, wait. Not praying. I'm an atheist. At least I think I am.

Or maybe that was always more about Carl than it was about me.

One More Thing

Nine nights later, I was standing on her street. Just above the subway. Just above the stairs down to our special place on our special
platform. Staring up at the moon. Don't ask me why. The subway
station just got too boring. Too painful. I hated the looks from the
people who saw me there every night. It made me feel pathetic.

So I stood outside. Looking up at the moon. It was closer to a
half moon than a crescent now. Taunting me with evidence of how
much time was slipping by.

I wanted to say something to the moon. Okay, I know that
sounds weird. But Delilah said at times like this I should be
thankful for my own life. But I wasn't. Because I felt I had no life.
Hadn't since I was seven. Except that handful of glorious days
when I was going to run away to a new life with Maria. But now,
when even that was in question, what exactly was I supposed to
be thankful for?

But then I thought, Maybe if I just said it. Maybe if I could say it
whether it felt true or not. Maybe it would start to feel truer later on.

I opened my mouth, but I couldn't bring myself to do it. I had
no gratitude because I had nothing to feel gratitude for. Then I
thought, That's not really fair. That's not really true. Grandma

Annie had a place for me in Mojave. That was something. But without Maria, I didn't feel I could go to Mojave. Still . . .

I opened my mouth again. But before I could say anything, I heard it.

"Tony?"

I whipped around. Yes. It was. It was her. It was Maria!

"Maria!" I said, and I lunged in to give her a hug. I was going to give her the biggest bear hug ever.

"No!" she said. "Don't!"

My heart fell right into my shoes.

I just stood there, dumbstruck, my face hot, wondering why I wasn't allowed to hug her. She looked into my face. I know she must have seen the devastation there.

"Oh, Tony," she said, and moved in slowly and gently, and put her arms around me. Set her head down against my shoulder. I just stood there with my arms at my sides, not sure what I was supposed to do. "Just be gentle," she said. "Hug me around my shoulders. Gently. Not around my ribs."

I put my arms around her shoulders. I could smell her hair. Some kind of fresh-smelling shampoo. It took a moment for two and two to come together in my confused brain and add up to four. "Are you hurt?"

"Just that my ribs are all taped up," she said.

I held her away from me at arm's length to look into her face. But she wouldn't meet my eyes. She looked away. "What happened to your ribs?"

"It's not as bad as it sounds," she said. "I just fell wrong. Over the table. And I broke four ribs and one of them punctured my lung. I can't believe you waited for me."

I took a deep breath and spoke out of what I believed. I let all the doubts and fears and swirling drop away. "I knew you'd come if you could."

"Thank you for waiting for me," she said.

She wasn't wearing her hat. She seemed smaller and more vulnerable without it.

"Let's go to Mojave right now," I said. "Not in four months. Now."

"That's what I was thinking. Now." She looked around her as if expecting suitcases to magically appear.

"Are you still at your sister's? Can you pack tomorrow? Or even tonight. How much stuff do you have? How much would you need to—"

"Tony—" she said, interrupting me. My heart sank again. It sounded like a bad "Tony." It sounded like a no.

"What?"

"There's something else. One more thing. That I didn't tell you yet. Because I wasn't sure how you would—"

"It doesn't matter," I said. "I want to go away with you. I never want to take a chance on losing you again. I don't care what it is. Will you go with me?"

I looked more closely into her face in the mostly-dark and saw that she was crying.

"Yes. I will. I just don't want you to change your mind if—"

"Never. I'll never change my mind. Can you go pack right now? How much stuff do you have?"

"I have a big duffel bag. I guess whatever doesn't fit in there I could just leave. I can only take what Stella brought over to her apartment, anyway. I wouldn't dare go back home for the rest of my stuff."

"Tomorrow. While he's at work."

"No. He might not go to work. And he might be out by tomorrow."

"Out? Out of what?"

"Tonight. In about two hours. Is that okay?"

"How will you carry that big duffel bag? You're hurt."

"I'll manage."

"I'll go with you and help."

"No. No, you can't. It's too risky. If he gets out, he'll kill you. I have to go alone. I'll carry the duffel bag. I'll do it because I have to. I'll be there."

I CAME BARGING back into Delilah's like a freight train. After running all the way home from the subway. She was still up. It was nearly midnight but she was still up. I felt so blessed.

"She came," I said. "She came. I asked her to leave with me right away. She said yes."

"Ho, ho, whoa," Delilah said. She was sitting in her big chair, reading a mystery novel. Wearing her little red half-glasses that sat way down on her nose. "I got the part about how you're happy. So, that's good. But the rest was just all gibberish as far as I could hear."

That's when I realized I was so out of breath she hadn't stood a chance of understanding.

I sat down on the couch. Breathed for a minute.

She closed up her book and gave me her complete attention. Watching me over the tops of her red reading glasses.

"She showed up. Maria."

"Oh, child! That's the best news! Did she say where she's been?"

"In the hospital."

Delilah frowned. Scowled, in fact. "He put her there?"

"I think so. I didn't exactly ask."

"Well, that explains a lot, anyway."

"I really banked on your good nature today," I said. "She's meeting me in a couple of hours. With all her stuff. Can I bring her here? Just till we figure out how to get to Mojave?"

"Well, now, child, you know you can. Won't have much privacy."

"It's okay. It's only for a day or two anyway. Oh, wait. How are we going to get to California?"

"We'll think of something," she said. "We'll work something out."

I was quiet for a time. Just thinking. My head spinning around, making circles of all the parts I would still need to work out. Like money. There was so much left to figure out.

I said, pretty much out of nowhere, "She said there's one more thing. That she's been putting off telling me. But I didn't give her a chance to say what it was. Now I wish I had."

"Well, let me ask you this, then. Would there be anything she could tell you that would really matter? I mean, are you sure? Or are you still in a place to let a thing get in your way?"

"I'm sure," I said. Without needing to think.

"Then put it out of your head. Because it won't even matter. If you're sure, you're sure."

I CALLED GRANDMA ANNIE right away. Because it wasn't as late in California. Praying she'd be there. That she'd pick up. She did. On the third ring.

"It's me," I said. "It's Sebastian. We can leave anytime after today. Sooner is better. The sooner we leave, the better. As far as I'm concerned. I'm not really sure how we'll get out there, though. I'm not sure how to get money from my father without starting trouble."

"Don't," she said. "Don't ask that man for anything. After what he did!"

"I feel like he owes it to me, though."

"Don't even open that can of worms. I'll wire you some money. It won't be much, I'm sorry to say. I can wire you about five hundred dollars. You'll have to go down to the Western Union office to pick it up. That sure won't get you out here on a plane or a train. Not both of you. Might do for the bus. If it's enough, go all the way to Bakersfield. I'll pick you up there. If it's not enough to get to Bakersfield, let me know. I'll drive farther."

I said nothing for a minute. I was too filled up with something to talk. A hard something to explain. It's like I was wondering why this stranger would do so much for me. But she was my blood family. My grandmother. I think it was dawning on me how weird and wrong it is that a member of your blood family should be a relative stranger. Not to mention two members of your family.

"This is so nice of you," I said. "I'll pay you back."

"Nonsense. I won't hear of it. Just tell me when to expect you. Soon as you know."

"Okay. Thanks. Really. Thanks."

"We can't wait to see you," she said. "Your mom has to work weekdays, but the very first Friday night she'll be here to see you."

"Grandma Annie . . ." I just stuck on the next thing for a long time. I had no words to put to it yet. No idea when I ever would. So why had I even opened my mouth?

"Yes?"

"Never mind. We'll talk a lot more when I get out there."

WHEN I GOT OFF THE PHONE, I got online on Delilah's computer and looked up the bus fare. The money she was sending was enough for both of us to get from New York to Bakersfield with more than a hundred dollars left over for food along the way. Now, if Maria just showed up like she promised she would, everything would work out perfectly.

Friends in Low Places

When I got back to Stella's, the apartment was all dark. I could hear Victor snoring from the bedroom.

I decided that before I went in there for Natalie I would have to write some notes.

I wrote most of the one to Stella in just a couple of minutes. That was easy. At least, the first part was.

At first I just said I was taking a chance on Tony. That we were going away to a place in California called the Mojave Desert. And that I thought it was nicer than it sounded by the name.

That I had to leave right now, with no notice, in the middle of the night, because otherwise Carl might get out on bail before I had my chance.

I also mentioned that there was a chance I'd be back by morning because maybe Tony would change his mind when he met Natalie.

I thought that was a diplomatic way to say it. Rather than, He might change his mind when he finds out there *is such a thing* as Natalie.

You learn after a while. How not to bring too much crap down onto your own head.

But that wasn't the hard part. The hard part was the part about C.J.

I tried a few things on in my head, but none of them worked out right. And I wasn't even packed yet. And I didn't want to keep Tony waiting any longer than what I promised.

I decided to ditch the Stella note for a while and work on the one for C.J. Now, there's another good little joke in my own head. Like that one would be easier. If I thought the second half of the Stella note was hard . . . The C.J. one was impossible.

I stared at the paper for what I thought was a couple of minutes, but when I looked at the clock I saw I only had about forty minutes left to pack and get Natalie and get down to the station with a duffel bag I probably couldn't even carry.

So I ditched the C.J. note altogether.

And I finished the Stella one like this:

When I get where I'm going I'll give you my address, and I'll also probably send you a letter and ask you to mail it to C.J. Because I can't mail it from California. I can't give Carl any clues. I wanted to leave a note for C.J., right now tonight. But I need a little more time to figure out what I need to say.

Please don't judge me. I am up against a wall here and doing the best I can.

Thank you for helping me,

Love,
Your Sister, Maria

P.S.: Maybe I won't give you my new address for the first six months or so, because then if Carl asks you can honestly say you don't know.

And another P.S.: I will try to send back the duffel bag, which I realize is actually yours, or at least send the money for you to buy another. I'm not sure exactly when I will be able to do this but I promise I'll try.

Oh. One more P.S.: I'm going to be rude and borrow
something without asking. But I will either give it back or
buy you a new one. I'm taking this VHS tape you have of
The Wizard of Oz. It just seems really important that Natalie
have at least one thing that feels familiar to her. If you weren't
family, that would just be too rude. But you are.

Love,
Maria

But I guess I said that part already.

I spent about ten minutes—time I didn't really have to spare—
searching for that tape among what seemed like about a thousand
others. How Stella navigated through that mass of videos was beyond me. But I couldn't give up, because it just felt too important.

By the time I found it I was late and pretty much stressed out.

I thought it would wake Stella up when I went to pull Natalie out
of their bed. She even fussed a little in her sleep when I took the
feather boa away from her. But I guess if Stella can sleep through
Victor's snoring, she can sleep through anything at all.

I HAD TO SORT OF DRAG the duffel bag down the stairs. Bumping
down one step at a time. I had Natalie half-sleeping on one shoulder, and that was painful enough. Just the way it pulled my rib cage
down on one side. Of course, I made sure it was not the bad side.
But it hurt just the same.

Trouble is, when I got to the lobby and had to pick up the bag, I
had to use my bad side.

"Ow," I said, and set it back down again. I can be really good at
understatements at a time like this.

"Hmmmm?" Natalie said. Or at least one syllable that added up
to that type of question.

"Nothing, honey. Go back to sleep."

I went back to dragging the bag by the corner. All the way across the linoleum floor of the lobby to Stella's outside door. Thinking that if I dragged it down to the subway, all down the rough concrete, it would have no bottom and no clothes by the time I got there.

And I was getting short on time, too.

I remembered telling Tony I could haul the bag down there. "I will because I have to," I said, or some bullshit like that. Something that sounded good at the time. Something that reminded me how I tend to bite off all kinds of stuff I can't really manage. Like I think I'm really powerful or something. Like I think my own will can work magic.

When I got through the doorway and out onto the landing, I saw Delores and another bag lady I didn't know, sleeping all huddled over each other on the curb.

Now, in my neighborhood, I say hi to the homeless people. But I never ask them their names and I never tell them mine. Because if one ever called me by my name in front of Carl, ho boy. It would really hit the fan.

But in Stella's neighborhood I feel a little freer. So in Stella's neighborhood, I know just about every street guy and lady personally. Except this one lady who was all curled up with Delores, who I think must have been new.

"Delores," I called in a sort of sharp, loud whisper.

Her head came up. "Yo, Maria," she said. "What you doin' out so late?"

"I need your help, Delores."

"Well, sure, honey. Anything for you."

Sometimes I give quarters to Delores and Sam and Mickey and Lois and some of the others, and even though a quarter wouldn't impress them a bit from some people, they know I don't have much. So it's the thought. You know. They know the good thought behind it. People don't forget things like that. The more people ignore them, the more they remember the ones who don't.

She came down the street to me, smoothing down her ripped skirt with the big yellow flowers on it.

"Bring your shopping cart," I said. "If I could just get you to put this big duffel bag on your cart. And then we can wheel it down to the subway."

She was surprisingly strong, Delores. Picked it up with one hand and threw it so it balanced across both sides of the cart. Then she lifted Natalie out of my hands, so gentle, like she was a newborn baby or something, and set her down in the seat. The seat they build into the cart for kids to ride in it.

And off we went. I was looking at her hair, and how it was formed into permanent mats in the back. Like extra-free-form dreadlocks. Like one of those psychiatric inkblot tests, only with hair.

I was also memorizing the look and feel of a city street in the dark. In case I never walked down one again.

"I don't think I have anything more than just change on me," I said.

"Don't matter to me," she said. "Not if it's you. Where you going?"

"I'm running away."

"From what?"

"My boyfriend."

"Sounds like a good move. Except how you gonna run away with nothing but change in your pocket?"

"Well, I got a friend," I said. "And we just have to do the best we can."

When we got to the subway stairs, she asked me if I wanted her to haul the bag and the girl downstairs for me. But I knew she didn't want to leave her shopping cart with its precious contents unattended. I mean, that was her life savings. So I told her I'd pull the bag down the stairs and it would be okay.

"Enjoy your new life," she said when she handed back Natalie.

"Thank you," I said, and tried to give her my miserable little pocketful of change.

She balled my hand back up into a fist and pushed it right back at me.

"Tonight you need this more than I do," she said.

Fatherhood Lessons

I paced the subway station for about forty-five minutes. Chewing on my lip. Biting my nails, which I almost never did.

Not that she was late. She wasn't. It's that I got there forty-five minutes early. Just in case she was early. I couldn't sit at Delilah's. I was too wound up.

So I just paced. And bit.

Then, finally, what seemed like hours later, I turned to pace back from the far end of the platform and there she was. Standing near our bench by the stairs. She had a big olive-green duffel bag lying on the platform by her feet. And in her arms was a kid. A girl. Bigger than a baby. Smaller than a child who would walk beside you all on her own.

I took two or three fast steps in her direction, then broke into a run.

The closer I got to her, the clearer I could see her face, and the more I saw her face, the more I saw something pleading. Something scared.

Meanwhile my brain was stupid and slow, and not catching up to all this. I was actually thinking, Why is she holding that kid? Whose kid? Where's the person who owns that kid and is about to take her back? There was no one else anywhere near them.

Then I remembered what she'd said. There's one more thing. That I haven't told you yet.

Then I knew.

I saw her face change the moment I got it. To even more scared. So she must have seen a lot of something bad in my eyes. Shock. What else can I call it? I thought it would just be the two of us. I had no idea how wrong I could be.

By now I was close enough to say something to her. But I didn't. Because I didn't know what to say. I slowed down to a fast walk again. Stopped a couple of steps in front of her.

I looked at Maria. Maria looked at me.

I looked at the kid. She looked back.

She was wearing a little dress. A purple dress. And bare feet. Her little bare legs were the tiniest, skinniest things. I couldn't imagine that even the bones of her legs all by themselves could be so skinny. She had dark hair, like her mother, but very thin. Just little wisps of soft-looking dark hair. And the biggest eyes I've ever seen on any face. I mean, the eyes just stole the whole show. They were huge. Dark, liquid brown.

She looked like a porcelain doll. Something desperately easy to break.

She was sucking her thumb.

I heard Maria say, "Tony, this is Natalie."

Natalie looked away again. Buried her face in the junction between Maria's neck and shoulder. Thumb and all.

"It's not you," Maria said. "She's shy. She's like this with everybody."

Then, with Natalie's face hidden, it was just the two of us again. Me and Maria. The pleading look on her face got stronger. Sadder.

I still had not managed to say so much as a word.

"If you want to change your mind," she said, "I'll understand. No hard feelings. Really. Either way."

I just stood mute. No words came. Not even thoughts, really. It was just a blank moment. Well, no it wasn't, really. It was a huge and very busy moment. But within that moment, I was just a blank.

"Please don't change your mind," she said. Her lower lip trembled when she said it. I could see it was all she could do to keep from crying.

It shook me out of my reverie. "I haven't changed my mind. Come on. Let's go."

I picked up her duffel bag. And we got on the train and headed for Delilah's.

DELILAH SWUNG THE DOOR WIDE, her face full of welcome. I expected that look to fall all the way to the carpet and hit hard when she saw the unexpected addition. But it didn't. If anything, she lit up even brighter.

"Well, now, who have we got here?" she said, clearly in a voice intended for a child's ears. "A very lovely little lady, I would say." Natalie buried her head, thumb and all. "You must be Maria," Delilah said. "Come in, come in. Are you hungry?"

We stepped inside, and life just seemed to go on from there. If Delilah was shocked, or even particularly surprised, she never let on.

"I had dinner," Maria said. "But thank you for asking."

She sat on the couch. Perched on the edge, a little nervous. She set Natalie next to her, and Natalie sucked her thumb and stared with wide eyes. Looked around the room for a minute. Then glued her eyes to Delilah.

I said nothing.

"What about that little girl? She eaten?"

"No, she won't eat when anything is different. She hates change. It's really hard to get her to eat even at home. She won't talk around anybody new, either. New people make her nervous. So don't take it personally if she's afraid of you."

"I'm going to make something I betcha she'll eat." And Delilah set to bustling about the kitchen. Opening cupboards and setting

food on counters. Setting pans on the stove. Into and out of the refrigerator, fetching things.

"Just promise me you won't be insulted if she won't eat it,"
Maria said.

Delilah hobbled back into the living room and stood in front of
the couch, looking down at Natalie and speaking directly to her.
Amazingly, Natalie did not bury her face or look away.

"Now, how about if I make something that's just so out-of-
this-world delicious that even the pickiest eater in the world
couldn't hardly resist it?" She gave Natalie a wink. Natalie just
stared. "Babies tend to like me," Delilah said. "I get along good
with babies."

Natalie took her thumb out of her mouth for the first time since
I'd made her acquaintance. "I'm not a baby," she said. Looking
right up into Delilah's big smiling face.

"Wow," Maria said. "That's a first."

Delilah scooped Natalie up into her arms. I expected her to
scream and cry and reach for her mother, but none of that happened. She just rode Delilah's hip into the kitchen. Sucking her
thumb. "You know, I think I was mistaken. You're right. You're not
a baby at all. You're a pretty darn big girl. I guess you must be,
what, maybe three years old?"

She shook her head, thumb and all.

"She'll be three in October," Maria said.

"Well, that *is* pretty big. That's a big girl. That's sure as heck no
baby. Can you forgive me for calling you a baby? Can you let that
big giant mistake go by?" I think Natalie might have nodded, but I
could barely see her head over Delilah's shoulder. They were in the
kitchen now, back to their cooking. "Now, you get a look at what
I'm making here. And you'll see you're hungrier than you think
you are. Just wait till you see."

I sat on the edge of Delilah's big chair. I looked at Maria, sitting
on the couch. And she looked at me. She smiled a weak little smile,
and I smiled back. It was the first real moment we'd had since I'd

lost her for all that time. The first chance we had to just be together, and say hello with our eyes. It made my stomach feel warm. Not hot, just warm. It was different, this smile. It was about a whole something else.

"Oh, child," I heard Delilah call from the kitchen, and I knew she meant me. "There's a phone message on my desk from your Grandma Annie. Has everything about where you need to go and what you need to do to pick up that money."

So that was the end of that moment.

I retrieved the message, and read it over. "I better go do this now," I said. "Then we can leave in the morning."

In my head I was thinking, Do two-year-olds ride the bus for free? Or is that a whole other bus fare? And will that whole other bus fare even fit into that leftover hundred-and-some dollars? And even if it does, what are we supposed to do for food for three or four days on the road? But I didn't ask any of that out loud. I just walked down to the Western Union office to pick up the money.

MARIA TOOK NATALIE into the bathroom to give her a bath before bed.

It was the first moment Delilah and I had alone together to talk.

"Sweet girl," Delilah said.

"Which one?"

"Well, I meant Maria. But both, I guess. Look, I didn't want to say this in front of her. But I called the bus company. While you was gone. It's gonna be an extra hundred and nine for the baby. It still all fits into five hundred. But it only leaves you twenty-five or thirty for food. That's not much for three people."

"We'll have to make do," I said.

"Why don't you let me give you fifty?"

"No. No way. Thanks, but you've done so much already."

"I can spare it."

"No, I couldn't take your money, Delilah. I wouldn't feel right."

"How about a loan?"

"No, please. I'd feel really guilty."

"Okay, how about this, then? How about I pack you some sand-wiches for the first day, and then some stuff that doesn't need to stay cool? Some nuts and dried fruit and candy bars and crackers? How would that be?"

"Well . . ." I still hated to take from her. When she'd given so much already. "That would be . . . nice."

"Done and done," she said, and got up to putter in the kitchen.

I got up and wandered in after her. Leaned on the counter and watched her work.

"Thanks," I said.

"It ain't hardly nothing."

"This is not exactly the way I pictured things."

"Life rarely is, honey. Like the old saying: If you want to hear God laugh, tell Her your plans. But she's here. And you're going. Isn't that the main thing?"

"Yeah. It is. I just feel like . . . it's so many people to be re-sponsible for."

"Honey, she been raising that child for years. She knows what to do. And she knows how to take care of herself, too. They each got their own Higher Power, and you are not It. You just put one foot in front of the other and don't worry so much."

"I just wish that kid wasn't so terrified of me."

"I would not take that personally if I was you."

Silence for a moment. I watched her spread peanut butter on six slices of whole wheat bread. Perfectly, and right to the edge, in about three smooth movements of the knife.

"She's not afraid of *you*," I said.

"That's because I'm not afraid of *her*. Think about that."

Then Maria came back out and asked permission to use one of Delilah's towels on the bed, on top of a rubber sheet she'd brought, because sometimes Natalie wets the bed.

So that was the end of my one and only fatherhood lesson. From that moment forth I was completely on my own.

A Painfully Obvious Question

I was in Tony's friend's bathroom, giving Natalie a bath, when the question first came up.

She doesn't talk a whole lot, Natalie. I mean, she's starting to. But she still chooses her moments carefully. When she said that thing to Tony's friend about not being a baby, I just about fell off the couch. That's about a month's worth of comments from her.

So I was not expecting her to ask any questions.

I was washing her hair, with real baby shampoo. Tony's friend had real baby shampoo. Which I thought was interesting. At home I had to wash her hair extra carefully with regular shampoo, because Carl thinks it's stupid to buy two kinds. Too expensive. I just had to be really careful not to get any in her eyes. But here I was in a house with no baby, and there was real baby shampoo. I felt like I'd landed in a place where everything I needed would appear before my eyes. I wondered if it would be that way from now on. Now that I had gotten brave enough to run away.

I was looking at Natalie's little ribs. How skinny she is. I think it's more than just normal skinny. Not that she's sick or anything. I know she's not. I took her to a doctor.

He said there was nothing wrong with her and I said, Well, then why is she so skinny? He said she had something called "failure to thrive." I asked him a lot about what that meant, but the most I could get was that there was no real physical cause. Like a fancy medical term for "it just *is* that way." Medicine is funny. Science, too. They have to think of names for things they can't explain, otherwise they'll never get any sleep at night.

Sometimes I feel like she's trying to disappear. Like she wants to subtract herself right out from under the world.

Maybe she'll eat more when we get there. Maybe we both will.

So I started telling her what it was going to be like, in this new place we were going to. Which was hard, because I didn't know much myself. So I just stuck with things I know. Like there wouldn't be any yelling and we could do what we wanted when we wanted.

I didn't mention hitting, even to tell her it was over, because that might just upset her more. Even bringing it up like that in conversation.

That's when she opened her mouth and asked that question I didn't expect.

"Where's C.J.?"

I was so surprised. It took me a minute to answer.

"Well, he's home. With Daddy. He's going to be with Daddy. And we're going to go someplace new."

She was quiet for a minute. I was rinsing the last of the baby shampoo out of her hair. She has beautiful hair, Natalie. Even though it's thin. But it's so soft and shiny. I could just touch it all day long.

"Where's C.J.?" She asked it again.

"He's at home, honey."

"Where's C.J.?"

That's when it hit me, everything that she was really trying to ask. She doesn't know thousands of words. She's only two. If she's going to try to get some information, she has a limit to the number of ways she can ask.

That's when it hit me that she wanted to know more than *where* C.J. was. She wanted to know *why*.

I was counting on not having to explain that. I thought I was headed somewhere where nobody I met would know enough to ask.

"He's just not coming with us, honey."

"Where's C.J.?"

Translation: Why on earth not?

Part of me wanted to tell her not to ask that in front of Tony. But I couldn't do that. That's the sort of thing Carl would do. Carl is the kind of person who would actually tell somebody else what they were and were not allowed to say. So I figured I wouldn't be.

I decided to just keep my fingers crossed that she had gotten the question out of her system.

But it stayed with me. It took away that nice happy feeling that everything was going to be okay now.

I guess I'm pretty good at pretending. If there's not a soul around who knows what's missing from this picture, I can pretty much pretend there's nothing missing. But all it takes is one person to remind me. I think I might be too sensitive about how I look through other people's eyes. What they think of me. At least, that's what a therapist told me once. Right after my mother died.

I thought it was only grown-up people, but it turns out you can look into the eyes of a two-year-old and feel a big sense of judgment come down on your head.

"Let's talk about something happy," I said.

But I did all the talking from that point on. She never said another word.

One Face in the World

Natalie wouldn't go to sleep on Delilah's bed unless Maria was there with her. And she wasn't all that quick to go to sleep. So the way it shook out, I bedded down on the couch alone. And the three of them ended up in Delilah's bed. Which I guess was okay. We'd never get two on the couch anyway. And I couldn't ask someone with broken ribs to sleep on the floor. And no matter where we slept there was no real privacy anyway.

But it felt lonely.

After midnight, I got up. Decided to go upstairs to my father's apartment. Make sure there wasn't anything else I cared to take along.

I'd been up there twice in the middle of the night. Taking clothes, mostly. A book or two. A few basic grooming items. I kept thinking something had to have sentimental value. But nothing did. It was all part of a life I didn't want to remember. If you could call it a life at all.

The only thing I really regretted leaving was my computer. But it was a desktop, and I just couldn't imagine any way to bring it along.

I stood in the hall outside his apartment door. What I'd called "our door" for all those years. It had only been a matter of a couple of weeks since I'd walked out. It was amazing how *over* that whole period of my life felt. How quickly it had become buried in the past.

I put my ear to the door and listened. Nothing. I opened it quietly.

The lights were all off. He'd taken his sleeping pill and gone to bed. Part of me felt relieved, and another part of me felt disappointed. Just all at once like that. I remembered Delilah saying two things can be true at the same time. That I would find that out. I think I knew now what she meant. Of course I didn't want to see him. Or talk to him. And yet part of me expected some kind of showdown. Some sense of conclusion. And instead the dark, quiet apartment just felt like an anticlimax.

The record cabinet lay empty. No record player, no records. But he hadn't put anything in the cabinet to take their place. It was just an empty, gaping hole I had created. Just for a minute I felt bad. To have done that to him.

I walked into my room. No note on the pillow. He must have been convinced I was really gone.

I poked around in my closet, but only managed to find one more shirt I wanted. The rest was just old stuff. Barely even me anymore.

I booted up my computer one last time. Deleted all the Internet history. So he couldn't see that I'd been looking up Mojave. If he got smart enough to check, and found someone who knew computers well enough to help him. None of which was likely. But I did it all the same. Then I shut it down for the last time. Ran my hand over the top of the monitor. Feeling sad. But then I realized the reason I loved it so much. Because it was my link with the world. But I wouldn't need a window onto the world where I was going. I'd be a part of it. For real.

When I turned to leave my bedroom, I expected to see him standing there in the doorway. Blocking me. It was like a sudden image that flashed in my head. But the doorway was empty. And it was time to go.

It felt weird to leave without saying good-bye. So I went into my bathroom, picked up a bar of soap, and wrote it on the mirror. I had no idea how long it would take him to go into my bathroom. If he ever did. But at least he could never claim I left without saying good-bye.

WHEN I GOT BACK DOWNSTAIRS, I peeked in the door to the bedroom.

Delilah was snoring like a buzz saw. I was amazed I hadn't heard her from the living room. Maria was in the middle, and she looked asleep. She was faced in my direction, and I just stood there looking at her face. Thinking about how it would feel to lie awake every night and every morning and watch her sleep.

Natalie was sleeping on the outside with her right thumb in her mouth. In her left hand she held one of Delilah's enormous fuzzy slippers. She'd managed to fall asleep with her cheek against it, and I could see her fingers move against the long fur even in her sleep. Stroking.

Then Maria opened her eyes. Not like she was waking up. Like she'd only been lying there with her eyes closed. Not sleeping at all.

I smiled at her, and she smiled back. I got that warm thing in my stomach again. But I didn't run away from it. I just stood there and smiled at her.

A minute later she lifted up the covers and climbed over Natalie without waking her. Tucked her back in, and then came to where I stood in the bedroom doorway and kissed me on the cheek. She was wearing a big checkered flannel shirt that came almost down to her knees, and it was hard not to stare at her legs. Beautiful long, thin legs. Woman legs. A new thing to me. I mean, like this. Not that I never saw a woman on the street in shorts or anything. But this was different.

"Can't sleep?" I whispered.

"No, how can I?"

"I know. The excitement and all."

"Oh, yeah. I meant the snoring. But that, too."

I took her hand and pulled her out into the living room and we sat down on my bed on the couch. For a few minutes we just sat that way, with my arm around her, and no one said a thing.

Then she said, "I'm lucky. That you're not most guys. Most guys would've changed their mind."

"My mind is pretty made up," I said.

"Your friend is really nice."

"Yeah, she is."

"I'm sorry I didn't tell you. I thought I had four months to tell you. And that if we got to know each other a little better . . . you know . . . it would be easier."

I didn't say anything because I didn't know what to say.

"She's a good girl. Really. And she'll get to like you. If you can just get to know her."

But I didn't really want to talk about that. I wanted to talk about us. So I said nothing.

After a while she turned her face up to me, so I kissed her. A little longer and deeper than anything we'd ever done before. Everything changed inside me, and the kisses got breathier, but I just kept my hands in her hair or on her neck or shoulders, because I was scared of hurting her. I couldn't think of any way to touch her with either my hands or my body without hurting her ribs. I thought about touching her legs, but if I did there'd be some sense of needing to move forward to something, and I just didn't see how we could. Not with her broken ribs and with two other people in the apartment. There was just nowhere to go.

So we just kissed.

I don't really remember stopping. I don't remember a moment when we decided, That's enough kissing. Like such a thing was even possible. I just remember Delilah in the kitchen, with the baby on her hip, waking us up by saying, "Honey, you best get up now so's you don't miss your bus."

It was morning, and light, and we were sleeping sitting up—mostly sitting up—with her head against my chest.

I whispered good morning to Maria. For the first time ever. A new tradition. A start on a new way to be.

LEAVING WAS HARD. It was a hard set of good-byes.

Natalie didn't want to let go of Delilah's slipper. And I didn't want to let go of Delilah.

Natalie fussed and cried. Not cried with tears, but cried out with indignant and unhappy noises. I mostly kept my thoughts to myself.

"I'm sorry," Maria said. "She's usually such a well-behaved girl."

"Well, honey," Delilah said, "cut her some slack. This is all so new to her. If my son hadn't given me those slippers . . ."

"No, they're yours. They need to stay here. She just misses her daddy's fur collar. This leather jacket with a fur collar that unsnaps. She used to carry it all over the house. But we had to leave it behind."

That rattled around in my brain in an unpleasant way. She misses her daddy's fur collar. Would she also miss her daddy? Did she have some kind of relationship with that man? Something good? Did he care about his daughter? And if so, how would that feel, to never know where she was or how to see her again?

Delilah broke up my thoughts by handing me a big paper grocery sack. "Food," she said. "For the small fry here, as well as the two of you. And there's an envelope in there. Make sure it doesn't get thrown out. It's got my address and phone number in San Diego. I'll be back there by the end of the month."

I took it, wanting to say thank you, but not able to say much of anything at all.

Natalie was still fussing. Making indignant noises. Not words, just sentiments.

"Now, call me if you miss that bus for some reason," she said. "Not that I think you will. But if I don't hear from you, I'll figure that's the bus you're on. And then I'll call your grandma and tell her. So she'll know when to come and get you."

It had never occurred to me that Delilah would call her for me. But I was thrilled. Because if I didn't talk to Grandma Annie until we saw her, then I wouldn't have to decide whether or not to warn her about the third party. Part of me felt like that might be the last straw. I hoped I was making too much out of it. Maybe Grandma Annie loved babies, like Delilah did.

I looked at Delilah and almost didn't want to go.

"What am I going to do without you?" I said.

"Oh, now, honey, don't go getting maudlin on me. It's not good-bye forever. It's just See you later. We're only three or four hours apart in California. You'll come visit."

"I know, but . . ."

"I know, child, I know. I'm sort of accustomed to having you around, too. Now don't make a long good-bye out of this. Just go on and don't look back. You got more waiting for you than what you're leaving behind. Go make a life, okay?"

I nodded. And decided to follow her advice.

"Okay, Delilah," I said. "Thanks for everything. See you later."

And we walked out together, the three of us. Two terrified barely-grown-ups and one fussy baby. And I didn't look back.

I LEARNED A COUPLE OF THINGS about Maria at the Port Authority bus station. Hanging out waiting to get on the bus and go. And it was funny, because she never opened her mouth to say a word. But I learned a couple of important things all the same.

First, I found out that there was only one face in the whole world, as far as I was concerned, and it was hers. Exactly hers. Nobody else's. It matched the one I had been trying so hard to remember, to see in my head, for so long. And it wasn't just her features, either. It was her smile. The way she cut her eyes away. The way she moved.

It was like a key that fit into a lock when no other key would.

And then everything was open. Everything that had been locked up all my life. Just open wide.

It was almost too much to bear.

I learned another thing, too. I really didn't know her.

That amazing face, those eyes, that hair, the smile, and the body language all belonged to a relative stranger. We had so much invested in each other. Yet most of who the other person actually *was* remained a mystery.

I also figured out that she was scared. So I guess that's three things, huh? But I guess I don't blame her. I was scared, too.

I want to say what I was scared of, but . . . No, wait, that was a stupid thing to say. I was scared of everything. I was leaving behind everything that had ever been familiar to me. The only parent I'd ever known. Such as he was. But still. My best friend, Delilah. The only city I could ever remember living in. All behind me. And in front of me, something entirely new. I wasn't even sure I knew exactly what.

But there was a bigger piece to it. Something more specific. And it's hard for me to talk about, because I was taught that there are some things a gentleman just does not say. It had to do with those delicate issues of our finally getting a moment to be alone together. You know what I'm saying. Those old habits die hard, so this is hard for me to say.

But it was about the broken ribs, and the kid. And having nothing but a fold-out couch at Grandma Annie's in front of us.

I felt like it was never going to happen.

I don't mean I was upset that it might be postponed. I mean I felt like it was *never* going to happen. Do you know the feeling I mean? When no matter how hard you chase something, it's always just beyond your reach? Always just disappearing around the corner? And you start to think it always will be? That in some ways it isn't even real?

Enough. I was making myself crazy with this. And we had a bus to catch. And a cranky little girl with no fur collar and no fuzzy slipper. And she was scared, too.

And I didn't blame her, either.

I walked over to the vending machines and got her a bottle of water. And brought it back, and opened it for her. But she pushed it away. And kept fussing.

I caught Maria's eye and saw how apologetic she felt. She wanted Natalie to behave, but you can't just will a thing like that and make it true. Besides, why should she behave? Her entire world was changing. I wasn't sure I felt like behaving myself.

I smiled at Maria, to try to help her feel better. And she smiled back. Just for a minute we decided to try to have a moment together. To try to pretend that Natalie wasn't haven't a semi-noisy tantrum.

"You look scared," I said. Because I guess saying it felt better than not saying it.

"Yeah." She nodded. "You?"

Just then they announced the boarding of our bus. So I didn't have to answer. Which is just as well.

WE WATCHED THE CITY CHANGE. Watched the heart of the city turn into the outskirts of the city. Factories. Wrecking yards. Train yards. Billboards. El train tracks.

If I had ever seen the outskirts of the city, I had sure forgotten it since.

I think we could both feel that we both had the same reaction to what we were seeing. What did I expect to see, after we left Manhattan? I hadn't thought much about it.

"Ever been out of the city?" I asked her.

"Not since I was a baby," she said. Speaking of babies, Natalie was still fussing. Little grunts and groans and angry-sounding bursts of air. "She might be hungry enough to eat something," Maria said. "At this point she might actually eat a tiny bit."

So I pulled out the big paper grocery sack full of food. I'd had it stashed under the seat in front of me. I wanted to be sure to pull out the envelope with Delilah's address. Save it in a safe place before I let either or both of them plow around in there.

I held the envelope tightly while Maria dug around and found a candy bar.

She unwrapped one end, and Natalie sucked on it. Never even took a bite, that I could see. Just ate it like it was a chocolate Popsicle.

The silence was a beautiful thing.

I looked away and opened the envelope.

Inside was a paper with Delilah's address on it, a note in her handwriting, and fifty dollars in cash.

I read the note. It said, "You are a brave warrior."

That's all it said. But it was enough to make me cry. I blocked it, though. I sat on it. I wouldn't let myself. But I scraped pretty close, all the same.

In my own head, I vowed to pay back that fifty dollars.

All through New Jersey, it was all I could do to keep from crying. It was a full-time job.

MARIA TOOK HER LAST PAINKILLER in Ohio. Vicodin, I think they were.

"That doesn't seem like very many," I said. "Wasn't that only about five or six days' worth?"

"Supposed to be a week," she said. "But they only lasted six days."

"Doesn't seem like much for all those broken ribs. And the thing with your lung."

"I was supposed to be able to refill it. But then I left."

"Oh."

I thought of maybe calling her doctor at the next stop. Or calling the pharmacy where she had the prescription filled. Seeing if they could somehow phone it in to a pharmacy on the road. But when would we stop near a pharmacy? And then I realized we didn't want to leave any trail to suggest which way she had gone.

So I said the only other thing I could think of. "Want me to get off at the next stop and see if I can get you some Tylenol or something? Advil?"

"Advil would be better than nothing," she said.

The next stop was pretty slim pickings, though. The bus station wasn't near anything except a couple of fast-food places.

By the time we stopped again, I knew she was in a lot of pain. She didn't say anything, but I knew. I could see it on her face. Plus she wouldn't let Natalie sit on her lap anymore. I guess she kept bumping her ribs. So Natalie had to wedge into the middle between our hips, and she was not a happy camper. Her grunts and complaints had turned to wails, and the other passengers kept sighing and giving us dirty looks.

This time, though, the bus station was right on the main street of this little town. What little town, I don't know. I couldn't even have told you what state we were in. But there was a little market a few doors down. And I ran for it.

I passed a hole-in-the-wall Italian restaurant and a Children's Hospital thrift store on the way there. Bought a big bottle of Advil, 120 count, with Delilah's money, which I still had in my jeans pocket. Wrapped around her warrior note.

On the way back, I stopped for a second in front of the thrift store.

In the window was a mannequin wearing a dark green cloth coat with a fur collar. I was wondering if it snapped off. On the mannequin's hands was some kind of piece of fur, too. White and brown in patches. Long fur. It seemed strangely out of place on a June afternoon.

I ran inside.

"What's that thing on the mannequin's hands?" I asked the woman behind the counter.

"That's a muff," she said.

"A what?"

"A muff. Something ladies put their hands in. To keep them warm. Never saw one before?"

"I don't think so."

"I guess its old-fashioned now."

She stepped into the window and pulled it off, to show me. I looked out through the window and kept an eye on the bus. Made sure the door was still open. That it wasn't about to take off without me.

She set it in my hands. "Rabbit fur," she said.

"Wow. It's so soft." I touched it to my cheek. Got a flash of insight into what made Natalie tick.

"It's got a bad spot on it, though," she said. "Right here." She pointed out a place near the seam where the fur had been rubbed or torn away.

"How much?"

"Well, it's not what you might call perfect. Six dollars?"

"Sold."

I counted out seven to cover tax and didn't wait for my change. I ran all the way back to the bus. I needn't have bothered. Nearly half the passengers hadn't gotten back on yet.

I could hear Natalie, but she was no longer wailing. Back to fussing. I wondered if she was happier when I wasn't around.

Maria's face was really showing the strain. From the pain or from the fussy baby, I wasn't sure which. Probably both.

"For you," I said, and gave her the Advil. "For you," I said to Natalie, and gave her the rabbit-fur muff.

Her eyes got even bigger, if such a thing was possible. She grabbed it out of my hands and held it to her cheek. Rubbed the side of her face against it. For the first time in hours, silence. I climbed over them to sit in the open window seat. Looked back at Maria.

"That was brilliant," she said. "Where did you get it?"

"That little thrift shop. It was right in the window."

"That was so sweet of you."

"It wasn't even very expensive."

"Natalie, tell Tony thank you." Nothing. "Natalie. Tony gave you a present. I know you like it. The least you can do is say thank you." Nothing.

"It's okay," I said. "She doesn't have to say anything. Don't force her. I can see she likes it."

The silence lasted. And with all that silence and the hypnotizing motion of the bus—even in daylight—it was surprisingly easy to sleep. It snuck up on us. And it was more than welcome.

I WOKE IN WHAT I THINK was the middle of the night to hear Natalie fussing again. Urgently, as if to alert us that something was suddenly very wrong.

I turned on my little overhead light. Maria was still asleep.

No muff. She must have dropped it.

I couldn't see it anywhere, but I managed to find it with my foot. But the seats were so small and I had so little leg room that I couldn't reach down to get it.

I heard a guy in the seat behind us say, "Not again."

I turned it around with my foot, stuck the toe of my shoe into it, flipped it up, and caught it with my left hand. Handed it back to Natalie, who held it to her cheek and stroked it with two fingers. Her thumb went back into her mouth. I turned off the light again.

Maria never had to wake up.

A minute or two later, I heard the soft, wet sound of Natalie's thumb being pulled out of her mouth. "Thank you, Tony," she said.

"You're welcome."

Then I couldn't get back to sleep right away, so I watched dark, flat landscape roll by for a few minutes. I was wishing Delilah were here, so I could ask two questions: Is love always confusing like this? And, Are you sure?

The Department of Stars

I've lived in the city my whole life.

I'm not saying I didn't know all this other stuff was out here. I knew. I went to school. I saw pictures of the country. I watched TV. And I saw some movies. So I knew it was out there. But that didn't exactly prepare me for this enormous world.

I know Mercury and Jupiter and Pluto are out there, too. I just hadn't planned on visiting anytime soon.

Now, I don't want to seem in any way like I'm not happy. Because I am. Very happy. And if there's one thing I really don't like, it's when people get everything they ever dreamed of and more, but they're still not happy. All they can do is complain.

I never want to be one of those people. So I will just say two things very quickly and then get back to being happy.

One. I am in a lot more pain than I realized. I didn't know how bad I was hurt until the Vicodin ran out. Tony was really nice to get me some ibuprofen, and I took about eight, I think, which helped a little but then it also made me sick to my stomach.

Okay, that's too much complaining. I don't like complaining.

Number two is not a complaint so much as a fear: I don't know if Tony's grandmother knows I'm coming. Not to mention me and Natalie. So what if, at the end of the line, she just says no?

I keep telling myself that Tony and I would work out that problem together. And that helps a little. But it keeps coming back into my head.

Enough of that. I'm going back to happy.

We made a stop late at night, after dark. It was one of those stops where they turn on the lights and you can get off the bus for fifteen minutes if you want. Go in the station. Walk around. You have no idea how much it means to walk around if you haven't ridden a bus for days.

I thought Tony was sleeping, so I got off by myself. Left Natalie sleeping draped over Tony's lap. Hoping she wouldn't wake up and find out that she had trusted someone in her sleep.

I didn't go inside.

I was just standing in this field near the bus station. Looking at the stars.

I'm pretty sure that, when Tony first told me about the stars, he thought I wasn't listening. You can always tell when someone thinks you're not listening. It makes them talk a lot harder. I was listening, but I was just worried about the thing with the two kids he didn't know existed, and I guess that's why I seemed far away.

I wanted to see so many stars. If that was really true.

Maybe it wouldn't be true until we got to his grandmother's house in the desert. But we had gone far enough that I thought it would pay to check.

I dropped my head back. It was a clear, clear night. There were more stars than I had ever seen in the city. Maybe not as many as Tony said to expect. But then again, we weren't half there yet. Maybe we were picking up stars all along the way.

I decided I could wait.

And, while I was waiting, this was enough in the star department to keep me busy for now.

After a minute I felt Tony move up against my shoulder.

I spun around real quick to see where Natalie was. If she was still on the bus. You can't just leave a baby on a bus. Sick people will steal a baby. But she was sleeping on Tony's shoulder. So I relaxed.

He put his arm around my waist. Soft. Careful not to hurt me. It hurt a little. Everything hurt a little. But I didn't say so, because I didn't want to make it go away.

I said, quiet so as not to wake Natalie, "Are there more stars than this in the desert?"

"Oh, yeah," he said. "Lots more."

I liked his voice. It was starting to sound familiar to me. I liked that he was not a guy who would leave Natalie on a bus.

"This is nice for now, though," I said.

And he said, "You can sort of think of it like a coming attraction."

Then we were going to get back on the bus, but just before we did, I saw this family—a guy and a lady and two kids—standing there, like they were seeing somebody off. And they had a golden retriever.

Sometimes I'm afraid of dogs, because where I lived in the city, they're not all nice. Not by a long shot. But golden retrievers are always nice. So far as I know. When I was a kid, my best friend, Stacy, had a golden retriever. I loved that dog. He died, though. She said he died of old age, but he was only twelve. That seems too young to die of old age, even though I know they say that's about right for dogs. And even though he did act kind of old. But it still doesn't seem fair.

I went up to the couple and asked if I could pet their dog, and they said I could.

The dog wagged his tail at me, and he licked my hand three times, so that made me feel good.

For a long time, not much has made me feel good, so when something does, I notice. It may be some weirdly small thing that somebody else wouldn't even bother to tell. Maybe wouldn't even notice. But I haven't had as much practice with this happy thing as they have.

I think Tony was afraid of the dog, but I told him to just reach his hand out. He did, and the dog licked the back of his hand, and he smiled.

Then, just as we were getting on the bus, this girl a few years older than me got on with a little boy. A little blond boy about five or six years old.

So, I don't mean to complain, but that's three.

I still did my best to get back to happy. But that little blond boy made it a much longer trip.

Real

There's something about a bus trip that makes you want to sleep. Maybe it's just the sheer boredom of it. The country is so big, and the bus is so slow. You start to ache to put more miles behind you, faster. Sleep is a blessing, because you wake up, and a piece of the trip is over. And you blessedly missed it.

But there's more to it than just that. There's also something about the bus that makes you *able* to sleep. Something about the rolling, vibrating motion. It hypnotizes you. The flat, monotonous scenery, rolling by the window. The farms and wheat fields that could just as easily be part of the last state, or the next. It's better than counting sheep.

Add to that the fact that I hadn't had one decent night's sleep in probably close to two weeks, and I think it forms a clear picture. I slept most of the first night and most of the second day. In fits and starts. With interruptions for walking dazed into bus stations, where the lights were always too bright, to use a real restroom or buy a bottle of orange juice. But, back on the bus, I'd be back to sleep.

Half the time when I woke up, Maria would be sleeping. Sometimes Natalie would be looking past me out the window. I wondered if she viewed it as something like a TV or movie screen. Or if she fully understood that we were moving miles away from everything we had ever known. My hope was that she didn't fully understand. Because that was a truth I was barely old enough and brave enough to handle myself.

The second night I woke up and knew that, unfortunately, I'd had enough sleep to last me for a while.

Maria was asleep with her head on my shoulder. Natalie was sleeping across both of our laps, her legs and feet on Maria's lap, her upper body on mine. Her thumb in her mouth, of course, and a death grip on that precious piece of fur. One of her elbows was digging into my thigh. It hurt a little, but I didn't want to disturb her.

Her hair was falling across her face, so I reached out and brushed it back again. It felt so soft. I got that feeling again, like when I stood in the thrift store touching that rabbit fur for the first time. The feeling that I understood Natalie and her needs.

So for a minute I just stroked her hair. Brushed my hand over it, enjoying not only the softness, but the peacefulness of her sleep.

Then I put my hand in the middle of her back and rubbed it softly. Because I knew how much it had meant to have my mother do that for me. Kids need to be touched. Loved in a way they can actually feel. If I was going to be one of the grown-ups in this kid's life, I was going to see to it that she had some of what every kid needs. It's only right. It's just the only decent way to be.

I felt Maria's head shift slightly on my shoulder. I looked over to see that she was awake and watching me.

"It makes me so happy to see you two getting along," she said.

"I want you to be happy," I said. And it was true. But we both knew I hadn't done it just for her, because I hadn't even known she was awake. Which, I guess, is part of why it made her so happy.

She kissed me softly, and then we fell under the spell of kissing again, the way we did on Delilah's couch. It went on for a long time.

Her tongue felt so velvety smooth against mine, and I remember thinking how real that was. And maybe if that was real, so was all the other stuff that seemed like it never would—never could—happen. But those were just disjointed thoughts in my head, and they didn't even last very long. Kisses like that fill up the whole world. Drive every thought out of your head. Pull you right down into the present moment. Which was probably a good place for me to stay.

In a few minutes we had to consciously force ourselves to stop, because it was pulling us toward a place we couldn't possibly go yet.

Instead she just leaned the side of her head against mine and we talked in a whisper.

"It's hard to stop," she said.

"Yeah."

"Does your grandmother know I'm coming? Or does she think it's just you? Tell me the truth, now. Please."

"She knows you're coming. She's fine with it."

"But she doesn't know about Natalie."

I got a little clutch in my stomach when she said that. "I'm not sure. Delilah is the only one who's talked to her since . . ." I trailed off, not quite knowing how to label that Meeting Natalie moment. "I'm not sure if that's something she would have mentioned or not." I tried to sound casual. I tried not to let on that I was worried about that, too.

"How long can we stay with her?"

"As long as we need, I guess. As long as we want to. She has this little guesthouse."

I was planning on saying more but she cut me off.

"We'll have our own house?"

"Well, a little one. But I have to warn you. She says it's a mess. It's going to take us probably a solid week of work to get it ready. We'll probably have to sleep on her fold-out couch until then. All three of us. So the first week could be hard."

"No, that'll be good," she said. "That'll give us something to do.

I'm good when I get to clean or something. Takes me out of myself."

We sat in silence for a few minutes. I was wondering if she could even help clean in her condition. I think we were both looking out the window. I know I was. I thought I could see the dark outlines of mountains in the distance. The scenery was changing. Suddenly it felt very real, being in a whole different part of the country. It felt foreign and strange and exposed. I reminded myself of Mojave, and the windmills, because it was something familiar. Something I held out to myself, for down the road. A place I already knew and loved. Even if I hadn't seen it for years.

Then I felt bad for Maria, because she didn't even have that.

"I never showed you the picture of the windmills," I said. "I brought it with me that first night. That first night you weren't there."

"Oh, God," she said. "I don't even want to think about that night."

"I'm sorry."

"It's not your fault. What did you do with the picture?"

"Oh. It's with me. But it's in my big bag. The one that's in the baggage compartment. Not the one under the seat."

"Oh," she said. "I guess it doesn't matter anyway. I'll see them with my own eyes soon enough." We watched the landscape roll by in silence for a little while longer. I remember wishing I could lie down. Get into some other position. My ankles and feet felt too big. They were blowing up like balloons. My back had a kink in it. I was beginning to hate the bus seat. It felt like a prison. And we still had so far to go.

I started thinking that maybe it was weird that Maria and I didn't talk much. That she hadn't asked me where we'd stay or how long until now. That she still wasn't telling me more about herself or asking more about me. It hit me that maybe that was weird.

I say maybe because how was I to know? Other than Delilah, I'd never gotten to know anybody. So how could I know if we were doing it the usual way or not? But something felt empty about it. And I couldn't bring it up, because I didn't know how a thing like this was supposed to be.

As if she was reading my mind, she said, "I don't even know your last name."

"Mundt," I said.

"Oh. Mine's Arquette. I just thought it was too weird to run away with somebody when you don't even know their last name."

"Easy enough to fix, though," I said. Liking that she and I seemed to have been in something of the same place in our heads.

Then she said, "Tell me again about it."

"What? The desert?"

"Yeah. The windmills and the heat and the mountains and the stars at night. Like you did that night on the subway."

So I ran through it all again, with all the detail I could possibly remember. I knew she needed it. So I tried to make it feel real.

THE LAST DAY AND A HALF WERE HELL. I don't know how to say it any better or any more plainly than that. It was torture.

First of all, I can barely describe how my body felt after three or four days of sitting in basically the same position. My back screamed with pain. I had a serious kink in my neck from sleeping wrong on it. My feet were so swollen it hurt just to wear my shoes. But I had to, because if I took them off, my feet would have swelled to the point where I doubt I could have gotten them back on again.

Then I had to try to translate my own pain into what Maria must be feeling. How would I feel if I had all this plus broken ribs?

I was pretty sure I could see the answer on her face. The skin of her face looked almost gray to me. She spent a lot of time with her eyes pressed shut. Once I saw her take nine Advil, all in one hand-ful. I wondered if even that helped much at all.

I started feeling apologetic about it. I never should have asked her to leave when she was still injured, and in pain. What was I thinking? How selfish was that?

"I'm really sorry I couldn't afford something better," I said. "Like a plane."

She looked at me strangely. Like that was the last thing in the world she expected me to say. "I couldn't even have afforded the bus," she said. "So don't feel bad."

But I think I mostly still did.

Then, to cap it all off, Natalie entered a new phase. She would pull her thumb out of her mouth. Look at me for a moment. Then turn to her mother and say, quietly—almost under her breath—"Where's C.J.?"

I had no idea who that was, and part of me wanted to ask, but I didn't. Maybe they had left a dog or a cat behind. Or a best friend. Maybe that was what she called her father. Which made me wonder again what kind of bond she had with her father. If she missed him.

I could tell it was hard for Maria to be forced to talk at all, but she usually said something vaguely comforting in return.

"Don't worry about it, honey, we're going to a new home."

"We'll be fine with just us. We're going to a really nice new place."

"Don't be afraid, honey. Everything is going to be fine."

Except for one time. There was this one time. I had been looking out the window. Noticing how the landscape had turned to desert. We were either in Arizona or New Mexico, I'm not sure which one. I wanted to point it out to Maria, because to me it was a source of comfort. We were already in the desert. But I'd seen her look out the window once or twice and not register much reaction. I didn't want to be like Natalie, forcing her to respond through her pain. So I just watched it myself, and took comfort.

After a while I closed my eyes. But I wasn't asleep. But I think maybe Maria thought I was. I heard Natalie's thumb pulling out of her mouth. That soft, wet sucking sound I'd heard so many times. And I braced for it.

"Where's C.J.?"

"I miss him too, honey," Maria said.

I sat still with my eyes closed for a long time. I didn't want her to know I'd been awake. I could feel this pain like a knife slicing into the vertical space between my ribs. Just under my heart. It was a radiating pain, almost a burning.

She might have been talking about a dog or a cat. She might not have been talking about *him.*

This tumbled around and around in my head for a long time. Finally I just had to put a stop to it. I just had to put it out of my mind. There was nothing else I could think to do. But the point of that knife never found its way out again. Every time I took a full, deep breath, I could feel that little knife point wedged underneath my ribs. Reminding me.

BY THE TIME WE PULLED INTO BAKERSFIELD, I was just full-on scared. What if Grandma Annie wasn't there? I hadn't even talked to her myself since finding out when our bus was arriving. Did I even have her phone number with me? If not, would it be listed? Could I get a listing for Delilah and then call Delilah and get Grandma Annie's number?

When I thought of Delilah, a strange feeling swayed through my stomach. If only I could be sitting on her couch right now. Where everything was familiar and safe.

Grandma Annie will be there, I told myself.

But that was scary, too. What if she was someone I could barely talk to? What if we didn't like each other much now that I was grown? What if she took one look at Natalie and said, "No way. That's just pushing a favor too far."

I tried to avoid Maria's eyes, because I didn't want her to see how scared I was. And I didn't want to see how scared she was. But I think we both knew that we both knew.

As the bus turned into the station, I saw a blue pickup truck with reddish-brown primer spots sitting more or less by itself in the parking lot. I couldn't have told you, until that exact moment, that Grandma Annie used to drive a blue pickup truck with red-dish-brown rust primer all over it. But I knew when I saw it. I didn't figure it was the same truck, though. She must've gotten a new car by now. It just reminded me.

Maria carried Natalie into the station. I carried the two enormous bags.

She was there. Waiting to see who got off the bus. Problem is, when you get to a station, it's like a break for everybody. A chance to get off the bus and eat or walk around or use the bathroom. So everybody got off the bus, whether they were going to Bakersfield or not.

So I was looking at Grandma Annie, knowing it was her—with her sun-damaged skin and her long, straight gray-blond hair and her unusual gray eyes—but she kept looking right through me. Looking at everybody to try to see somebody who could be me.

I dropped the heavy bags, raised one hand. Caught her eye. I watched her face change. I wish I could describe how it changed, but it's hard. It started out as worry, that's easy enough. But it turned into something deeper and harder to pinpoint. If I had to try, I'd say it turned into pleasure at seeing me, mixed with sadness over not seeing me for so long. After all, I'd grown a good three feet since then. I was like walking, breathing evidence of all that water under the bridge.

She ran to me, and threw her arms around me, and I picked her up. It wasn't hard. She was little and light. I didn't know I was about to do that. But her head barely came up to about my shoulder, so I just grabbed her around the ribs and picked her up to hug her, and we both laughed.

"Oh, my God, look at you," she said. "You're a grown man."

I put her down and saw she was crying.

"Grandma, this is Maria."

She wiped at her eyes, like she was ashamed of her own tears. Extended a hand for Maria to shake. At this point she must have made some kind of mental note, even in her current over-emotional state, of the fact that Maria was holding a kid. But nothing got said out loud. Nothing registered to the degree that I could see it.

"And Natalie," I said.

"Hello, Maria. Hello, Natalie. Pleased to meet you."

She shook Maria's hand, then offered to do the same for Natalie, who buried her face in her mother's neck.

"She's just shy," Maria said. "Please don't take it personally."

I watched Grandma Annie take a big, deep breath. Settle herself into the moment.

"Well," she said, "let's go." I grabbed the big bags again, and we walked. "We'll be a little crowded in the front of that truck," she said. "But I guess we'll manage."

We said nothing in response. I wasn't sure what to say. I wasn't sure if I had just been told there was a problem or not. But one way or another, it was a problem I couldn't solve.

We walked out of the bus station together and out into the desert morning heat. I guess it was about eighty. Not so bad as it would be later that afternoon. But it felt like the desert. It wasn't New York City. You could know that with your eyes closed.

"Remember this old truck?" I heard her ask. And, sure enough, she walked us right up to the blue pickup truck with the rust-primer spots.

"This truck is kind of hard to forget," I said.

"Still runs great. And that's what counts, right?"

The truck didn't have air-conditioning. Which is tough in the desert. But I guess that's not what counts.

"It has two-sixty air-conditioning," she said.

"I never heard of that," I said. "What is it?"

"Roll down two windows and drive sixty miles per hour."

So that's what we did.

WHEN WE GOT TO THE PLACE where I could first see the windmills on the pass up ahead, I pointed them out to Natalie. First, I mean. I mean, it was a general announcement. An overall announcement. I wanted Maria to see them, too, of course.

But what I said was, "Look, Natalie. Look at the windmills."

I'm not sure why. Tradition, I guess. Kids need to see windmills.

Maria was sitting in the middle, between me and Grandma Annie, and she ducked her head down to see. "Wow," she said. "Wow. Somehow that's not what I was picturing. I mean . . . I don't know what I was picturing. But, I mean . . . wow."

Natalie just stared at first. Blinked. Then she decided she wanted to see them out the window, so she launched off Maria's lap, pushed off with both hands and landed on my lap, and it hurt Maria's ribs. We could all hear it. She let out a sound like a cross between a grunt and a roar. I could feel the rabbit-fur muff land lightly on my feet.

Natalie hung her whole head out the window, her thin hair blowing back in the hot wind, and I instinctively held her around the waist, as if she might fly away like a bit of paper.

"You okay?" I asked Maria.

She nodded gravely. "My ribs are taped up," she said to Grandma Annie.

"Oh," Grandma Annie said. A note of something in her voice. One of those things you can hear even when the person isn't saying it. "Had an accident?"

I looked at her quickly and cut my eyes away and Maria never met her eyes.

"Yeah," Maria said. "An accident."

But after that things were weirdly uncomfortable. And I wasn't sure why. So I did the only thing I could think to do. I hung my head out the window and looked at the windmills with Natalie. It made me happy, like something you thought was only a dream, and now here it is. I think Natalie could tell I was happy. I'm not even sure what makes me say that. But I'm still pretty sure it was true.

I noticed that she didn't have her thumb in her mouth for maybe the first time since I'd met her.

I said, "Natalie, do you like the windmills?"

"Yeah," she said.

Word number four from Natalie to me.

The Wind

I never really stopped to think about the desert. I mean, even after I knew I was going to go live there. I thought about being with Tony. And that there would be a lot more stars at night. I maybe even wanted to see what he meant about windmills.

But the desert itself—I not only didn't give it any thought, I guess I figured there was nothing really to think about. I mean, it's a desert. Right? It's like outer space. Just a big void. And it's dry. So, what's to think about?

I was so wrong.

I was so blown away when we drove away from Bakersfield in Tony's grandmother's old truck. First of all, there were hills and mountains, but not like the kind you see in pictures. Some looked like huge rocks, all eroded in sections, and others looked like regular smooth hills but with thousands of little rocks scattered all over them. And the trees were more like cactus trees, reaching up with two arms, and then with these little balls of cactus-type leaves at the ends, like the cactus were holding what they grew in their hands. Everything was sort of one color, which was tan, but in shades, so you started thinking tan was the only color you even needed.

And the wind. It was different. It had some kind of energy that I never felt at home. Maybe because it was a hot wind. Where I come from, when it's windy it's usually cold. But there was something else different about it, and I couldn't quite put my finger on what. Maybe wind changes when it bumps into too many buildings. I don't know. I just know I had this feeling like if there was still some stuff in me I didn't want, some old crap I'd carried along for the ride, I could just throw it out and the wind would make it gone.

Probably that was just imagination. But I liked it, so I stuck with that thought.

It was so beautiful it almost made me cry. Well, that's not quite right. It's not so much because it was beautiful that I got a lump in my throat. It's because I never thought I'd get to see anyplace like this. Never in a million years.

You know what the best part was? Not a tall building in site. Most of where we drove, not a *building* in site. Not any kind of one. But now and then there'd be a house or a gas station or a little store, but only one floor. Not an upstairs anything as far as the eye could see.

The sky was bluer than I've ever seen a sky be, so I started thinking that maybe the idea was not to block the sky. That the people who built houses and stores out here knew they had a better sky than anybody else's. So they made sure not to get in the way.

People must be a lot smarter out here in the desert. In the city, anybody'll get in the way of anything. They don't really care.

Then after we had been driving awhile we came to this pass over the mountains, and there were the windmills that Tony had been trying to tell me about for so long. They made me suck in a big breath that I almost forgot to let out again. I'm not sure what I was picturing, but whatever it was, it was not as good as what I saw.

I had this funny feeling in my stomach, and it took me a minute to realize it was good. A good feeling.

Everything was really perfect until Natalie hurt my ribs and I had to say out loud that my ribs were taped up.

That bothered Tony's grandmother. A lot. And I have no idea why. I mean, you're either hurt or you're not. It's not like it hurts *her* any. But she got real quiet after that. And even though she'd been pretty quiet before, this quiet was different.

I can read people. When they get tense, I always know it. I don't even have to be looking at their face. And even if they say they're not upset, I still know. I can't even tell you what it is I know by, but I always turn out to be right. I'm like a weather vane for what's happening with the insides of other people. I can always feel the wind change.

I decided there was only one possible reason I could think of. Somehow the fact that I was beat up was like a red flag to let her know that I was from the land of trouble. That I was nothing but trouble, like my father always said.

I guess normal people don't get beat up as much as people like me.

So then I started thinking again that maybe she wouldn't let us stay. Maybe we'd even have to go back to the city. Which I hated to think. Because I already loved it here in the desert. I know it sounds like I wasn't even there long enough to love it yet. But it was like love at first sight. Really, like falling in love, only with a place.

Even if we had to go back, I decided it was worth it to ride that bus all the way out here. It was worth it just for Natalie to see the windmills. Even if she never saw anything like this again. Maybe at least she could hang on to the idea that there's something better out there, somewhere.

Maybe she would remember.

You can't want something for yourself if you don't even know it exists.

I tried to just relax and enjoy the view. And enjoy the fact that Tony was being so sweet with Natalie, and that they were getting along. I had a lot to feel good about.

But I can always tell when someone's upset. It's hard for me to relax unless everybody else will, too.

What We've Dreamed Of

When I opened the door to the little guesthouse, I thought I was pre-pared for anything. I told myself I wouldn't be shocked. No matter how worn down, run-down, torn down it was, I would be ready.

But I was in no way prepared for what we saw.

It was perfect.

The carpeting was brand-new. The walls looked like they had been painted in about the last ten minutes. It even smelled a little like fresh paint. The windows sparkled.

It was really just one room with a bathroom and a tiny nook of a kitchen. Miniature appliances that looked like they belonged in a trailer or an RV. But they must have been brand-new. If they weren't, they sure knew how to do a good imitation.

The main room had a couch and two stuffed chairs. I wondered if the couch folded out. I figured it must. They might not have been brand-new but they were in great condition.

Over the little mantel hung a banner. A long paper banner. It said, "Welcome home, Sebastian." There were little bits of other things written on in pen, but I couldn't read them from the door.

It was warm inside, but not sweltering, and I could hear the sound of a blowing motor.

I looked at Grandma Annie. "This is our little surprise," she said. I still got the feeling that there was something she wasn't saying. I got the sense that something was wrong.

"Who's we?"

"Word got around that I'd heard from you, and you were coming, and everybody put together a team to fix this place up. Paint and carpet and new appliances and furniture. And they even fixed the swamp cooler. It'll never be as good as real air-conditioning but it's something. I couldn't believe anybody could get it done in time but they were determined. One day there were fifteen people here at once. Mostly people from the motel. But a few townspeople, too. A lot of them met you when you were little. The others just know you from hearing so much about you."

A silence fell. Well, maybe *fell* is the wrong word. Because it seemed to ricochet off the walls and hit my ears again and again.

There was so much happening to me at once, I couldn't break it all down to something that could be said. I couldn't isolate anything.

"The couch folds out," she said. "If you children want to take a nap. You must be beat."

It seemed odd to me that in Grandma Annie's eyes we were all three children.

She bustled off and left us alone.

I pulled the cushions off the couch and pulled out the bed. It had clean white sheets on it. I wondered if there were blankets anywhere. Pillows. In a closet or a drawer. But we didn't need them right now and I was too tired and overwhelmed to stay with that thought.

I sat down on the edge of the bed and Maria came and sat down close beside me. I could feel her hip bump up against mine, and it felt good. A purposely familiar gesture. She laid Natalie down beside her and Natalie just lay there, eyes wide open, her thumb in her mouth, a death grip on the fur.

I brushed the hair back off Maria's forehead.

"You okay?" I said. Quietly. Feeling like we were no longer strangers in any way.

"Yeah. Tired."

"You want to take a nap?"

"Yeah. I think it would do Natalie good, too."

"Okay."

I was wondering where Natalie was going to sleep. Not for a nap that day, but in general. Always. But it didn't seem like the time to bring it up.

"You should go talk to your grandmother," she said. I could hear the note of tension in her voice. Fear. Or was *fear* too big a word? No, I don't think so. Fear. "See what's wrong."

"She *was* acting a little funny," I said, picking up the fear like something contagious.

"It's the three of us. It's too many. She's going to ask us to leave."

"No. I don't think so. It was something that happened on the drive. She was fine at the bus station. Something happened later on, but I don't know what it was."

"Maybe you better go talk to her," she said.

"Okay." I said it calmly. At least I hope I did. But I didn't feel calm.

On the way out I stopped and looked at the banner close up. The people who had fixed up this house for us had all signed it. It said things like, "Welcome back to Mojave! Jerry Argenaut." "Your grandmother loves you and so do we. Minnie Binch." "Enjoy the new place. We're glad you're here!!! Todd and Dora Martin." I just read a few. Then it all got to be too much for me.

A couple of months ago, I would've told you there wasn't more than one person in the world who really loved me. Maybe not even that. Then I met Delilah, and I knew she did. I knew it nearly from the start. Now here was this declaration—no, more than a declaration, concrete proof—of love from dozens of people, and I didn't even know them.

I looked back at Maria. She was lying on the bed beside Natalie. Faced away. I wondered if Maria loved me. She'd never exactly said so. But she was here. And maybe that's concrete proof. But as I walked out into the baking heat of the Mojave day, I couldn't help feeling that—as with my father—we were still on the fence about that.

THE BOARDS ON THE STAIRS up to Grandma Annie's back porch creaked under my weight. They announced me before I was ready to be announced. I could see into the kitchen, and she was working in there. Puttering between the fridge and the counter. I saw her look up at the sound, then look away again.

I raised my right hand to knock but she spared me the trouble.

"Come on in, hon."

I stepped into her kitchen. The linoleum was so faded it looked as if the design had been walked right off. But it was clean, and had a nice fresh coat of wax on it. Maybe good wax jobs run in the family. I could tell the house had only a swamp cooler, too. It was about twenty degrees cooler inside, but not the icy shock of air-conditioning. And I could hear it blowing.

"I was making some lemonade for later," she said. "For when you kids woke up. But you can have some now if you want."

I looked at the little hand juicer on the counter in front of her. It had a red plastic top. Delilah's was all glass. But it was still the familiar sight of cut lemons and a hand juicer.

She was working with her back to me.

"Delilah used to make me lemonade from scratch," I said.

"Well, I'm glad you like it, hon."

Another long silence.

I sat down on a kitchen chair and looked at the refrigerator, with its four or five dozen magnets. Some were shaped like fruit, some like hot-air balloons, some like seashells or fish. Some were from places like the Grand Canyon and Carlsbad Caverns. Most held some small scrap of paper underneath. A newspaper clipping or snapshot or recipe. Her counters were lined two deep with glass canisters of peas and beans and pasta.

"Did I do something wrong?" I just said it out of nowhere. Without even really wasting any time gearing up to speak. No answer. "Because everything seemed fine at first, and then it wasn't anymore, and I don't know what happened or how to fix it."

Suddenly Grandma Annie's face was right in mine, filling my whole field of vision. I tried to push back but the chair legs stuck on the linoleum under my weight.

"You want to fix it? I'll tell you how to fix it. You look me right straight in the eye and tell me you didn't break that girl's ribs."

At first I was too stunned to speak. But I think my face might have spoken for me. Because her face softened when she saw my reaction.

After a horrible moment's pause I said, "I would never do that."

And I think she believed me. I think I could see that she did.

"Well, then why did you look away like that? When I asked if it was an accident?"

"Like what?" But I had a bad feeling I knew.

"Like you were ashamed of something."

"Oh," I said. And felt ashamed all over again. "It was nothing *that* bad."

Her face retreated, and she sat down on one of the other kitchen chairs. They had hard, straight wood backs, and I could feel the wood digging into my shoulder blades. I tried to relax a little. Grandma Annie looked guilty and sad, like she wished she had never said it out loud.

"I'm sorry," she said. "It's just, you looked like you had something to hide around that."

I took a deep breath. It struck me suddenly that this is what it meant to be out in the world. You had to make your way with people. You had to hit big bumps in the road. "I was ashamed for you to know that a few days before we got on that bus together she was living with some other guy. This guy named Carl who had a bad temper."

"Why, honey? Why would you be ashamed of that?"

I was surprised. To say the least. I thought it went without saying. "I guess it just seemed kind of pathetic. Here I am asking you if I can bring my girlfriend, and she really isn't even my girlfriend, I just want her to be. You know?"

"Oh, honey, I don't care about stuff like that. Just so long as your heart's in a good place. Just so long as I can trust you."

I wanted to say something. I wanted to know how she could have thought something so awful about me. But I couldn't say that. Could I? Then I had another thought: If she can say what she's really thinking, so can I. And if she's going to, then I almost have to.

"How could you think I would do a thing like that?"

That hurt, guilty look again. "Well, honey, I don't really know you."

"Oh. That's true."

We sat at the table in silence for a while. A beam of light from the window fell across the table, and I watched little particles of dust float around in it. They looked so bright and so detailed. Like some kind of kinetic art. Beyond that I saw the lemon halves still lying on the counter. Not yet squeezed.

When she spoke again, it made me jump.

"It's just that, the one fear your mother and I've had all this time . . ." Enough time went by that I thought I might never know what it was. "All these years . . . was that . . . you might grow up to be . . ." The longest pause of all. The longest pause in the history of pauses. ". . . like your father."

"I'm nothing like my father." I spit it out like something poisonous had just landed in my mouth. I was surprised at my own voice. A vehemence almost bordering on hatred. "I will never be like him. Never."

"Good," she said. "Then can we just let that whole thing go by?"

"Yes." I said it with some firmness. And I meant it. It was gone, left behind. I was letting it go by.

"I'll just finish up this lemonade. And then we can go sit on the porch with it. Unless it's too hot out there for you. Oh. It's probably too hot out there."

"I like the heat. I've been looking forward to the heat."

It was a true thing, but a hard thing to explain. I guess I was trusting the heat to make me feel alive, and to remind me that I was really here. At last.

"I FEEL LIKE I'VE DREAMED OF THIS PLACE my whole life," I said. We were sitting on her front-porch swing. I could feel sweat trickling down between my shoulder blades. The big round thermometer on the front of her house said it was 105 degrees. And it was in the shade. "It's weird to think that it was only a few weeks ago that I even remembered I'd ever been here. Because it doesn't feel like a place I've been dreaming of for a few weeks. It feels like a place I've been dreaming of all my life." I stared at the windmills for a while in silence. Watched them spin, whole sections out of rhythm with whole other sections, through the shimmery distortion of the rising bands of heat. "Do you think you can miss a place even if you don't consciously remember it?"

"I don't know," she said. "But I would allow for the possibility."

I took another sip of the lemonade. It was not as sweet as Delilah's. But it was refreshing.

Then she said, "He called here."

My stomach turned to ice. It flowed in my blood. Made my brain tingle. "My father?" But there was no other "he" she could have meant.

She nodded. "Said he just wanted to know you're okay."

"So he knows I'm here?"

"I doubt it. I think he figures you went to Celia's. But he would never call there. Never. I just said you weren't here. And you weren't yet. So that was true. But I said I'd spoken to you and I knew for a fact you were all right. And he swore that was all he wanted to know."

"Do you believe him?"

"I never know what to believe from that man. But he sounded relieved to hear you were okay."

Then we didn't talk for a long time. Some kind of little insect was circling my head, and I swatted at it, but it never seemed to do much good. I could feel the sweat on my face. The spinning windmills were beginning to hypnotize me in some subtle way.

"Do you think he loves me?" I asked after a while.

"To the degree he's even able to love, yeah. I figure he does." She swatted her own little insect. "Sometimes people can give you the very best they got and it's still no damn good."

"Yeah. I know what you mean." I thought about Delilah, telling me that two or more things can be true at the same time. I missed Delilah. "Do you think he loved my mother?"

"Oh yeah, he did. I can say for a fact he did. Tell you how I know. Because only love can turn into that kind of hate."

More silence. But it didn't feel awkward. The windmills seemed to fill up the space. As if I were experiencing them with all five of my senses. Not just my eyes.

"I feel like I've been dreaming about this place all my life," I said. I knew I'd said it before, but it didn't matter. I needed to say it again.

We sat in silence for a few minutes, until a new-looking SUV pulled into Grandma Annie's dirt driveway. I watched a plume of dust follow it, and slowly digested what I was waiting to know, and what I knew already.

It wasn't close enough that I could see the driver. Not yet. But I had a feeling I knew what I would see.

"Is that my mother?"

"You don't say that like it's a good thing."

"You said she was coming on Friday."

"I said she'd be coming every Friday. In general. But of course she wanted to see you first thing. She even got a couple days off work for you."

I could hear the strain in her voice. In the thick of all my other thoughts and feelings, I remember being vaguely sorry that she had to get stuck in the middle of this.

Meanwhile the driver had come into plain view. I was looking right at her. And she was looking right at me.

"I'm not ready for this," I heard myself say out loud. I think I had only meant to say it in my head. "You should have warned me."

If she answered, I didn't hear, or don't remember.

My mother was getting out of the car.

She was so beautiful. Even though she looked older. But she still had that beauty that comes from the inside of a person and shines out through their eyes. It made me angry. Because of how much of it I had missed.

We were still holding each other's eyes.

I felt myself stand. "I'm not ready. You should have told me. It wasn't fair to spring this on me." The words came out louder than I had intended. Plenty loud enough for my mother, who was still standing beside her car, to hear.

Then I walked away. Off the porch and back down the path to the guesthouse.

I faintly heard Grandma Annie say, "No, Celia. Don't. Give him time."

I let myself into the little guesthouse, and Maria looked up at me. I could see the shock on her face. It was almost like looking in a mirror. I didn't realize how upset I was until I saw it reflected in her.

"Tony. What's wrong?"

"My mother is here."

"Oh. Aren't you going to go talk to her?"

"No."

She seemed a little surprised that I would say that. But she didn't ask any questions. And she didn't bring it up again.

GRANDMA ANNIE CALLED UP SOME NEIGHBORS, and by the end of the day she'd managed to find us a crib. Not that Natalie was young enough to really need a crib, but the size was okay, and the bars on the sides came down, anyway. Grandma Annie loaned us a Japanese folding screen from her bedroom, and we used it to turn one corner of the guesthouse into a tiny makeshift bedroom for the kid.

I thought it would take Maria forever to get Natalie to sleep, but I guess she was worn out from all the newness and the travel. She fussed for a few minutes as though she'd never stop, and then suddenly all went silent.

I was lying on the folded-out bed, waiting. I'd made it up with a blanket and pillows. I was just lying on it, fully dressed. Because I had no idea what to do. I'd feel stupid getting into pajamas. Like we were just going to go to sleep together, like some old married couple. But I didn't want to just take off my clothes. I didn't want to assume much of anything. There was still the matter of her broken ribs.

When the fussing stopped, my stomach got scared. Well, all of me got scared, I guess. But I felt it in my stomach. I lay very quiet and still and waited. The icy feeling in my stomach was spreading into my arms and legs. I was out in the world, having a life, and I had no experience and no instructions. I had never felt so completely lost.

I squeezed my eyes shut and kept them shut for a long time.

Then I felt the bed move as she lay down beside me. I felt her move up against me and put her head down on my shoulder. I put my arm around her, but I still didn't open my eyes.

I heard her say, "Alone at last, huh?"

I opened my eyes. She propped up on one elbow and we looked at each other. It was a way nobody had ever looked at me before, not even Maria. My muscles got so melty that I said a silent thank you for the fact that I was lying down on the bed. Otherwise I think I might have crumpled and landed on the floor. I doubt I had one limb capable of holding me up.

"What about your ribs?"

"We can be careful. I mean . . . we can be gentle, right?"

"I'm not sure I know . . ." The rest of that sentence never really happened. I think the correct word would have been "anything." I didn't know anything. I didn't know what I was supposed to do even in a normal situation. And now with her ribs adding another challenge . . .

But we had never broached the subject of my inexperience. We had left it as kind of a "don't ask, don't tell" proposition. I didn't know if she'd guessed, and I had no idea how or if I should talk about it. Finally I just said, "I don't know how to do this without hurting you."

"I'll show you," she said. Her voice was low. Warm.

That's when it hit me that I had received a strange example of a blessing. No matter how awkward or tentative I seemed, she would assume it was because I didn't want to hurt her. I could stand back and wait for directions. She would interpret whatever I did—or didn't do—as the newness of this unique intimate situation, not the newness of any intimacy at all. What Delilah would have labeled "Life or whatever-you-want-to-call-it" had cut me a break. I was grateful beyond words.

I can't say any more about that night. I'm sorry. But a gentleman wouldn't say more.

Naked

I never made love with anybody before.

And yes, in a minute I'll go on to say exactly what I mean by that, but first I want to set the record straight on one thing. Before this, the only guy in my life, ever, was Carl. There's this big misconception that if you have a kid when you're very young then you must be some kind of whore and you probably slept with every guy on the planet. Me, I just fell in love with Carl when I was barely fifteen, and then I got pregnant. I'm not saying that wasn't a mistake, but at least it was only one.

This was different.

This was like something that two people do together. Not like something one person does to somebody else.

I really only offered to do this tonight for Tony. Because, poor Tony. He waited so long. And I'm pretty sure he was a virgin. So, when you're a virgin, it feels like the most important thing in the world, I think. Especially if you're a guy.

But it was for me, too, the way it turned out. And it was nice.

It was also a little scary, though. Because it felt sort of like being naked on the inside, too. Like you're really there and there's no place to hide.

Maybe I'll get used to that in time.

And he was so careful not to hurt me. Even a little bit.

Speaking of things I need to get used to.

I guess I shouldn't say too much more about that night. After all, it's a personal thing. So I think that's all I'm willing to say. I think the rest is between Tony and me.

Sebastian | *Sixteen*

You Don't Know How it Feels

I think it was around two or three in the morning. We were lying outside looking at the stars. On a lounge chair. I had one of my legs on either side of her, and she was lying on me with her back against my chest. I had my arms around her, but way up by her collarbone so I wouldn't hurt her.

It was surprisingly cool. I had forgotten about that part of desert weather. No matter how hot it gets during the day, it cools down nicely at night.

I was feeling my lack of sleep, feeling exhausted, yet so wide awake that it seemed like I might never sleep again.

"I see what you mean about the stars," she said.

I said nothing. Because nothing felt like it needed saying. For the first time in my life, everything felt complete. *I* felt complete. I felt like I'd found something I'd always wanted, but in some strange way I'd never even known what it was. I guess I'm not saying it right. It's like all my life I'd been missing something, but not knowing what I was missing. And now it seemed amazing that I had found it. Having had so little to go on.

I knew I was different. I could feel the difference in me. And I knew that, whatever you want to call the change, it was never changing back. I had woken up, or grown up. Or both. And once you grow up, you'll never be a child again. And sometimes when you wake up there's just no getting back to sleep.

At first I couldn't even think of a way to describe what I was feeling. But then it hit me. The simplest possible word. I was happy. For the first time in my life, I was happy.

And nothing needed saying.

Maybe that was why Maria didn't talk much. Maybe nothing needed saying.

"How can there be more stars in the desert?" she asked. "That doesn't really make sense."

"There aren't," I said. "There are the same number of stars everywhere. But the city lights wash them out so you can't see them. So the farther out you get from the city, the more stars you can see."

"Oh. That makes sense. So, are you ever going to talk to your mother?"

I tensed up a little at the question. But I tried to relax my chest and my breathing, so she wouldn't know that by feel. "I guess. I don't know."

"But she's your mother."

"Then where was she? If she's my mother, why haven't I seen her for ten years?"

I thought I felt something tighten in Maria right about then. But maybe she was just in pain. A weird thought came into my head out of nowhere. All of a sudden it hit me to ask her who this C.J. is. But I didn't. I just waited to see what she would say.

"She was afraid of your father. That's why."

"I'm not sure that's good enough," I said. "I know that's what everybody says. But it just doesn't feel like enough. *I'm* afraid of my father. But I wouldn't have given up seeing her. I would have faced up to him, if I'd known she was there for me to see. I loved her enough to take that chance. Why didn't she face up to him for me? He wasn't going to kill her."

A long silence. I wondered if I was upsetting her. Though I'm not sure why what I'd just said should upset her. Maybe because I was getting a little mad.

"You don't know that for a fact," she said.

"He wouldn't have."

"Well, maybe *she* didn't know that for a fact."

I was feeling vaguely irritated, because this was my situation, and I didn't see why she had any cause to argue a different position. Why was she on my mother's side and not mine?

"I think you just don't realize what it feels like to be left by your own mother."

"Well. I sort of do. My mother died. But I guess that's different."

"Oh. I'm sorry. How did she die?"

"My father killed her."

"Oh, God. That's awful. I'm so sorry."

Silence. So, that explained a lot. I didn't want to talk anymore, because it didn't feel right. I felt it would be insensitive to say more.

After a long silence, she said, "It's okay. My mother died a long time ago. You still get to talk if you want."

"You want to talk about it?"

"Oh, God no. I'd definitely rather talk about your mother. Please."

Another respectful silence. Then I said, "What's weird is that I sort of know how you feel. I had to get used to the fact that my mother was dead, too. But when I found out she'd been around all this time, I just can't explain how bad that felt. I don't expect anybody else to understand it. How it feels to find out that your mother could have been with you the whole time you were growing up, but she just wasn't. She just decided to be somewhere else. No matter what the reason. I mean, I know. She had a good reason. Pretty good. I mean, I guess it's good. But I just wish she'd fought for me. I guess I just wish she'd stood up to him to get me. I wish

I'd meant so much to her that she just had to. No matter what she thought might happen."

Then we were quiet for another long time. A very long time. I guess she was thinking about what we'd said. But what she was thinking about it, I didn't know.

My thoughts wandered. I found myself watching the stars again.

I started to wonder again if Maria loved me. As soon as I wondered, I wished I could push the thought away. Because it left a nasty little crack in my moment of happiness. And I couldn't get it to go back to how it had been before.

She had never told me she loved me.

I had told her once. I think. I think I told her I loved her that night I asked her to run away with me. But I think I said it in a big rush, like, "I love you run away with me." And then she was left to answer the "run away with me" part. Which is different than just saying I love you and then waiting to see what the other person will say.

Then again, maybe I hadn't said I loved her. Maybe I'd only thought it. Because everything that happened that night happened so fast. It was hard to remember.

What would she say if I told her I loved her now? And just waited? I was too afraid to find out. So we just lay there, looking at the stars together. But now I wasn't happy anymore. Now I was bothered by not knowing if she loved me or not.

All of a sudden I remembered the tone of my voice when I told Grandma Annie, "I am nothing like my father." The vehemence of that statement. And even though I tried not to have this next thought, I couldn't help knowing that being too afraid to tell Maria I loved her was being something like my father.

"Maria." Then I froze a long time. But I had to do it. I had to. "I love you."

The pause seemed to last forever. I could actually feel my head spin. My lungs felt like they'd been vacuumed out, like I couldn't get any air. I thought she was never going to answer. I thought the world would end if she didn't answer, and it seemed like she never would.

"I love you too, Tony."

I guess the pause was really only a couple of seconds.

I watched the stars shine even more than they'd shone a moment before. Nothing more needed to be said.

I was happy.

Maria | Sixteen

Things That Fly Away

I'm getting too good at writing notes that say good-bye. It's nice to feel like you're talented at something in life, but I'm not sure this is such a great thing to add to the list.

I didn't tell Tony why I was leaving. In the note, I mean. Just that I was. I couldn't bring myself to tell him about C.J. I guess it was partly because then he would know I lied to him. Even more than he already thought I did. But that wasn't most of it. Most of it was because then he would know I was just like his mother. That I was a mother who would leave her little boy with a father she knew was terrible. Like passing him off for the sake of my own safety. Like sacrificing him to some big angry God to save myself.

Then Tony would hate me. For being so much like his mother.

I could almost live with losing Tony. I can do losing. I've been doing it all my life. But if he hated me . . . I could never live with that. Same with C.J., I guess.

I woke Natalie with a finger to her lips, and she stayed silent. She was good at silent, Natalie. She knew all about what not to say and when not to say it.

Maybe that's why she's nearly three and almost never talks. Maybe she's afraid of saying the wrong thing at the wrong time.

I pulled the duffel bag across the carpet. Thank God for the new carpet. It hardly made a sound.

THE SUN WAS ONLY JUST BARELY UP. We couldn't see it or anything. We could just see that the sky was starting to get light.

I barely knew this place, but it was breaking my heart to have to leave it behind. But I had to go get C.J. I knew that now. Where I would go after I got him, well, I hadn't quite figured that out. But I had to get him. Now. Before he grew up and learned to hate me for what I didn't have the guts to do.

The morning air was already warm. More than warm, really. Not hot exactly, but sort of like hot in waiting. Like hot gearing up to go.

And it was clean.

It was different from the air in the city. Like you could blindfold me and plug my ears and I'd still know where I was. Just by the feel of the air.

I looked at the windmills again. For a long time.

I was wondering how I would ever be able to live without this place that I'd only known for about a day.

Turns out some places leave a tattoo on you that never goes away. And I hadn't known that. Because I hadn't known many places. Please don't ask me how I knew it would never go away. I just knew.

I guess Tony was mixed into that tattoo somewhere. But standing there on the highway, watching those windmills spin and smelling the desert air, I got the sense that this place could mark me forever all on its own.

I stuck out my thumb and we got a ride from an old man in a big Chrysler from the sixties. I was almost sorry he came along.

Kind of glad and sorry at the same time.

He smiled and said good morning and Natalie buried her head in my neck.

"Where to?" he asked.

I said we were going to the bus station.

I didn't have money for the bus. But I still had my pocketful of change. So I could call Stella, though I might have to call her collect. And she would probably buy me a ticket with Victor's credit card. Victor and Stella had plenty of money, especially since Victor never wanted to go anywhere and spend it.

We rolled down the windows because it was getting too warm already.

About a couple of miles later down the highway, Natalie's fur muff took off and flew. I guess she started to drift off to sleep and sort of loosed up her vise grip on it. It flew right out the window. I looked at it in the side-view mirror and watched it land on the center line of the highway.

Natalie started to cry right away.

"Want me to turn around and go back for that?" the old man asked. He was a pretty nice old guy, I think.

"No, thank you," I said. "It'll be okay."

I'd been wondering how I'd ever be able to bring myself to keep looking at that beautiful piece of fur. The only thing anybody—at least, anybody who wasn't me—ever gave Natalie. The constant reminder that this guy I left behind, the one I blew my chance with, had been sweet.

Not the best way to solve a problem, but at least it was solved.

The story of my life.

The Shot

When I woke up, it was barely light. Not even quite dawn. But it was light. I think it was the light that woke me.

I was still on the lounge chair outside. But Maria wasn't lying on me anymore.

I got up, stretched. Went inside.

I could still feel that new feeling. That sense that everything had changed. That I had changed. And that there was no changing back.

And it's a good thing, too. Because Maria wasn't there.

The bathroom door was standing open, so I swung it wider and looked in. In case she was in the tub or something. No Maria.

I peeked around the screen, but Natalie's crib bed was empty, too.

I was just about to go up to the house to look for them when my eyes landed on the closet. The doors stood open wide, and Maria's clothes were no longer hanging there. And her duffel bag was no longer lying on the floor. I just kept looking for a long time, trying to catch up to a place in my mind where I would know what that meant. But I guess I must have wanted not to catch up to that place. I must have wanted that a lot. Because it's pretty obvious. I mean, there aren't a lot of things that could mean. Really just the one. But I just kept staring.

Then I looked at our bed. And, you know, before I even did, I think I knew what I would see there. I don't think it was even a surprise. Not by then.

I must've walked over and picked up the note. But I don't remember doing that. I just remember sitting with it, on the edge of the bed. I have no idea how long.

She said she had to go back.

She said it was true what she said about loving me, but she had to go back.

She said she was sorry.

That's all she said.

I can't tell you how long I sat there holding the note, or what I was thinking. I'm not even sure I *was* thinking. I think my brain was switched off in a way I couldn't completely control. But I remember my first thought after that long gap. She might only have left a few minutes ago. It might not be too late to catch her.

I ran out to the street. A neighbor was watering in his front yard. The house right across the way. An older guy maybe in his sixties, bald, in his bathrobe.

"Hi, Sebastian," he called to me. "We're really glad you're here." And he waved.

I had never met him or seen him, and at first I had no idea how he knew my name or why he was glad I was here. But I guess everyone in town had been expecting me. Which I don't think I could have wrapped my brain around at any time. Just then it was all quite beyond me.

I ran up to his fence. "Did you see a woman and a little girl leave here this morning?"

"Sure, just a few minutes ago," he said. "She walked down to the corner of the highway there and caught a ride."

"Caught a ride?"

"You know. Stuck out her thumb."

"Oh. Right. Thanks."

I started running in the direction of the highway. Why, I guess, is hard to explain. Because I had just missed her. Because the ride would have to let her off somewhere. Because the alternative was to do nothing. Because I had to change the ending of the story.

What good is a love story without a happy ending?

Halfway to the highway I realized I hadn't even asked which way she had gone. But I didn't even need to, really. West. The bus station was west. So, when I hit the highway, I went west.

Now, this highway is really just a road with a lane in each direction. And there was nobody out at that hour, anyway. So I ran right down the center line. For about two miles. Could even have been three. I think at some point I might have questioned myself about what I was doing. But, if so, it was in a muddy sort of way. Mostly I just ran. I thought I was going to run forever. I could have. I was into something that was hard to stop. I don't think I could have stopped if I hadn't seen something lying in the middle of the road.

At first I thought it was an animal. I thought it was a rabbit or a cat that had been killed by a car. But when I got closer, I saw it had no head. No feet. No shape to identify it as a living thing. It was just a piece of fur. I stopped in front of it. Squatted down and picked it up.

It was the rabbit-fur muff.

I just squatted there for a minute or two, holding it in my hands. Feeling the softness. In the distance I saw the windmills spinning, but really more in my peripheral vision. But I was aware of them.

Then a car went by, swerving around me and blaring its horn. I didn't move.

First I thought maybe she threw it away on purpose. Not Natalie. She wouldn't. But maybe Maria did. Maybe she didn't want anything to remind her of me.

But then I had another thought, and I liked this one better. I decided that Natalie threw herself half out the window again, to see the windmills. And this time the fur muff didn't land on anybody's feet. This time it flew out the window and landed on the road. And Maria was too timid and shy to ask the driver to stop and go back.

I would never know which was true. But I burned the image of the second story into my brain. I wrote it like a piece of history, so I would always remember it just that way.

I couldn't get up and run anymore, because I knew it wouldn't do any good. And because all the energy and all the fight had drained out of me. As a direct result of knowing it wouldn't do any good.

I stood up and turned around and saw Grandma Annie in her old blue and rust-primer truck. She was just sitting off on the shoulder of the road, watching me.

I got up and walked over. "What are you doing here?" I asked her.

"I saw you running down the road."

"Aren't you even going to ask me why?"

"Don't really have to." A long silence. I was looking down at the tarmac. "Come on," she said. "Get in."

I walked around and climbed in the passenger's side. Pulled the door shut behind me. The window was rolled down, so I leaned partway out and watched the windmills. So I wouldn't have to look at her. I was waiting for her to turn around and drive us home.

"Did she have any money?" I heard her ask me. Her voice sounded strangely far away. Like I was partly asleep.

"I don't think so. Why?"

"Maybe she's at the bus station."

"Your neighbor said she hitched a ride."

"Maybe she hitched a ride to the bus station. Let's go see."

"Did my mother go home?"

"No, honey. She's still here."

A few miles later she looked over at me. Looked at the rabbit-fur muff I was holding tightly in both hands. "She must've dropped it by accident. No way she'd let it go on purpose."

"Yeah," I said. "That's what I was thinking, too."

MAYBE IT'S BECAUSE I WAS SO UPSET. Because the morning was playing out like a dream. A weird, bad dream. But I fell into my Tony role. When I jumped out of Grandma Annie's truck and ran into the bus station, I felt like the Tony in the movie, running up and down the streets calling for Maria. But I guess I rewrote a little history there, because I realize now he wasn't calling for Maria in the movie. He thought she was dead. He was calling for Chino to come kill him, too.

But he found his Maria all the same. And I found mine.

She was sitting on a hard wooden bench with Natalie by her side. Sitting up stiff, with her back weirdly straight. Looking at something right in front of her, maybe, or maybe at nothing. I couldn't tell.

It was Natalie who saw me. And gave me away.

She pulled her thumb out of her mouth and said, "Hi, Tony." Clear as a bell.

Maria looked up at me, her face dissolving into layers of shame and guilt and regret. All the things I never wanted to see on her face. There they all were. It was all I could do not to look away.

I sat down next to her. Gave Natalie back her rabbit-fur muff.

"Thank you, Tony," Natalie said.

Nobody had said a word so far except Natalie.

"You're welcome. Come home with us." But of course I said this second part to Maria.

She shook her head. "I can't."

"You had money for the bus? Why didn't you tell me?"

"No. I didn't have any money. I called my sister. And she bought me a ticket."

"You don't have to go back. Come home with us."

"No. I can't. I have to go back."

"Why?"

"I have to go get C.J."

My stomach cramped painfully at the mention of that name.

But then I also started thinking that it probably wasn't Carl. The way she said she had to go get him.

"Who's C.J.?"

She wouldn't look at me. Just kept looking down at the linoleum of the bus station floor. "Carl Jr.," she said. I still didn't get it, and I guess she could tell. "C.J. is my little boy."

"You have a son?"

I heard myself asking the question, as if from the outside. Like a voice that sounded enough like mine, but didn't feel connected.

"I'm sorry I didn't tell you. I knew you wouldn't take me with you if you knew I had two kids. I didn't even think you'd take me and Natalie. But I couldn't leave Natalie. But I thought I could leave C.J. But I can't. I have to fight for him. No matter what I think will happen."

I sat back on the hard wooden bus bench. Felt the cool, smooth wood against the hard knobs of my spine. The conversation under the stars came into my head again. It's weird how something that's already happened can change. Just by keying in some new information.

After about an eternity I said, "Why did you leave a note that made it sound like you were leaving forever?"

Her eyes came up to mine and I saw she was crying. But silently. I hadn't even known.

"Well, I can't just come back and live here with two kids."

"Why can't you?"

She looked into my eyes for a strangely long period of time. I tried not to squirm.

"We can't fit four of us in that tiny little place."

"Then I'll get a job, and we'll get a bigger place."

"Really, Tony? Two kids?"

"Is this dangerous?"

She looked down at the dirty floor again. Didn't answer.

"Maybe you should leave Natalie here with me."

For two reasons. So Natalie couldn't get hurt by Carl, or taken away by Carl. And so I knew for a fact that Maria would have to come back to me.

Three reasons. So I wouldn't be all alone in my tiny new house in the waiting.

"She wouldn't stay with you."

"We like each other."

"She might cry the whole time."

"Better that than take a chance on her getting hurt."

A long silence.

Then Maria said, "Natalie, would you be okay with Tony for a while? I promise I'll come back as soon as I get C.J."

"When?" Natalie asked.

"About a week, I think. Will you be okay with Tony?"

She didn't answer. Just stuck her thumb in her mouth.

I lifted her gently off the seat beside Maria, and she didn't object. Just buried her face in my neck.

"Please be careful," I said.

"I will. I'll call you at your grandmother's when I get there. And when I get C.J. So you'll know I'm okay."

I started getting scared, thinking about what had happened last time she saw Carl. I started thinking that maybe leaving C.J. where he was had been good logic in the first place.

"Maybe—"

"No," she said. "I have to do this. I have to."

She dug around in the duffel bag and pulled out a few things. Made a neat little stack on the bench beside her.

Two little dresses.

Three pairs of clean white underwear, unbelievably tiny.

A soft-bristled hairbrush.

A toothbrush with a plastic handle shaped like a teddy bear.

A VHS tape of *The Wizard of Oz*.

"Why do you have to do this again?"

"So C.J. will never talk about me the way you were talking about your mother last night."

"Oh," I said.

I scooped up the pile of Natalie's things.

What else could I say? It had been the truth. All of it. It was way too late to take any of my words back now.

GRANDMA ANNIE WAS WAITING FOR ME in the truck, with the engine still running. I climbed in and set Natalie on my lap. Carefully laid Natalie's things on the passenger side floor at my feet. Put the seat belt around both of us.

"It's a long story," I said.

She just nodded, and then put the truck in gear.

"HE'S GOING TO KILL HER," I said. "Why did I let her go? It was so stupid. He'll kill her. She'll never make it back here in one piece. I should have gone with. At least tried to protect her."

I was sitting at the breakfast table with Grandma Annie and my mother, who had joined us silently and without warning. Or permission. I was staring at a glass of orange juice I had no intention of drinking. My stomach felt like someone was squeezing it with pliers and then twisting. I was holding Natalie on my lap, her thumb in her mouth, her eyes shut tight and pressed against my neck. Her usual death grip on the fur muff. I realized too late that I probably shouldn't have said those things in front of her. I was feeling bad about that.

It was the first time I had spoken. And the words had just gone out in general. Just flowed out to fill the kitchen. I had not been speaking directly to my mother. And I had not looked at her once.

Grandma Annie said, "She was right, though. When she said you had to stay out of it. He'd kill you quicker than anybody."

First there was just a long silence. Longer than a normal lag in conversation. Also quieter than your average silence. I didn't know it was an important silence. At the time. Although I guess in a way I could feel something starting to build.

Then, out of nowhere, my mother said, "He can kill *me*."

I only knew it was my mother because it wasn't Grandma Annie and it wasn't me. I hadn't heard her voice since I was seven. I couldn't even decide if it sounded familiar or not.

"*What?*" I looked up at her. I couldn't help it. It had just been such a weird thing to say. "What does that mean?"

"It means just what I said. I'll go with her and try to protect her. If he wants to kill somebody he can kill me."

Another long silence. I'm pretty sure no one else knew what to say, either.

Then my mother said, "I better hurry, if I'm going to catch her."

Grandma Annie followed her away from the table. Out into the hall by the front door. I could hear quiet whispers of their voices. Just a few sentences each. I was about to get up and move closer. I wanted to hear what they were saying.

Before I could, I heard the jingle of car keys as my mother grabbed them up off the hall table. I heard the door open and then slam shut.

I looked up to see Grandma Annie in the kitchen doorway. She looked worried and far away.

I said, "What just happened?"

"You were here as much as I was, honey."

"But why would she do that?"

"Oh, honey. Use your head."

I felt insulted. Belittled. But I figured she was just worried, so I worked on letting it go by.

I tried to understand what had just happened with my mother. I really tried. But I still didn't get it. "I'm sorry. Maybe this stuff is obvious to everyone. But it's not obvious to me. I really don't understand. She doesn't even know Maria."

A long silence. I was beginning to think she would never answer me.

Then she said, "Longer you live, honey, the more you see

everybody's just running around looking for a do-over. Chance to go back to their worst mistake and get it right this time."

I said, "Oh."

Then I spent the rest of the morning being afraid that Carl would kill Maria *and* my mother. But I never said so out loud.

Maria | Seventeen

Brave

I was so close to being on the bus. Another couple of minutes, and I would have been on already. And then I guess everything would have turned out different.

I was standing outside, where the buses are. In the boarding place, hearing that really familiar roar of the bus engine idling. It fills up your head in a special way. It's something you could almost get used to. And there's a smell to the exhaust from those big engines, also, but that's not as nice.

I had my duffel bag beside me. A guy was throwing people's bags into the space under the bus and I was waiting for him to help me. If it hadn't hurt so much to try to pick up that big bag, I'd have hauled it up to the front of the line myself. Then I would've been on that bus already, and then maybe I never would have heard this lady, this total stranger I'd never met before, calling my name.

That's not usually a good sign, when somebody yells your name. Usually, in my world, when nobody notices me at all that's the good news. When somebody calls me out, that makes my guts freeze up. Makes me want to go the other way. Fast.

But then I looked closer and I started to think it was Tony's mom.

See, I was looking out the window when Tony's mom first drove up. I was looking out because I heard a car come up the driveway, and that scared the crap out of me. I knew Carl could never really find me. But I still had to look.

And even though I hadn't seen her very close up, I saw just enough of what she looked like to be thinking this was probably her calling me.

So I said, "I'm Maria."

And she came up to me and looked straight in my eyes. Or she tried anyway.

I'm not good at looking in people's eyes. Once in grade school I went trick-or-treating in my building, and I was wearing this Dracula costume, and there was no way anybody could tell who I was. Except three of my neighbors opened their doors and said, "Oh, hi Maria." And when I asked them how they knew, they said they could tell because I always looked down a certain way.

But I don't mean to get off track.

"Come on," she said. "Let's go."

"I can't. I have to go get C.J."

"I know. That's where we're going."

She picked up my duffel bag and started walking, so I walked with her. Even though I totally still didn't get it.

She had a not-too-big SUV, real nice and new, and she threw my bag in the back.

I said, "Wait. We're going to New York to get C.J. in your car?"

"That's right," she said.

"But I have a bus ticket. My sister, Stella, bought me a bus ticket."

"Why don't you go inside and cash it in?" she said. "We can use the money for food and gas on the road."

I'm not so good at talking to strangers. I think it goes along with that thing about not looking in people's eyes. Anyway, it was about twenty miles or so before I said anything to her. Maybe thirty.

"Why are you doing this with me again?" I asked. Even though there was really no "again" about it. She hadn't even told me once. But with strangers it's easier to go the long way around a thing than it is to hit it dead on.

"Because it's a lot harder to kill two people than one."

"So you get that this is probably really dangerous."

"Oh, yeah."

A few more quiet miles.

"But you don't even know me," I said.

She didn't answer right away. Then after a while she said, "If you let go of the idea that I'm doing it just for you . . . and think of it as something I need to do for myself, too . . . then it might make more sense."

It's a long drive from California to New York. So I figured I'd have time to work that one out in my head. And, truthfully, I had some sense of what she meant already.

WE WERE ON ROUTE 40, where you can drive really fast, when she talked to me again. We were close outside Kingman, Arizona. According to the signs, anyway. I had nothing better to do than read the signs.

She asked me if I drove.

"Oh," I said. "No. I never learned to drive." Silence. I wondered if she was asking just to make conversation. Probably not. Because we hadn't made much conversation so far. "You know. Growing up in the city and all. We never had a car."

"Okay."

"Sorry." Even though I wasn't sure what I was being sorry for. But I tend to be, as sort of a default mood. "Why?"

"It's okay. It would just go faster, is all. With two drivers. But it just means we'll need to stop more. I'll need to sleep. I was just thinking we could save money on motels. You know, if you drove while I napped. But it's okay. So I run up my credit card a little. Motels on the road will be cheap enough. It's when we get to the city that I'm worried about. It's so expensive in the city."

"We can stay at my sister Stella's."

"Oh. That's good to know. That helps."

Then we were all the way through Kingman before I got up the nerve to say, "Mrs. . . . Mundt? That's probably not your name anymore. Is it?"

"No. It's not."

"So . . . what's your name?"

"Celia."

"What should *I* call you?"

"Celia."

"Isn't that sort of . . . disrespectful?"

"No. Not if that's what I say I want. What were you about to ask me?"

"Oh. Right." I had almost forgotten. "You were going to let me drive your car?"

"Well, yeah. If you knew how to drive."

"Wow," I said.

That was all the talking we did for Arizona.

THAT WOMAN HAD SOME STAMINA for driving. We didn't stop to let her sleep until we got to Gallup, New Mexico.

Before we could settle in to go to sleep, we had to go find a store so she could buy a toothbrush and some underwear and stuff like that. I guess she hadn't bothered to have any of that with her when she took off to find me.

On the way to find a motel, I was staring at the side of her face. I'm not sure why. I was tired, that might have been part of it. And I guess I felt like I could get away with it because it was dark. I could only really see her when we passed a streetlight.

I was looking at the way she wore her hair back in a loose braid, even though it had a lot of gray in it. I never saw somebody wear their hair in a braid when it had so much gray. At least, not a big loose braid like that. Like the way somebody young would wear their hair. And I was looking at the little lines at the corners of her eyes.

I thought she didn't know I was staring. I don't know how she could tell.

"What?" she said.

I was so tired, I told her the truth. "I was just trying to picture what my mother would look like. If she hadn't died. She would have been so many years older now. I was just wondering how she would have looked."

"I'm sorry you lost your mother," she said.

I waited for her to ask me how she died. When she didn't, I was really relieved.

WE ONLY HAD ONE CONVERSATION that made me feel laid bare. On the way out east, that is. Most of the time we talked very small, or didn't even bother.

All of a sudden she looked over at me and said, "You get to know somebody pretty well when you're driving cross-country with them."

I tried to hide the fact that a thing like that makes me nervous. "But we barely even talk."

"It's not always about talking. Just watching the way a person functions night and day for three or four days running."

I took a deep breath. "So what do you know about me?"

"That you're a lot like I was ten years ago. Even though ten years ago I was a lot older than you are now. But when I was just getting out of that horrible marriage, and I had a kid. I was a lot like you."

"I'm not sure what you mean," I said after a while. "Because I'm not sure what you think I'm like."

"Scared. Willing to do anything to avoid a confrontation. Peace at any price."

"Well. Peace is good. Right?"

"Real peace is great. But peace at any price is not real peace."

I thought about that across maybe a few more miles of Ohio before I said, "How did you get from that to what you are now? Because you don't seem scared now at all."

"I just handle fear differently."

"Really? You don't seem scared at all."

"Everybody's scared."

"Really? I thought it was mostly me."

"Everybody. If they say they're not, they're lying. Either to you or themselves."

"You still didn't tell me how you got to here."

"Just took a lot of time with myself, I guess. After I left that awful marriage. Learned to live with myself and learned something about myself instead of spending all my time figuring out how to live with somebody else."

"Oh," I said.

And I guess that was enough serious talking, because we went back to being two people who hardly know each other for the rest of the trip.

"YOU CAN'T DO THIS," Stella said. "It's suicide."

"I have to do this," I said.

Celia said nothing at all.

We were sitting in Stella's living room. The light was starting to fade, and no one had bothered to turn on any lamps or anything. So we could only see each other a little bit, which made talking easier. I was holding Ferdy so he wouldn't rub all over Celia because Celia is allergic to cats. I felt really sorry for her. New York hotel rooms must be awful damned expensive to make a person who's allergic to cats stay at Stella's.

Stella said, "You can't. You have to go through the courts. I wouldn't even have bought you a bus ticket if I knew you were going to do this. It's crazy."

We all ignored the fact that I obviously got here anyway. Without the bus ticket.

"I have to surprise him. If I just get an attorney and serve him with custody papers, he'll run away. He'll take C.J. and hide where I can't get to him. I'll never find them. And then I'll never have my chance."

"And this way? You think you're going to beat him in a fistfight? He'll kill you for leaving him to run off with another man."

I had to wait to answer while she went off to get a box of tissues for poor Celia.

As soon as she got back I said, "I'm thinking maybe he doesn't even know that yet. Because maybe he just watched your window the whole time I was away. And maybe he has no way of knowing I was even gone."

Silence. Way too much silence.

"When he got out of jail," Stella said, "we had a little . . . confrontation. I told him it served him right that you found somebody new."

A big storm of tingling hit my brain and belly. My thoughts moved further away. Like a milky glass wall was forming between my thoughts and me. So I could hardly get to them when I reached out to try. I made sure to avoid Celia's eyes.

I loved my sister, Stella. She was my whole living family. But I had been counting heavily on Carl's not knowing I had ever been gone. It was my whole plan. My only plan. It just seemed too cruelly familiar, to find out that my one and only plan would never hold water.

I never answered Stella. I would never want to say anything unkind.

"I'm so sorry," she said. "Oh, Maria. I'm so sorry. I thought you were gone and safe and it wouldn't matter. I just wanted to rub his face in it a little. I didn't think he could do anything to you now."

"It doesn't matter," I said. But it did. And we all three knew it.

"Don't go in."

"I have to. If it doesn't work, at least C.J. will know I tried."

"I don't want to lose you," she said. She sounded like Stella at about sixteen years old. When we were losing everything. All our cornerstones, right and left.

"For one time in my whole life I need to do something brave. Besides. At least there'll be two of us."

"No, there'll be three of us," Stella said. "I'm going in with you. I dare that son of a bitch to kill all three of us at once."

That was sort of a conversation stopper, so we didn't talk for a while, and then Stella fixed us some Swiss cheese–and–avocado sandwiches.

"I have to call Tony," I said. "Stella, can I call Tony on your phone?"

"Yeah, but don't talk all night," she said.

Celia said, "Who's Tony?"

"Oh. I mean Sebastian. I call him Tony."

She didn't ask why, and I was kind of worried that she would take offense to that, because it might have been her idea to name him Sebastian in the first place.

I ended up having to call pretty much right in front of them. Because Stella still hadn't replaced the phone Carl smashed through the window. There was just the kitchen phone, and it only worked right if you kept it pretty close to the base. So we didn't say much. I just told him we made it to New York, and that I'd call him as soon as we had C.J. and were out safe. And he said to be careful about seven times.

And then, when I hung up the phone, my stomach felt weird, even more so than usual, and I couldn't figure out why.

I DIDN'T SLEEP MUCH, if I slept at all. But I think they might have thought I was asleep.

I was lying on the couch, which was my bed that night. So I could give Celia the spare room, so she could close the door and be away from the cats. But she was in the kitchen talking to Stella. Talking and blowing her nose. And I was just lying there, not really letting on that I was awake.

They were talking about what kind of guy Carl was. They had been for a while.

I heard Stella say, "More of a coward, really. You know, one of those bullies who are really just cowards at heart."

Celia said, "Oh, yes. I know them."

Then Stella said, "Cowards can be really dangerous, though."

And Celia said, "Don't I know it." Then, after a pause, she said, "We should just go pick C.J. up straight from school."

Stella told her what I already knew. "School just let out for the summer. I'm afraid he'll be home with Carl all day."

Then they didn't say much else, or maybe they just lowered their voices. Or maybe I even fell asleep for a minute or two. But I doubt it.

WHILE THE THREE OF US WERE WALKING up the stairs together, actually purposely headed in the direction of Carl, I said, "I think I finally get it."

Stella said, "Get what?"

I tried to think of a way to explain what it is I got. But it was tricky.

Kind of everything. I think I finally got everything.

Then we were standing there in front of my old place, waiting to knock on the door, and it was like my whole life was falling into place. I could only hope this was not another example of my life flashing before my eyes.

It just seemed so clear, how every time I picked something in my life, there was a price. Like life is some big store. Most of my life I guess I thought I could only afford certain things. Like there were some things I just couldn't have. But now it seemed like maybe I could have had more.

Maybe the cheap stuff is cheap for a reason.

I guess most of the time I didn't pick at all. But now I could see that not picking is a type of picking. You're still choosing what you want, only in this case you're choosing to take the stuff you get by default when you don't choose.

Default merchandise is the worst.

I think you get a whole different set of stuff in life if you're brave.

I hope that makes any kind of sense at all. It did to me. But I didn't try to explain it. It wouldn't have come out right. And besides, everybody was all nervous and focused and not wanting to talk.

It's a strange experience to voluntarily walk into a situation where you could very likely get hurt or killed. Soldiers are the only ones I know who do it all the time. I guess a person has to have a really good reason. Something worth maybe dying for. I'm not sure what a soldier's good reason is. Because I've never been a soldier, so I don't know.

And I don't know what Celia and Stella's reasons were. I can only guess, because we hadn't been saying much all morning, and I wasn't inside their heads. Stella, I think it was because she hated Carl and she loved me. Celia, I think she felt really bad that she didn't go back for her own kid. So instead she was going to go back for mine. I didn't know if it would help her any. But I was happy to let her try.

For me, it was this: Whatever happened, C.J. would know he meant everything to me. If you can't get that much from your own mother, you start thinking it doesn't exist anywhere in the world. And that can really mess up a kid. Look what it did to poor Sebastian.

I called him Sebastian in my head. Not Tony. I'm not sure what that meant.

I said a quick prayer that I'd see him again.

I looked at the other two, like to make sure they were really ready. Then I raised my hand and knocked on the door. It was brave.

WHEN CARL OPENED THE DOOR I was shocked. Really shocked. He looked like he hadn't shaved in about a week. His hair wasn't combed. The clothes he was wearing didn't look ironed. In fact, they didn't even look clean. His eyes looked dead.

Until he saw me. Then his eyes just went all on fire and he came lunging in my direction, yelling, "I can't believe—"

But I never got to find out what it was he couldn't believe, because Celia threw herself right in between us. She just kept walking at Carl, and he kept stumbling back, and she was saying things to him that were quiet but sounded very strong. But I couldn't make them out because her mouth was about two inches from his nose. She walked him all the way backwards to the couch and pushed him down into a sit, which didn't look very hard. Then the three of us just stood there in front of him, and I could see him try to take us all in at once, like he was trying to figure out if he had any opening at all. But we outnumbered him. Even Carl wasn't stupid enough to miss that.

Celia said, "Now, you feel free to try to take one of us out, but remember, the minute you do you'll have the other two all over you. This isn't going to be easy like it used to be."

He did nothing. He said nothing. He just sat there.

So Celia said, "Yeah, that's what I figured. I figured you for one of those bullies who just goes after the easy target. The one who doesn't ever dare fight you back."

He still did nothing.

That's when I figured I better hurry up and get C.J. He was sitting in front of the TV, watching all this play out. I'd been watching him out of the corner of my eye, but I hadn't really dared take my eyes off Carl. But sooner or later I would have to.

I grabbed C.J. by the hand and pulled him to his feet.

"Ow," he said. "Where have you been? Where's Nattie?"

"Come on." I said it to him but also to Stella and Celia. "We're going."

We all headed for the door. For about three beautiful seconds I thought that was it. I thought we were just home free. That it was over, and we had won, just that easily.

But then I heard Carl's mad voice, that full-on bellow, from behind us. "Hell, no! You're not taking C.J.!"

I picked up my pace, trying to get to the door, but it wasn't good enough.

Celia tried to wedge herself between Carl and me, but he threw her aside like an old sock doll. We all heard this big horrible thud as she hit the wall near the front door.

I turned, and just as I did Carl got hold of C.J. and tried to pull him away.

Now, Carl is stronger than me. Much stronger. But for a few seconds I managed to hang on in spite of my broken ribs. Probably because I wanted to so badly. Like one of those mothers who picks up a car because her kid is trapped under it. But then the pain got bigger than that rush of adrenaline, and I felt C.J. slipping away.

That was when Stella maced Carl right in the eyes. I heard the sound of the spray, and Carl's screaming, and we left him there on the entry-hall floor yelling and rubbing his eyes. He was yelling that he would get me for this, when he found me. But I didn't care, because I knew he would never find me. Celia grabbed my sleeve with her left hand and pulled me hard out the door and that was it. We were all out safe.

So far as we could tell, Carl couldn't even see well enough to follow.

NOT TWENTY MINUTES LATER, Celia and C.J. and I were driving over the bridge and headed west. We didn't even dare go back to Stella's, because that's the first place he would think to look. In fact, it was the only place he would know to look. So we were home free. Except Celia's shoulder was hurt. Her car was a standard shift, and she had hurt her right shoulder bad enough that I had to keep holding the steering wheel steady so she could shift with her left.

"Maybe we should stop at a hospital," I said.

"I don't think it's that bad. I think it's just bruised."

But I could tell she wasn't sure.

I looked around at C.J., buckled into the back seat. He was looking down at the car floor. I could tell he was upset. He clams up when he's upset.

"You okay, C.J.?"

He never answered. He was a terrible mess. His hair was

greasy. He looked like he hadn't taken a bath for weeks. I'm not even sure he'd been brushing his teeth.

"We have to stop soon so I can call Tony," I said. "I mean Sebastian."

"Tell me why you call him Tony again?"

Aha. See? We *were* a little bit alike. She was going the long way around a thing. We both knew I had never told her even once. "So we could be Tony and Maria, like in *West Side Story*." I waited to see if she would say anything. Then I said, "I thought I would die in there. Because it was getting to be more and more like *West Side Story*, and in that movie they don't get to be together because one of them dies."

"Well, in *Romeo and Juliet* they *both* died."

I had no idea what that had to do with what I'd just said. So I didn't answer.

"You know *West Side Story* is a retelling of *Romeo and Juliet*."

"Oh. No. I didn't know that."

"So they did a modern version of it in *West Side Story*, but only one of the lovers died. So I guess in your story nobody has to."

"Thank God," I said. "Since it's my story and all."

Funny thing is, I didn't know that I thought I was going to die until after it was over. I guess that's not the kind of thing you dwell on at the time.

BY THE FOLLOWING MORNING, C.J. was talking again. And boy, was he pissed.

"Where are we going?" he kept asking. I'd tell him, but he'd still ask again. "Why didn't we bring Pops? When do I get to see Pops?"

He was clean, at least. We'd spent the night in a motel, where I'd made him take a bath, wash his hair, and brush his teeth. "Pops didn't make me do it if I didn't want." That was all he'd had to say at the time. But in the light of day, he had more complaints.

"Do I have to go to a new school in the fall? A new school sucks.

You have a new boyfriend, don't you? That sucks. That sucks that you did that. I hate him."

"You don't even know him, C.J."

"I don't care. I hate him."

This went on—well, truthfully, off and on—for hours, until finally he complained himself right into a state of exhaustion and fell asleep. The silence was a beautiful thing.

Celia said, "Tell you a secret. It wouldn't have made sense if I told you any sooner. But I think you'll understand now. It wasn't just that I was afraid of Sebastian's father. I was afraid of Sebastian, too. I mean, not in general. But if I took him away."

She was driving with her left hand, her right arm hanging straight down into her lap. I felt bad for her, because I knew she must be in pain. Then it hit me. I was in pain, too. I hadn't forgotten it, exactly. My ribs were always happy to remind me. I had just almost gotten used to it. I didn't think much about it. And I sure never thought to feel bad for myself because of it.

"I wish I could do what you did," I said out of nowhere, surprising even me. "I wish I could spend years just living with myself." Then I got this huge wash of shame, because this was Tony's mother. How much would she hate me for not wanting to move right in and spend the rest of my life with her son?

"Well . . . you can."

"No, I can't."

"Why can't you?"

"That would hurt him."

"But if it's what you need to do . . ."

"But he did so much for me."

"You don't have to spend the rest of your life with somebody just because they're nice to you. Or just because they want you to."

"I don't?"

She laughed a little. "No. You don't."

"How do you know all this stuff? Oh, never mind. I remember. You lived by yourself and figured it out. I feel like I could figure out some stuff, too, if I lived on my own. I'd still have the kids, though."

"That's a little different."

"I guess. What do you think I should do?"

"I don't know what you should do."

Silence. I was disappointed. I guess I was hoping she would. Either that, or I wanted her to give me permission.

"Sorry," she said.

"Yeah, me too."

"Well, we're still about twenty-two hundred miles from home," she said. "So at least you have plenty of time to think."

Sebastian | Eighteen

Hunter Moon

I should have known there was a problem when they called me from the motel. The Tehachapi Mountain View Inn, where Grandma Annie worked for so many years.

It's only about a twenty-minute drive from here.

I was the one to answer, because I'd been sitting by the phone. For days.

It was Maria who called. My mother and I had still not said more than a couple of sentences to each other. So Maria called to tell me they'd be home in the morning.

She sounded strange.

I kept saying, "You're almost here. Why don't you just come home now?"

She just kept giving the same answer. "We'll be back in the morning." Ignoring the "why" entirely.

So I put Natalie to bed, telling her about thirty times that she'd see her mother in the morning. And then I sat up all night. Waiting for them. And wondering why.

I FELT LIKE HELL because I hadn't slept. But of course the minute I heard the car drive up, I ran to greet them, holding Natalie against my shoulder.

Maria didn't look at me right away, which didn't help my stomach settle.

My mother got out of the car first, and as she walked past me into the house, I took hold of her elbow lightly. To stop her and turn her around.

"Thank you," I said.

"You're welcome," she said, and walked up onto the porch and inside. I think she found it as hard to communicate as I did.

Then Maria got out of the car, and unbuckled C.J. from the back seat. They walked up to where I was standing. My stomach sagged down in my shoes, waiting for her to look happy to see me. The boy was giving me really hateful looks. Exaggerated hateful looks, as if he was afraid I wouldn't notice a more subtle form of hate.

I handed Natalie back, and she reached for her mother gratefully. I felt a pull of pain as I let her go. As if she had been literally, physically attached to me, and it hurt to yank those strings until they broke.

I was too terrified to open my mouth, so Maria spoke first. "C.J., this is Tony."

He intensified his hateful look, if such a thing was possible. "How *old* are you?"

I didn't have to answer, because Maria said, "C.J, be polite or go wait in the car."

"I don't have to be nice to him. He's not my father. I can ask him anything I want."

"Okay, go wait in the car, then."

He did. But just before climbing in again, he gave me the finger behind his mother's back.

I finally found it in myself to speak. "He can't stay in there forever. Sooner or later he has to come into the house."

"Sebastian," she said. "I need to talk to you."

I'd like to say my heart and my stomach dropped even lower. But, truthfully, I'm not sure they had any more downward space. I think they went a little more blank and numb, waiting for the worst. She walked with me up to the porch swing, and then finally, almost mercifully, pulled the trigger.

"We're going to be living at the motel for a while."

"Why?"

"They have a room that an employee can use. It comes out of my pay, of course. But, anyway, it's a place. I'm going to be cleaning rooms there."

"But why wouldn't you live here?"

"I just feel like I need to be on my own. Not because of you. It's not you. I've just never been on my own. I spent all these years with Carl, just thinking whatever he said I should think, and now I don't even know what *I* think anymore."

"But I would never tell you what to think."

"I know that. I know. But I'd still think whatever you did. Don't you see? I would automatically think your thoughts because I never figured out my own."

I sank into a quiet space where I stopped arguing. She had obviously thought this out. Made up her mind. I clearly was not about to change it. "How long is a while?"

"I don't know. Until I can live someplace bigger and nicer."

"But not here with me."

"Not with anybody. Except my kids. Not for a really long time, anyway."

A moment without talking. A moment of desert wind in my ears. The motion of the windmills at the corner of one eye.

"Will I even see you? And Natalie? Natalie and I have gotten kind of attached."

"Well, sure. Yeah. I mean, we won't be that far. Neither one of us has a car. Or even drives. But we'll figure out a way to visit sometimes. That's nice, that you and Natalie like each other. I really like that she has a guy she knows who's nice. You know. Not like the one she used to know."

I didn't know what to say next. Part of me wished she would just hurry up and go away. So I could fall apart. "Well . . ."

"Yeah. I'll go tell Celia we're ready to go."

"In a minute," I said. "Maybe you could wait in the car for a minute. I need to have a talk with my mother."

"WHAT THE HELL DID YOU SAY to her?" I asked, not two seconds after we'd closed ourselves inside my little guesthouse.

"What do you mean?"

"She's leaving me to go off and be on her own. Everything was fine between us when she left. What did you say to her all that time you two were together?"

She sighed. Kind of sadly, I thought. "Sebastian. I didn't tell her she needed to be on her own. She told me. But she's right. Really. She has no idea how to have a relationship."

"But she was all ready to try. Until you came into the picture."

We were still standing up. Just hovering by the door. Both looking and feeling uncomfortable. I mean, as much as I can judge how someone else feels. I noticed she was holding her right arm against her belly, as if to support it. But I didn't want to interrupt the more important proceedings to ask why.

"She wasn't really ready, honey. She just didn't know she had a choice."

"And you told her. Great. So she doesn't know how to have a relationship. Big deal. Neither do I. We would have figured it out together."

"It's not the same thing, honey. It's like . . . It's like the difference between no credit and bad credit. You just don't have any track record. But she's got repossessions and bankruptcies. She's learned how to do it completely wrong. It takes a long time to sort that out again."

A long time. Just like Maria said. The hopelessness of my situation descended like a guillotine. I felt like I might be about to cry. But I refused to cry in front of my mother, because I didn't even trust her enough to let her see my weakness.

"But I love her." Which was not the tough thing I intended to say.

"Oh, honey. I know you do. First love is so hard. I know you love her enough to want to be with her. But do you love her enough to want her to do what's actually the right thing for her? I mean, even if you're not in that picture?"

I tried to think about that, but my mind just curled in on itself and gave up, like when I used to sit in front of my computer and try to understand the concept of infinity.

I said the most honest thing I could find. "But that's so hard."

She did something unexpected. She took three steps in and put her arms around me. Well, her arm. Her left arm. She pulled me into an awkward one-armed hug. I wanted to pull away. I wanted to yell at her and tell her not to do that. How dare you hold me? Can't you see I'm still angry? Can't you see I'm trying to take you to task for something?

Then I felt her rubbing my back, and I started to cry. There was no holding it in.

"Yes. It is. It's the hardest thing in the world. For everybody. I know people four times your age who haven't even begun to learn it."

"Then how come I have to do it?" I was a little embarrassed by the childlike misery I heard in my own voice.

"So you can be happy," she said.

And she rubbed my back for a few minutes while I tried to stop crying.

Just before she opened the door to leave, just before she drove my first and only girlfriend and my little buddy Natalie out of my life, she paused with her hand on the doorknob. Her left hand.

"I know what I did was wrong, Sebastian. You don't have to convince me. I plead no contest. I hurt you by leaving, and it was wrong. I'm going to ask you to try to get beyond that with me. The good news is, there's no time limit. Take a decade. More, if you need it. But if you could just try. That's all I ask."

"It's a lot," I said.

"I know. I know it is. I have to get home, but I'll be back next Friday. And we can talk about it some more. If you're willing."

She didn't wait, to see if I was willing. She just left me alone to think.

NO SOONER HAD SHE WALKED out of my house than Grandma Annie came jogging down the path and held a phone in front of my face. "It's your friend Delilah," she said. "I took the liberty of telling her about Maria going off on her own. She asked how everything was. I hope that's okay."

Oh, thank God, I thought. Now I wouldn't have to dredge up those words myself.

I took the phone. "Hello, Delilah."

"I'll be there as quick as I can."

"Wait. Where are you?"

"I'm home. In San Diego. I got home a little early. Been here for a day and a half. Now I'm getting in the car right now. I'll be there as quick as I can."

I held the phone for a long time. Wondering how she did that. Where she'd learned that uncanny knack for being exactly where she was needed at exactly the right time.

I DECIDED THAT WHILE I WAS WAITING I'd remake the guesthouse a little. Take away the crib, and anything else that would keep rubbing my nose in the past.

The minute I did, that's when it hit me. It was a nasty surprise. The shock parted, and there was the real bulk of the pain. It almost brought me to my knees. The empty closet. The empty crib.

I started straightening the place up as a way of holding myself together. I folded up the bed into a couch. Wheeled the crib outside. Folded up the Japanese screen to take back to Grandma Annie. I felt almost like I wanted to cry again, but I wasn't going there. I just somehow managed to stay up above it all. I just kept moving.

I gathered up my clothes so I could do a load of wash. Made sure to empty out the pockets of everything. In the pocket of the pants I'd worn on the bus, I found a wad of money. The rest of Delilah's fifty dollars. I saw a scrap of paper wrapped in with it, but I couldn't initially put my finger on what it was. I unfolded it.

It was the warrior note. I was a brave warrior.

I didn't straighten up anymore after that. I didn't stay up above it all. I lay on the rug and held still and let the tears catch up with me. I just let it happen.

"WHAT GOOD IS A LOVE STORY without a happy ending?" I asked Delilah.

We were sitting in my little house. She was fanning herself with the Japanese fan I'd given her, despite the best efforts of the swamp cooler.

"Well, I told you when you first asked that. Do you remember? I said not all of them end happy, and even you know enough to know that. But you tried. Anyway. You gambled everything for love. You were brave enough to try. In spite of everything your father taught you. He did his best to make sure you'd never be alive. But you are alive. In spite of him."

"I'm beginning to see his point. Why take a gamble if it turns out like this?'

"You don't get to know how it'll turn out, child. That's why they call it gambling."

"But I lost everything. Maybe he was right." A terrible thing to say. I know. But that's how broken I felt.

"No," she said. "Wrong. You did not lose everything. You got your own place. And a grandmother who loves you. And you got your freedom. You got a whole new life. And you got your mother coming to know you again. You got a lot. Don't make the mistake of failing to see that. You want to know who lost everything? Your father. That's who. Lost any chance he ever had to get anything in this life except you. Then in the end he lost you. That's where all that caution got him. Now, where is that big brave Tony I remember?"

"Tony's dead. Remember? That's how the story ends. Tony gets shot dead."

"Well," she said, "good thing for you Sebastian is still alive, then. Isn't it?"

I didn't answer. I was looking at the huge banner signed by all the neighbors who fixed up this house for me. Part of me could feel the truth in what she was saying. I had that, at least. I had this place I'd dreamed of.

"You catch my drift about that?"

"Yes," I said. "I catch your drift about that."

"And, Sebastian . . ." She had never called me by my actual name before. As far as I could remember. "I know this is hard for you to believe. But everybody had a first love and everybody got hurt a few times on the way to the one that lasts. So people are going to tell you they know just how you feel. That's true and it's not true, both. Because unless you're right in the middle of it, you really can't know how much it hurts. You forget in time. So the bad news is, they don't exactly know how bad you hurt. Because they forgot. Only, that's the good news, too. In time they forgot how awful it is. And so will you. In time."

"I don't think I'm ever going to get over this," I said. I was being blazingly, painfully honest. Because it was Delilah. And I felt like I could with her. In fact, I felt I owed her no less. I expected her to argue with me. Tell me I was wrong. I was used to being told I was wrong.

"I didn't say you would," she said. "It's not exactly something you get over. It's like those steel spikes they drive into a tree. If the tree doesn't die, it just sort of grows around it. You sort of make it part of you. You learn how to live around it after a while."

I was grateful to her for telling me that. Because it was something I could almost believe.

IT WAS AFTER MIDNIGHT, and I still hadn't slept.

Delilah was asleep on the fold-out couch in the main house. I knew she'd be leaving in the morning, which made me feel alone.

I went outside and looked at the stars. Lay on the lounge chair, just the way I had with Maria that first night. But this time, I was in it by myself.

I still felt different, though. Whatever I had gained had not entirely left me. I felt scraped out. Sore in my gut. I had a headache. My eyes burned and ached from crying. My sinuses hadn't quite cleared. I hadn't slept. In short, I felt like hell. But I was alive. Not even a hundred percent sure that was the good news. But I was definitely alive.

After a while the moon came up over the horizon. I had never seen a moon like it before. It was almost full. Just one edge was a little lopsided. Not sharp and clear like the rest of it. But nearly full. It was about three times the size of any moon I had ever seen before. And it was yellow. Not really white. Yellow.

At first I couldn't figure out why. Especially I couldn't understand why it was so big. But the higher it rose, the closer it got to the way I was used to seeing it. I guess it's biggest when it's just over the horizon. You never really see the horizon in Manhattan. You see the moon when it's up above the skyscrapers. You never really see it rise.

I thought about the time Delilah told me to go out into nature. Find something that was not man-made. I thought about the times I looked up at the moon before I left New York. And told it, *Thanks for nothing.* Couldn't thank it for my life because I didn't have one. Back then I didn't.

"Thank you for my life," I said. Out loud.

And here's the part that might be hard to explain: I meant it.

At least I *had* a life. I'd never had one before, so it was painfully easy to tell.

So, now what? What had Delilah said I was supposed to do next?

It didn't take long to remember. She said I was supposed to put one foot in front of the other and see what life had in store for me next.

I looked at the windmills in the moonlight, and wondered if

Maria was looking at them, too, from the other side of the mountain. Maybe not, but she always could be.

I don't know if I'm that guy my mother talked about. If I could love her enough to send her away, if away is best. But I know I want to be. And maybe that'll have to be enough for now.

I decided the best thing I could do for right now would be to go inside and get some sleep.

Me

It was the first night in our new place. I was sitting there watching my children sleep. It's just a room. Like the size of a normal motel room. So it's hard not to be right there with them all the time.

That's okay, though.

Just before he went to bed, this is the last thing C.J. said to me: "I hate you for making me come here."

And you know what I said? "I'm sorry you feel that way, C.J. But this is the way it has to be."

I thought that was big progress for me.

I really know what Celia meant about being afraid of her own kid. Not like afraid he would hurt her or anything. I think she meant afraid he wouldn't like her. Like he would say "I hate you" or something.

I've been afraid of my kids. In some ways I guess I still am. But I didn't act afraid when he said that. So I had to give myself a pat on the back for just looking him right in the eye and saying it's going to be that way anyway. For acting like I'm the mother.

It's the decision I made. It's what *I* thought was right. Now that I get to do the thinking.

If he ever asks me why we can't live with his father, I'll tell him the truth. But I don't think he'll ask. Because he knows the truth. Already.

Then I couldn't help worrying about how much stuff I still needed to find out, figure out. Do. I had to find day care, and it had to be something that would fit into what I'd be making. I had to figure out how soon I could actually work with my ribs and all. But fortunately the people at the motel pretty much made it clear that I could have the room until then. They said I was a friend of the family.

I'm pretty sure once I pay for day care and buy our food, there won't be a cent left over. I won't be making much because the room is part of the pay.

But, anyway, we won't die.

AFTER A WHILE I went outside and sat in this little plastic chair outside our sliding glass door. Close enough to hear my kids if they cried.

I looked at the windmills and thought about Sebastian. And, also, I thought about how it felt to be free.

Terrifying. It was so scary it hurt. But on the other hand, there was something about it. Like, I wasn't going to trade it back.

I thought about how Sebastian is free now, too. And I think that puts him in a much better place than if he was trying to earn enough money for four people, and trying to learn how to be a boyfriend and a father at the same time, not to mention trying to raise a boy who would never give him a break.

I wonder if he sees it that way. If he feels like I do, like the part of life down the road is an empty blackboard just waiting for me to pick up a piece of chalk.

Probably not. But I still think it's true. I still think it's best.

I wish I could see him more, but probably that would just make it harder for me not to change my mind. Besides, I can always look at the windmills in the moonlight from where I am, and know that he's looking at the same windmills in the light of the same moon. And in a weird sort of way, that might tie us together well enough.

Anyway, that's what *I* think.